DEATH IS NOW MY NEIGHBOR

An Inspector Morse Novel

COLIN DEXTER

Published by Random House Large Print
in association with Crown Publishers, Inc.
New York 1997

Library of Congress Cataloging-in-Publication Data
Dexter, Colin.
[Death is now my neighbour]
Death is now my neighbor / Colin Dexter.
p. cm.
Originally published: Death is now my neighbour.
London : Macmillan, 1996.
ISBN 0-679-77417-3
1. Morse, Inspector (Fictitious character)—Fiction.
2. Police—England—Oxford—Fiction.
3. Large type books. I. Title.
PR6054.E96D43 1997b
823'.914—DC20 96-41563 CIP

Random House Web Address: http://www.randomhouse.com/
Printed in the United States of America
FIRST LARGE PRINT EDITION

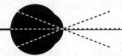

**This Large Print Book carries the
Seal of Approval of N.A.V.H.**

For
Joan Templeton
with gratitude

Acknowledgments

The author and publishers wish to thank the following who have kindly given permission for use of copyright materials: Extract from *The Dance* by Philip Larkin reproduced by permission of Faber & Faber Ltd.;

Extract from the *News of the World* reproduced by permission of the *News of the World;*

Extract from Fowler's *Modern English Usage* reproduced by permission of Oxford University Press;

Ace Reporter by Helen Peacocke reproduced by kind permission of the author;

Extract from *Major Barbara* by Bernard Shaw reproduced by permission of The Society of Authors on behalf of the Bernard Shaw Estate;

Extract from *The Brontës* by Juliet Barker reproduced by permission of Weidenfeld and Nicolson;

Extract from *The Dry Salvages* by T. S. Eliot reproduced by permission of Faber & Faber Ltd.;

Extract from *Summoned by Bells* by John Betjaman reproduced by permission of John Murray (Publishers) Ltd.;

Extract from *Aubade* by Philip Larkin reproduced by permission of Faber & Faber Ltd.;

Extract from *May-Day Song for North Oxford* by John Betjaman, from *Collected Poems of John Betjaman,* reproduced by permission of John Murray (Publishers) Ltd.;

Extract from *This Be the Verse* by Philip Larkin reproduced by permission of Faber & Faber Ltd.;

Extract by Philip Larkin on p. 426 reproduced by permission of Faber & Faber Ltd.

Quickly, bring me a beaker of wine,
so that I may wet my mind and say
something clever.

—ARISTOPHANES

DEATH IS NOW
MY NEIGHBOR

January 1996

A decided boon, therefore, are any multiple-choice items for those pupils in our classrooms who are either inured to idleness, or guilty of willful ignorance. Such pupils, if simply and appropriately instructed, have only to plump for the same answer on each occasion—let us say, choice (a) from choices (a) (b) (c) (d)—in order to achieve a reasonably regular score of some 25% of the total marks available. This is a wholly satisfactory return for academic incompetence.

—*Crosscurrents in Assessment Criteria: Theory and Practice,* HMSO, 1983

"WHAT TIME DO you call this, Lewis?"

"The missus's fault. Not like her to be late with the breakfast."

Morse made no answer as he stared down at the one remaining unsolved clue:

"Stand for soldiers?—5, 4"

Lewis took the chair opposite his chief and sat waiting for some considerable while, leafing through a magazine.

"Stuck, sir?" he asked finally.

"If I was—if I *were*—I doubt I'd get much help from you."

"You never know," suggested Lewis good-naturedly. "Perhaps—"

"Ah!" burst out Morse triumphantly, as he wrote in TOAST RACK. He folded *The Times* away and beamed across at his sergeant.

"You—are—a—genius, Lewis."

"So you've often told me, sir."

"*And* I bet you had a boiled egg for breakfast—with soldiers. Am I right?"

"What's that got—?"

"What are you reading there?"

Lewis held up the title page of his magazine.

"Lew-is! There are more important things in life than the *Thames Valley Police Gazette*."

"Just thought you might be interested in one of the articles here . . ."

Morse rose to the bait. "Such as?"

"There's a sort of test—you know, see how many points you can score: ARE YOU REALLY WISE AND CULTURED?"

"Very doubtful in your case, I should think."

"You reckon you could do better than I did?"

"Quite certain of it."

Lewis grinned. "*Quite* certain, sir?"

"Absolutely."

"Want to have a go, then?" Lewis's mouth betrayed

gentle amusement as Morse shrugged his indifference.

"Multiple-choice questions—you know all about—?"

"Get *on* with it!"

"All you've got to do is imagine the world's going to end in exactly one week's time, okay? Then you've got to answer five questions, as honestly as you can."

"And you've already answered these questions yourself?"

Lewis nodded.

"Well, if *you* can answer them . . . Fire away!"

Lewis read aloud from the article:

Question One
Given the choice of only four CDs or cassettes, which one of the following would you be likely to play at least once?

  (a) A Beatles album
  (b) Fauré's Requiem
  (c) An Evening with Victor Borge
  (d) The complete overtures to Wagner's operas

With a swift flourish, Morse wrote down a letter.

Question Two
Which of these videos would you want to watch?

  (a) Casablanca *(the film)*
  (b) England's World Cup victory (1966)
  (c) Copenhagen Red-Hot Sex *(2 hours)*
  (d) The Habitat of the Kingfisher *(RSPB)*

A second swift flourish from Morse.

Question Three
With which of the following women would you wish to spend some, if not all, of your surviving hours?
(a) Lady Thatcher
(b) Kim Basinger
(c) Mother Teresa
(d) Princess Diana

A third swift flourish.

Question Four
If you could gladden your final days with one of the following, which would it be?
(a) Two dozen bottles of vintage champagne
(b) Five hundred cigarettes
(c) A large bottle of tranquilizers
(d) A barrel of real ale

Flourish number four, and the candidate (confident of imminent success, it appeared) sat back in the black-leather armchair.

Question Five
Which of the following would you read during this period?
(a) Cervantes' Don Quixote
(b) Dante's The Divine Comedy
(c) A bound volume of Private Eye *(1995)*
(d) Homer's Iliad

This time Morse hesitated some while before writing on the pad in front of him. "You did the test yourself, you say?"

Lewis nodded. "Victor Borge; the football; Princess Diana; the champagne; and *Private Eye*. Just hope Princess Di likes Champers, that's all."

"There must be worse ways of spending your last week on earth," admitted Morse.

"I didn't do so well, though—not on the marking. I'm not up there among the cultured and the wise, I'm afraid."

"Did you expect to be?"

"Wouldn't you?"

"Of course."

"Let's hear what you picked, then."

"My preferences, Lewis," Morse articulated his words with precision, "were as follows: (b); (c); (b); (c); none of them."

Turning to the back page, Lewis reminded himself of the answers putatively adjudged to be correct.

"I don't believe it," he whispered to himself. Then, to Morse: "You scored the maximum!"

"Are you surprised?"

Lewis shook his head in mild bewilderment.

"You chose, what, the *Requiem*?"

"Well?"

"But you've never believed in all that religious stuff."

"It's important if it's *true*, though, isn't it? Let's just say it's a bit like an insurance policy. A beautiful work, anyway."

"Says here: 'Score four marks for (b). Sufficient recommendation that it was chosen by three of the last four Popes for their funerals.'"

Morse lifted his eyebrows. "You didn't know that?"

Lewis ignored the question and continued:

"Then you chose the sex video!"

"Well, it was either that or the kingfisher. I've already seen *Casablanca* a couple of times—and no one's ever going to make me watch a football match again."

"But I mean, a sex video . . ."

Morse, however, was clearly unimpressed by such obvious disapprobation. "It'd be the choice of those three Popes as well, like as not."

"But it all gets—well, it gets so plain *boring* after a while."

"So you keep telling me, Lewis. And all I'm asking is the chance to get as bored as everybody else. I've only got a *week,* remember."

"I like your next choice, though. Beautiful girl, Kim Basinger. Beautiful."

"Something of a toss-up, that—between her and Mother Teresa. But I'd already played the God card."

"Then," Lewis considered the next answer, "Arrghh, come off it, sir! You didn't even go for the beer! You're supposed to answer these questions *honestly.*"

"I've already got plenty of booze in," said Morse. "Certainly enough to see me through to Judgment Day. And I don't fancy facing the Great Beyond with a blinding hangover. It'll be a new experience for me —tranquilizers . . ."

Lewis looked down again, and proceeded to read

out the reasons for Morse's greatest triumph. "It says here, on Question Five, 'Those choosing any of the suggested titles are clearly unfit for high honors. If any choice whatsoever is made, four marks will therefore be deducted from the final score. If the answer is a timid dash—or similar—no marks will be awarded, but no marks will be deducted. A more positively negative answer—e.g. "Come off it!"—will be rewarded with a bonus of four marks.'" Again Lewis shook his head. "Nonsense, isn't it? 'Positively negative,' I mean."

"Rather nicely put, I'd've thought," said Morse.

"Anyway," conceded Lewis, "you score twenty out of twenty according to this fellow who seems to have all the answers." Lewis looked again at the name printed below the article. "'Rhadamanthus'—whoever he is."

"Lord Chief Justice of Appeal in the Underworld."

Lewis frowned, then grinned. "You've been cheating! You've got a copy—"

"No!" Morse's blue eyes gazed fiercely across at his sergeant. "The first I saw of that *Gazette* was when you brought it in just now."

"If you say so." But Lewis sounded less than convinced.

"Not surprised, are you, to find me perched up there on the topmost twig amongst the intelligentsia?"

"'The wise and the cultured,' actually."

"And that's another thing. I think I shall go crackers if I hear three things in my life much more: 'Hark the Herald Angels Sing'; *Eine Kleine Nachtmusik;* and that wretched bloody word 'actually.'"

"Sorry, sir."

Suddenly Morse grinned. "No need to be, old friend. And at least you're right about one thing. I did cheat —in a way."

"You don't mean *you* . . . ?"

Morse nodded.

>‹

It had been a playful, pleasant interlude. Yet it would have warranted no inclusion in this chronicle had it not been that one or two of the details recorded herein were to linger significantly in the memory of Chief Inspector E. Morse, of the Thames Valley Police HQ.

Part One

Chapter One

In hypothetical sentences introduced by "if" and referring to past time, where conditions are deemed to be "unfulfilled," the verb will regularly be found in the pluperfect subjunctive, in both protasis and apodosis.

—Donet, *Principles of Elementary Latin Syntax*

IT IS PERHAPS unusual to begin a tale of murder with a reminder to the reader of the rules governing conditional sentences in a language that is incontrovertibly dead. In the present case, however, such a course appears not wholly inappropriate.

If (*if*) Chief Inspector Morse had been on hand to observe the receptionist's dress—an irregularly triangled affair in blues, grays, and reds—he might have been reminded of the uniform issued to a British Airways stewardess. More probably, though, he might not, since he had never flown on British Airways. His only flight during the previous decade had occasioned so many fears concerning his personal survival that he had determined to restrict all future travel to those statistically far more precarious means of conveyance— the car, the coach, the train, and the steamer.

Yet almost certainly the Chief Inspector would have noted, with approval, the receptionist herself, for in

Yorkshire she would have been reckoned a bonny lass: a vivacious, dark-eyed woman, long-legged and well-figured; a woman—judging from her ringless, well-manicured fingers—not overtly advertising any marital commitment, and not averse, perhaps, to the occasional overture from the occasional man.

Pinned at the top left of her colorful dress was a name tag: "Dawn Charles."

Unlike several of her friends (certainly unlike Morse) she was quite content with her Christian name. Sometimes she'd felt *slightly* dubious about it; but no longer. Out with some friends in the Bird and Baby the previous month, she'd been introduced to a rather dashing, rather dishy undergraduate from Pembroke College. And when, a little later, she'd found herself doodling inconsequentially on a Burton beer mat, the young man, on observing her sinistrality, had initiated a wholly memorable conversation.

"Dawn? That *is* your name?"

She'd nodded.

"Left-handed?"

She'd nodded.

"Do you know that line from Omar Khayyam? 'Dreaming when Dawn's left hand was in the sky. . . .' Lovely, isn't it?"

Yes, it was. Lovely.

She'd peeled the top off the beer mat and made him write it down for her.

Then, very quietly, he'd asked her if he could see her again. At the start of the new term, perhaps?

She'd known it was silly, for there must have been at least twenty years' difference in their ages. If only . . . if only he'd been ten, a dozen years older . . .

But people *did* do silly things, and hoped their silly hopes. And that very day, January 15, was the first full day of the new Hilary Term in the University of Oxford.

Her Monday–Friday job, 6–10 P.M., at the clinic on the Banbury Road (just north of St. Giles') was really quite enjoyable. Over three years of it now, and she was becoming a fixture there. Most of the consultants greeted her with a genuine smile; several of them, these days, with her Christian name.

Nice.

She'd once stayed at a four-star hotel which offered a glass of sherry to incoming guests; and although the private Harvey Clinic was unwilling (perhaps on medical grounds?) to provide such laudable hospitality, Dawn ever kept two jugs of genuine coffee piping hot for her clients, most of them soberly suited and well-heeled gentlemen. A number of whom, as she well knew, were most seriously ill.

Yes, there had been several occasions when she had heard a few brief passages of conversation between consultant and client which she *shouldn't* have heard; or which, having heard, she should have forgotten; and which she should never have been willing to report to anyone.

Not even to the police.

Quite certainly not to the Press . . .

As it happened, January 15 was to prove a day unusually easy for her to recall, since it marked the twenty-fifth anniversary of the clinic's opening in 1971. By prior negotiation and arrangement, the clinic was visited that evening, between 7 P.M. and 8:30 P.M., by Radio Oxford, by the local press, and by Mr. Wesley Smith and his crew from the Central TV studios out at Abingdon. And particularly memorable for Dawn had been those precious moments when the camera had focused upon her: first, when (as instructed) she had poured a cup of genuine coffee for a wholly bogus "client"; second, when the cameraman had moved behind her left shoulder as she ran a felt-tipped pen through a name on the appointments list in front of her—but only, of course, after a full assurance that no viewer would be able to read the name itself when the feature was shown the following evening.

Yet Dawn Charles was always to remember the name:

Mr. J. C. Storrs.

It had been a fairly new name to her—another of those patients, as Dawn suspected correctly, whose influence and affluence afforded the necessary leverage and money to jump the queues awaiting their calls to the hospitals up in Headington.

There was something else she would always remember, too. . . .

By one of those minor coincidences (so commonplace in Morse's life) it had been just as most of the personnel from the media were preparing to leave, at almost exactly 8:30 P.M., that Mr. Robert Turnbull, the Senior Cancer Consultant, had passed her desk, nodded a greeting, and walked slowly to the exit, his right hand resting on the shoulder of Mr. J. C. Storrs. The two men were talking quietly together for some while—Dawn was certain of that. But certain of little else. The look on the consultant's face, as far as she could recall, had been neither that of a judge who has just condemned a man to death, nor that of one just granting a prisoner his freedom.

No obvious grimness.

No obvious joy.

And indeed there was adequate cause for such uncertainty on Dawn's part, since the scene had been partially masked from her by the continued presence of several persons: a ponytailed reporter scribbling a furious shorthand as he interviewed a nurse; the TV crew packing away its camera and tripods; the Lord Mayor speaking some congratulatory words into a Radio Oxford microphone—all of them standing between her and the top of the three blue-carpeted stairs which led down to the double-doored exit, outside which were affixed the vertical banks of well-polished brass plates, ten on each side, the fourth from the top on the left reading:

> ROBERT H. TURNBULL

If only Dawn Charles could have recalled a little more.

"If"—that little conjunction introducing those unfulfilled conditions in past time which, as Donet reminds us, demand the pluperfect subjunctive in both clauses—a syntactical rule which Morse himself had mastered early on in an education which had been far more fortunate than that enjoyed by the receptionist at the Harvey Clinic.

>‹

Indeed, over the next two weeks, most people in Oxford were destined to be considerably more fortunate than Dawn Charles: she received no communication from the poetry lover of Pembroke; her mother was admitted to a psychiatric ward out at Littlemore; she was twice reminded by her bank manager of the increasing problems arising from the large margin of negative equity on her small flat; and finally, on Monday morning, January 29, she was to hear on Fox FM Radio that her favorite consultant, Mr. Robert H. Turnbull, MB, ChB, FRCS, had been fatally injured in a car accident on Cumnor Hill.

Chapter Two

The Master shall not continue in his post beyond
the age of sixty-seven. As a simple rule, therefore,
the incumbent Master will be requested to give
notice of impending retirement during the University term immediately prior to that birthday.
Where, however, such an accommodation does not
present itself, the Master is required to propose a
particular date not later than the end of the first
week of the second full term after the statutory ter-
mination (*vide supra*).

> —Paragraph 2 (a), translated from the
> Latin, from the Founders' Statutes
> of Lonsdale College, Oxford

SIR CLIXBY BREAM would be almost sixty-nine years
old when he retired as Master of Lonsdale. A committee of Senior Fellows, including two eminent
Latin scholars, had found itself unable to interpret
the gobbledegook of the Founders' Statutes (*vide
supra*); and since no "accommodation" (whatever
that was) had presented itself, Sir Clixby had first
been persuaded to stay on for a short while—then
for a longer while.

Yet this involved no hardship.

He was subject to none of the normal pressures
about moving to somewhere nearer the children or

the grandchildren, since his marriage to Lady Muriel had been *sine prole*. Moreover, he was blessedly free from the usual uxorial bleatings about a nice little thatched cottage in Dorset or Devon, since Lady Muriel had been in her grave these past three years.

The position of Head of House at any of the Oxbridge Colleges was just about the acme of academic ambition; and since three of the last four Masters had been knighted within eighteen months of their appointments, it had been natural for him to be attracted by the opportunity of such pleasing preferment. And he *had* been so attracted; as, even more strongly, had the late Lady Muriel.

Indeed, the incumbent Master, a distinguished mathematician in his earlier days, had never enjoyed living anywhere as much as in Oxford—ten years of it now. He'd learned to love the old city more and more the longer he was there: It was as simple as that. Of course he was somewhat saddened by the thought of his imminent retirement: He would miss the College—miss the challenges of running the place—and he knew that the sight of the furniture van outside the wisteria-clad front of the Master's Lodge would occasion some aching regret. But there were a few unexpected consolations, perhaps. In particular, he would be able (he supposed) to sit back and survey with a degree of detachment and sardonic amusement the infighting that would doubtless arise among his potential successors.

It was the duty of the Fellows' Appointments Committee (its legality long established by one of the more readily comprehensible of the College Statutes) to stipulate three conditions for those seeking election as Master: first, that any candidate should be "of sound mind and in good health"; second, that the candidate should "not have taken Holy Orders"; third, that the candidate should have no criminal record within "the territories administered under the governance of His (or Her) Most Glorious Majesty."

Such stipulations had often amused the present Master.

If one judged by the longevity of almost all the Masters appointed during the twentieth century, physical well-being had seldom posed much of a problem; yet mental stability had never been a particularly prominent feature of his immediate predecessor, nor (by all accounts) of his predecessor's predecessor. And occasionally Sir Clixby wondered what the College would say of himself once he was gone. . . . With regard to the exclusion of the clergy, he assumed that the Founders (like Edward Gibbon three centuries later) had managed to trace the source of all human wickedness back to the Popes and the Prelates, and had rallied to the cause of anticlericalism. . . . But it was the possibility of the candidate's criminality which was the most amusing. Presumably any convictions for murder, rape, sodomy, treason, or similar misdemeanors, were to be discounted if shown to have taken place *outside* the jurisdiction of His (or Her) Most Glorious Majesty. Very strange.

Strangest of all, however, was the absence of any mention in the original Statute of academic pedigree; and, at least theoretically, there could be no bar to a candidate presenting himself with only a Grade E in GCSE Media Studies. Nor was there any stipulation that the successful candidate should be a senior (or, for that matter, a junior) member of the College, and on several occasions "outsiders" had been appointed. Indeed, he himself, Sir Clixby, had been imported into Oxford from "the other place," and then (chiefly) in recognition of his reputation as a resourceful fund-raiser.

On this occasion, however, outsiders seemed out of favor. The College itself could offer at least two candidates, each of whom would be an admirable choice; or so it was thought. In the Senior Common Room the consensus was most decidedly in favor of such "internal" preferment, and the betting had hardened accordingly.

By some curious omission no entry had hitherto been granted to either of these ante-post favorites in the pages of *Who's Who*. From which one may be forgiven for concluding that the aforesaid work is rather more concerned with the third cousins of secondary aristocrats than with eminent academics. Happily, however, both of these personages had been considered worthy of mention in Debrett's *People of Today 1995*:

STORRS, Julian Charles; *b* July 9, 1935; *Educ* Christ's Hosp, Emmanuel Coll Cambridge (BA, MA); *m* Angela Miriam Martin March 31, 1974; *Career* Capt RA (Indian Army Reserve); Pitt Rivers Reader in Social Anthropology and Senior Fellow Lonsdale Coll Oxford; *Recreations* taking taxis, playing bridge.

CORNFORD, Denis Jack; *b* April 23, 1942; *Educ* Wyggeston GS Leicester, Magdalen Coll Oxford (MA, DPhil); *m* Shelly Ann Benson May 28, 1994; *Career* University Reader in Medieval History and Fellow Lonsdale Coll Oxford; *Recreations* kite flying, cultivation of orchids.

Each of these entries may appear comparatively uninformative. Yet perhaps in the more perceptive reader they may provoke one or two interesting considerations.

Was, for example, the Senior Fellow of Lonsdale so affluent that he could afford to take a taxi everywhere? Did he never travel by car, coach, or train? Well, quite certainly on special occasions he would travel by train.

Oh, yes.

As we shall see.

And why was Dr. Cornford, soon to be fifty-four years old, so recently converted to the advantages of latter-day matrimony? Had he met some worthy woman of comparable age?

Oh, no.

As we shall see.

Chapter Three

> How right
> I should have been to keep away, and let
> You have your innocent–guilty–innocent night
> Of switching partners in your own sad set:
> How useless to invite
> The sickening breathlessness of being young
> Into my life again.
>
> —Philip Larkin, *The Dance*

DENIS CORNFORD, *omnium consensu*, was a fine historian. Allied with a mind both sharp and rigorously honest was a capacity for the assemblage and interpretation of evidence that was the envy of the History Faculty at Oxford. Yet in spite of such qualities, he was best known for a brief monograph on the Battle of Hastings, in which he maintained that the momentous conflict between Harold of England and William of Normandy had taken place one year earlier than universally acknowledged. In 1065.

In the Trinity Term of 1994, Cornford—a slimly built, smallish, pleasantly featured man—had taken sabbatical leave at Harvard; and there—somehow and somewhere, in Cambridge, Massachusetts— something quite extraordinary had occurred. For six months later, to the amazement and amusement of his colleagues, the confirmed bachelor of Lonsdale had returned to Oxford with a woman who had agreed to change her name from Shelly Benson to Shelly Cornford: a student from Harvard who had just gained her Master's degree in American History, twenty-six years old—exactly half the age of her new husband (for this was her second marriage).

It is perhaps not likely that Shelly would have reached the semifinal heats of any Miss Massachusetts beauty competition: her jawline was slightly too square, her shoulders rather too strong, her legs perhaps a little on the sturdy side. Yet there were a good many in Lonsdale College—both dons and undergraduates—who were to experience a curious attraction to the woman now putting in fairly regular appearances in Chapel, at Guest Nights, and at College functions during the Michaelmas Term of 1994. Her wavy, shoulder-length brown hair framed a face in which the widely set dark brown eyes seemed sometimes to convey the half-promise of a potential intimacy, while her quietly voiced New England accent could occasionally sound as sweetly sensual as some enchantress's.

Many were the comments made about the former Shelly Benson during those first few terms. But no one could ever doubt what Denis Cornford had seen in her, for it was simply what others could now so clearly see for themselves. So from the start Shelly Cornford was regularly lusted after; her husband secretly envied. But the couple themselves appeared perfectly happy: no hint of infidelity on her part; no cause for jealousy on his.

Not yet.

Frequently during those days they were to be seen walking hand-in-hand the short distances from their rooms in Holywell Street to the King's Arms, or the Turf Tavern ("Find Us If You Can!"), where in bars blessedly free from jukebox and fruit-machine Shelly had quickly acquired a taste for real ale and a love for the ambience of the English public house.

Occasionally the two of them ventured further afield in and around Oxford; and one evening, just before Christmas 1994, they had taken the No. 2 bus from Cornmarket up to another King's Arms, the one in the Banbury road, where amid many unashamedly festive young revelers Cornford watched as his (equally young) wife, with eyes half-closed, had rocked her shoulders sensuously to the thudding rhythm of some pop music, her black-stockinged thighs alternately lifted and lowered as though she were mentally disco dancing. And at that point he was conscious of being the oldest person in the bar, by about twenty years; inhabiting alien territory there; wholly excluded from the magic circle of the night; and suddenly sadly aware that he could never even begin to share the girlish animality of the woman he had married.

Cornford had said nothing that evening.

Nor had he said anything when, three months later, at the end-of-term Gaudy, he had noticed, beneath the table, the left hand of Julian Storrs pressed briefly against Shelly's right thigh as she sat drinking rather a lot of Madeira, after drinking rather a lot of red wine at dinner, after drinking rather a lot of gin at the earlier reception . . . her chair perhaps unnecessarily close to the Senior Fellow seated on her right, the laughing pair leaning together in some whispered, mutual, mouth-to-ear,exchange. Perhaps it was all perfectly harmless; and Cornford sought to make little of it. Yet he ought (he knew it!) to have said a few words on that occasion—lightly, with a heavy heart.

It was only late in the Michaelmas Term 1995 that Cornford finally did say something to his wife . . .

❊

They had been seated one Tuesday lunchtime in the Turf Tavern, he immediately opposite his wife as she sat in one of the wooden wall seats in the main bar, each of them enjoying a pint of London Pride. He was eagerly expounding to her his growing conviction that the statistical evidence concerning the number of deaths resultant from the Black Death in 1348 had been wildly misinterpreted, and that the supposed demographic effects consequent upon that plague were—most decidedly!—extremely suspect. It should all have been of some interest, surely? And yet Cornford was conscious of a semipreoccupied gaze in Shelly's eyes as she stared over his left shoulder into some more fascinating area.

All right. She *ought* to have been interested—but she wasn't. Not everyone, not even a trained historian like his wife, was going to be automatically enthralled by any reevaluation of some abstruse medieval evidence.

He'd thought little of it.

And had drunk his ale.

They were about to leave when a man, in his early thirties or so, walked over to them—a tall, dark, slimly built Arab with a bushy mustache. Looking directly into Shelly's eyes, he spoke softly to her:

"Madame! You are the most beautiful lady I see!"

Then, turning to Cornford: "Please excuse, sir!" With which, picking up Shelly's right hand, he imprinted his full-lipped mouth most earnestly upon the back of her wrist.

After the pair of them had emerged into the cobbled lane that led up again into Holywell Street, Cornford stopped and so roughly pushed his wife's shoulder that she had no choice but to stand there facing him.

"You—are—a—bloody—flirt! Did you know that? All the time we were in there—all the time I was telling you—"

But he got no further.

The tall figure of Sir Clixby Bream was striding down toward them.

"Hell-*o*! You're both just off, I can see that. But what about another little snifter? Just to please me?"

"Not for me, Master." Cornford trusted that he'd

masked the bitterness of his earlier tone. "But if . . . ?" He turned to his wife.

"No. Not now. Another time. Thank you, Master."

With Shelly still beside him, Cornford walked rather blindly on, suspecting (how otherwise?) that the Master had witnessed the awkward, angry scene. And then, a few steps later—almost miraculously—he felt his wife's arm link with his own; heard the wonderful words spoken in her quiet voice: "Denis, I'm so very sorry. Do please forgive me, my darling."

><

As the Master stooped slightly to pass beneath the entrance of the Turf Tavern, an observer skilled in the art of labiomancy would have read the two words on his smoothly smiling mouth:

"Well! Well!"

Chapter Four

Wednesday, February 7

> Disciple (weeping): O Master, I disturb thy meditations.
>
> MASTER: Thy tears are plural; the Divine Will is one.
>
> DISCIPLE: I seek wisdom and truth, yet my thoughts are ever of lust and the necessary pleasures of a woman.
>
> MASTER: Seek not wisdom and truth, my son; seek rather forgiveness. Now go in peace, for verily hast thou disturbed my meditations—of lust and of the necessary pleasures of a woman.
>
> —K'ung-Fu-Tsu, from *Analects XXIII*

"WELL, AT LEAST it's *left* on time."

"Not surprising, is it? The bloody thing *starts* from Oxford. Give it a chance, though. We'll probably run into signaling failure somewhere along the line."

She smiled, attractively. "Funny, really. They've been signaling on the railways for—what?—a hundred and fifty years, and with all these computers and things . . ."

"Over one hundred and seventy years, if we want

to be accurate—and why shouldn't we? Eighteen twenty-five when the Stockton to Darlington line was opened."

"Yeah. We learned about that in school. You know, Stephenson's *Rocket* and all that."

"No, my dear girl. A few years later, that was. Stephenson's first locomotive was called *The Locomotive*—not very difficult to remember, is it?"

"No."

The monosyllable was quietly spoken, and he knew that he'd made her feel inadequate again.

She turned away from him to look through the carriage window, spotting the great sandstone house in Nuneham Park, up toward the skyline on the left. More than once he'd told her something of its history, and about Capability Brown and Somebody Adams; but she was never able to remember things as accurately as he seemed to expect. He'd told her on their last train journey, for example, about the nationalization of the railways after World War II: 1947 (or was it 1948?).

So what?

Yet there was one year she would *never* forget: the year the network changed its name to "British Rail." Her father had told her about that; told her she'd been born on that very same day. In that very same year, too.

In 1965.

"Drinks? Refreshments?"

An overloaded trolley was squeezing a squeaky

passage along the aisle; and the man looked at his wristwatch (10:40 A.M.) as it came alongside, before turning to the elegantly suited woman seated next to him:

"Fancy anything? Coffee? Bit too early for anything stronger, perhaps?"

"Gin and tonic for me. And a packet of plain crisps."

Sod him! He'd been pretty insufferable so far.

A few minutes later, after pouring half his can of McEwan's Export Ale into a plastic container, he turned toward her again; and she felt his dry, slightly cracked lips pressed upon her right cheek. Then she heard him say the wonderful word that someone else had heard a month or two before; heard him say "Sorry."

She opened her white-leather handbag and took out a tube of lip salve. As she passed it to him, she felt his firm, slim fingers move against the back of her wrist; then move along her lower arm, beneath the sleeve of her light mauve Jaeger jacket: the fingers of a pianist. And she knew that very soon—the Turbo Express had just left Reading—the pianist would have been granted the licence to play with her body once more, as though he were rejoicing in a gentle Schubert melody.

She had never known a man so much in control of himself.

Or of her.

><

The train stopped just before Slough.

When, ten minutes later, it slowly began to move forward again, the Senior Conductor decided to introduce himself over the intercom.

"Ladies and Gentlemen. Due to a signaling failure at Slough, this train will now arrive at Paddington approximately fifteen minutes late. We apologize to customers for this delay."

The man and the woman, seated now more closely together, turned to each other—and smiled.

"What are you thinking?" she asked.

"You often ask me that, you know. Sometimes I'm not thinking of anything."

"Well?"

"I was only thinking that our Senior Conductor doesn't seem to know the difference between 'due to' and 'owing to.' "

"Not sure *I* do. Does it matter?"

"Of course it matters."

"But you won't let it come between us?"

"I won't let anything come between us," he whispered into her ear. For a few seconds they looked lovingly at each other. Then he lowered his eyes, removed a splayed left hand from her stockinged thigh, and drank his last mouthful of beer.

"Just before we get into Paddington, Rachel, there's something important I ought to tell you."

She turned to him—her eyes suddenly alarmed.

He wanted to put a stop to the affair?

He wanted to get rid of her?

He'd found another woman? (Apart from his wife, of course.)

"Tickets, please!"

He looked as if he might be making his maiden voyage, the young ticket collector, for he was scrutinizing each ticket proffered to him with preternatural concentration.

The man took both his own and the young woman's ticket from his wallet: cheap-day returns.

"This yours, sir?"

"Yes."

"You an OAP?"

"As a matter of fact I am not, no." (The tone of his voice was quietly arrogant.) "To draw a senior citizen pension in the United Kingdom a man has to be sixty-five years of age. But a Senior Railcard is available to a man who has passed his sixtieth birthday— as doubtless you know."

"Could I see your Railcard, sir?"

With a sigh of resignation, the man produced his card. And the slightly flustered, spotty-faced youth duly studied the details.

Valid:	until MAY 7, 1996
Issued to:	Mr J. C. Storrs

"How the hell does he think I got my ticket at Oxford without showing *that*?" asked the Senior Fellow of Lonsdale.

"He's only doing his duty, poor lad. And he's got awful acne."

"You're right, yes."

She took his hand in hers, moving more closely again. And within a few minutes the PADDINGTON sign passed by as the train drew slowly into the long platform. In a rather sad voice, the Senior Conductor now made his second announcement: "All change, please! All change! This train has now terminated."

They waited until their fellow passengers had alighted; and happily, just as at Oxford, there seemed to be no one on the train whom either of them knew.

In the Brunel Bar of the Station Hotel, Storrs ordered a large brandy (two pieces of ice) for his young companion, and half a pint of Smith's bitter for himself. Then, leaving his own drink temporarily untouched, he walked out into Praed Street, thence making his way down to the cluster of small hotels in and around Sussex Gardens, several of them displaying VACANCIES signs. He had "used" (was that the word?) two of them previously, but this time he decided to explore new territory.

"Double room?"

"One left, yeah. Just the one night, is it?"

"How much?"

"Seventy-five pounds for the two—with breakfast."

"How much without breakfast?"

Storrs sensed that the middle-aged peroxide blonde was attuned to his intentions, for her eyes hardened knowingly behind the cigarette-stained reception counter.

"Seventy-five pounds."

One experienced campaigner nodded to another experienced campaigner. "Well, thank you, madam. I promise I'll call back and take the room—after I've had a look at it—if I can't find anything a little less expensive."

He turned to go.

"Just a minute! . . . No breakfast, you say?"

"No. We're catching the sleeper to Inverness, and we just want a room for the day—you know?—a sort of habitation and a place."

She squinted up at him through her cigarette smoke. "Sixty-five?"

"Sixty."

"Okay."

He counted out six ten-pound notes as, pushing the register forward, she reached behind her for Key Number 10.

It was, one may say, a satisfactory transaction.

>←

Her glass was empty, and without seating himself he drained his own beer at a draught.

"Same again?"

"Please!" She pushed over the globed glass in which the semi-melted ice-cubes still remained.

Feeling most pleasantly relaxed, she looked around the thinly populated bar, and noticed (again!) the eyes of the middle-aged man seated across the room. But she gave no sign that she was aware of his interest, switching her glance instead to the balding, gray-white head of the man leaning nonchalantly at the bar as he ordered their drinks.

⇥⇤

Beside her once more, he clinked their glasses, feeling (just as she did) most pleasantly relaxed.

"Quite a while since we sat here," he volunteered.

"Couple o' months?"

"Ten weeks, if we wish to be exact."

"Which, of course, we do, sir."

Smiling, she sipped her second large brandy. Feeling good; feeling increasingly good.

"Hungry?" he asked.

"What for?"

He grinned. "An hour in bed, perhaps—before we have a bite to eat?"

"Wine thrown in?"

"I'm trying to bribe you."

"Well . . . if you *want* to go to bed for a little while first . . ."

"I *think* I'd quite enjoy that."

"One condition, though."

"What?"

"You tell me what you were going to tell me—on the train."

He nodded seriously. "I'll tell you over the wine."

It was, one may say, a satisfactory arrangement.

As they got up to leave, Storrs moved ahead of her to push open one of the swing doors; and Rachel James (for such was she), a freelance physiotherapist practicing up in North Oxford, was conscious of the same man's eyes upon her. Almost involuntarily she leaned her body backward, thrusting her breasts against the smooth white silk of her blouse as she lifted both her hands behind her head to tighten the ring which held her light brown hair in its ponytail.

A ponytail ten inches long.

Chapter Five

Then the smiling hookers turned their attention to our shocked reporters.

"Don't be shy! You paid for a good time, and that's what we want to give you."

Our men feigned jet lag, and declined.

—Extract from the *News of the World*, February 5, 1995

GEOFFREY OWENS had a better knowledge of Soho than most people.

He'd been only nineteen when first he'd gone to London as a junior reporter, when he'd rented a room just off Soho Square, and when during his first few months he'd regularly walked around the area there, experiencing the curiously compulsive attraction of names like Brewer Street, Greek Street, Old Compton Street, Wardour Street . . . a sort of litany of seediness and sleaze.

In those days, the mid-seventies, the striptease parlors, the porno cinemas, the topless bars—all somehow had been more wholesomely sinful, in the best sense of that word (or was it the worst?). Now, Soho had quite definitely changed for the better (or was it the worse?): more furtive and tawdry, more dishonest in its exploitation of the lonely, unloved men who would ever pace the pavements there and occasionally stop like rabbits in the headlights.

Yet Owens appeared far from mesmerized when in the early evening of February 7 he stopped outside Le Club Sexy. The first part of this establishment's name was intended (it must be assumed) to convey that *je-ne-sais-quoi* quality of Gallic eroticism; yet the other two parts perhaps suggested that the range of the proprietor's French was somewhat limited.

"Lookin' for a bit o' fun, love?"

The heavily mascara'd brunette appeared to be in her early twenties—quite a tall girl in her red high-heels, wearing black stockings, a minimal black skirt, and a low-cut, heavily sequined blouse stretched tightly over a large bosom—largely exposed—beneath the winking lightbulbs.

Déjà vu.

And, ever the voyeur, Owens was momentarily aware of all the old weaknesses.

"Come in! Come down and join the fun!"

She took a step toward him and he felt the long, blood-red fingernails curling pleasingly in his palm.

It was a good routine, and one that worked with many and many a man.

One that seemed to be working with Owens.

"How much?"

"Only three-pound membership, that's all. It's a private club, see—know wha' I mean?" For a few seconds she raised the eyes beneath the empurpled lids toward Elysium.

"Is Gloria still here?"

The earthbound eyes were suddenly suspicious—
yet curious, too.

"Who?"

"If Gloria's still here, she'll let me in for nothing."

"Lots o' names 'ere, mistah: real names—stage
names . . ."

"So what's your name, beautiful?"

"Look, you wanna come in? Three pound—okay?"

"You're not being much help, you know."

"Why don't you just fuck off?"

"You don't know Gloria?"

"What the 'ell do you *want*, mate?" she asked
fiercely.

His voice was very quiet as he replied. "I used to
live fairly close by. And she used to work here, then
—Gloria did. She was a stripper—one of the best in
the business, so everybody said."

For the second time the eyes in their lurid sockets
seemed to betray some interest.

"When was that?"

"Twenty-odd years ago."

"Christ! She must be a bloody granny by now!"

"Dunno. She had a child, though, I know that—a
daughter . . ."

A surprisingly tall, smartly suited Japanese man
had been drawn into the magnetic field of Le Club
Sexy.

"Come in! Come down and—"

"How much is charge?"

"Only three pound. It's a private club, see—and you gotta be a member."

With a strangely trusting, wonderfully polite smile, the man took a crisp ten-pound note from his large wallet and handed it to the hostess, bowing graciously as she reached a hand behind her and parted the multicolored vertical strips which masked from public view the threadbare carpeting on the narrow stairs leading down to the secret delights.

"You give me change, please? I give you ten pound."

"Just tell 'em downstairs, okay?"

"Why you not give me seven pound?"

"It'll be okay—okay?"

"Okay."

Halfway down the stairs, the newly initiated member made a little note in a little black book, smiling (we may say) scrutably. He was a member of a Home Office Committee licensing all "entertainment premises" in the district of Soho.

His expenses were generous: needed to be.

Sometimes he enjoyed his job.

"Don't you ever feel bad about that sort of thing?"

"What d'you mean?"

"He'll never get his change, will he?"

"Like I said, why don't you just fuck off!"

"Gloria used to feel bad sometimes—quite a civilized streak in that woman somewhere. You'd have liked her . . . Anyway, if you do come across her, just say you met me, Geoff Owens, will you? She'll remember me—certain to. Just tell her I've got a little proposition for her. She may be a bit down on her luck. You never know these days, and I wouldn't want to think she was on her uppers . . . or her daughter was, for that matter."

"What's her daughter got to do with it?" The voice was sharp.

Owens smiled, confidently now, lightly rubbing the back of his right wrist across her blouse.

"Quite a lot, perhaps. You may have quite a lot to do with it, sweetheart!"

She made no attempt to contradict him. "In the pub," she pointed across the street, "half an hour, okay?"

She watched him go, the man with a five o'clock shadow who said his name was Owens. She'd never seen him before; but she'd recognize him again immediately, the dark hair drawn back above his ears, and tied in a ponytail about eight or nine inches long.

>←

Apart from the midnight "milk float," which gave passengers the impression that it called at almost every hamlet along the line, the 11:20 P.M. was the last train from Paddington. And a panting Owens jumped into its rear coach as the Turbo Express suddenly juddered and began to move forward. The train was only half-full, and he found a seat immediately.

He felt pleased with himself. The assignation in the pub had proved to be even more interesting than he'd dared to expect; and he leaned back and closed his

eyes contentedly as he pondered the possible impli-
cations of what he had just learned . . .

He jolted awake at Didcot, wondering where he
was—realizing that he had missed the Reading stop
completely. Determined to stay awake for the last
twelve minutes of the journey, he picked up an
Evening Standard someone had left on the seat opposite, and was reading the sports page when over the
top of the newspaper he saw a man walking back
down the carriage—*almost* to where he himself was
sitting—before taking his place next to a woman.
And Owens recognized him.

Recognized Mr. Julian Storrs of Lonsdale.

Well! Well! Well!

At Oxford, his head still stuck behind the *Evening
Standard*, Owens waited until everyone else had left
the rear carriage. Then, himself alighting, he
observed Storrs arm-in-arm with his companion as
they climbed the steps of the footbridge which led
over the tracks to Platform One. And suddenly, for
the second time that evening, Owens felt a shiver of
excitement—for he immediately recognized the
woman, too.

How could he fail to recognize her?

She was his next-door neighbor.

Chapter Six

Monday, February 19

Many is the gracious form that is covered with a veil; but on withdrawing this thou discoverest a grandmother.

—Musharrif-Uddin, *Gulistan*

PAINSTAKINGLY, in block capitals, the Chief Inspector wrote his name, E. MORSE; and was beginning to write his address when Lewis came into the office at 8:35 A.M. on Monday, February 19.

"What's that, sir?"

Morse looked down at a full page torn from one of the previous day's color supplements.

"Special offer: two free CDs when you apply to join the Music Club Library."

Lewis looked dubious. "Don't forget you have to buy a book every month with that sort of thing. Life's not all freebies, you know."

"Well, it is in this case. You've just got to have a look at the first thing they send you, that's all—then send it back if you don't like it. I think they even refund the postage."

Lewis watched as Morse completed and snipped out the application form.

"Wouldn't it be fairer if you agreed to have *some* of the books?"

"You think so?"

"At least *one* of them."

Intense blue eyes, slightly pained, looked innocently across the desk at Sergeant Lewis.

"But I've already got this month's book—I bought it for myself for Christmas."

He inserted the form into an envelope, on which he now wrote the Club's address. Then he took from his wallet a sheaf of plastic cards: Bodleian Library ticket; Lloyds payment card; RAC Breakdown Service; blood donor card; Blackwell's Bookshops; Oxford City Library ticket; phonecard . . . but there appeared to be no booklet of first-class stamps there. Or of second-class.

"You don't, by any chance, happen to have a stamp on you, Lewis?"

"What CDs are you going for?"

"I've ordered Janáček, the *Glagolitic Mass*—you may not know it. Splendid work—beautifully recorded by Simon Rattle. And Richard Strauss, *Four Last Songs*—Jessye Norman. I've got several recordings by other sopranos, of course."

Of course . . .

Lewis nodded and looked for a stamp.

It was not infrequent for Lewis to be reminded of

what he had lost in life; or rather, what he'd never had in the first place. The one Strauss he knew was the "Blue Danube" man. And he'd only recently learned there were two of *those*, as well—Senior and Junior; and which was which he'd no idea.

"Perhaps you'll be in for a bit of a letdown, sir. Some of these offers—they're not exactly up to what they promise."

"You're an expert on these things?"

"No . . . but . . . take Sergeant—" Lewis stopped himself in time. Just as well to leave a colleague's weakness cloaked in anonymity. "Take this chap I know. He read this advert in one of the tabloids about a free video—sex video—sent in a brown envelope with no address to say where it had come from. You know, in case the wife . . ."

"No, I don't know, Lewis. But please continue."

"Well, he sent for one of the choices—"

"Copenhagen Red-Hot Sex?"

"No. *Housewives on the Job*—that was the title; and he expected, you know . . ."

Morse nodded. "Housewives 'on the job' with the milkman, the postman, the itinerant button-salesmen . . ."

Lewis grinned. "But it wasn't, no. It just showed all these fully dressed Swedish housewives washing up the plates and peeling the potatoes."

"Serves Sergeant Dixon right."

"You won't mention it, sir!"

"Of course I won't. And you're probably right. You never really get something for nothing in this life. I never seem to, anyway."

"Really, sir?"

Morse licked the flap of the white envelope. Then licked the back of the first-class stamp that Lewis had just given him.

The phone had been ringing for several seconds, and Lewis now took the call, listening briefly but carefully, before putting his hand over the mouthpiece:

"There's been a murder, sir. On the doorstep, really —up in Bloxham Drive."

Part Two

Chapter Seven

In addition to your loyal support on the ballot
paper, we shall be grateful if you can agree to display the enclosed sticker in one of your windows.

—Extract from a 1994 local election leaflet
distributed by the East Oxford Labor Party

IT REMINDED Morse of something—that rear window
of Number 17.

As a young lad he'd been fascinated by a photograph in one of his junior school textbooks of the
apparatus frequently fixed round the necks of slaves
in the southern states of America: an iron ring from
whose circumference, at regular intervals, there
emanated lengthy, fearsome spikes, also of iron. The
caption, as Morse recalled, had maintained that such
a device readily prevented any absconding cotton
picker from passing himself off as an enfranchised
citizen.

Morse had never really understood the caption.

Nor indeed, for some considerable while, was he
fully to understand the meaning of the neat bullet
hole in the center of the shattered glass, and the
cracks that radiated from it regularly, like a young
child's crayoning the rays of the sun.

Looking around him, Morse surveyed the area from the wobbly paving slabs which formed a pathway at the rear of the row of terraced houses stretching along the northern side of Bloxham Drive, Kidlington, Oxfordshire. About half of the thirty-odd young trees originally planted in a staggered design beside and behind this path had been vandalized to varying degrees: some of them wholly extirpated; some cruelly snapped in the middle of their gradually firming stems; others, with many of their burgeoning branches torn off, standing wounded and forlorn amid the unkempt litter-strewn area, once planned by some Environmental Officer as a small addendum to England's green and pleasant land.

Morse felt saddened.

As did Sergeant Lewis, standing beside him.

><

Yet it is appropriate here to enter one important qualification. Bloxham Drive, in the view of most of its residents, was showing some few signs of unmistakable improvement. The installation of sleeping policemen had virtually eliminated the possibilities of joyriding; many denizens were now lying more peacefully in their beds after the eviction of one notoriously antisocial household; and over the previous two or three years the properties had fallen in price to such an extent as to form an attractive proposition to those few of the professional classes who were prepared to give the street the benefit of the doubt.

To be more specific, three such persons had taken out mortgages on properties there: the properties standing at Number 1, Number 15, and Number 17.

But—yes, agreed!—Bloxham Drive and the surrounding streets was still an area a league from the peaceful, leafy lanes of Gerrards Cross; and still the scene of some considerable crime.

Crime which now included murder . . .

>‹

The call had come through to Lewis at 8:40 A.M.

Just over one hour previously, while the sky was still unusually dark, Mrs. Queenie Norris, from Number 11, had (as was her wont) taken out her eight-year-old Cavalier King Charles along the rear of the terrace, ignoring (as was her wont) the notices forbidding the fouling of pavements and verges. That was when she'd noticed it: noticed the cracked back window at Number 17—yet failed to register too much surprise, since (as we have seen) vandalism there had become commonplace, and any missile, be it bottle or brick, would have left some similar traces of damage.

Back from her walk, Mrs. Norris, as she was later to explain to the police, had felt increasingly uneasy. And just before the weather forecast on Radio 4, she had stepped out once again, now minus the duly defecated Samson, and seen that the light in the kitchen of Number 17 was still on, the blind still drawn down to the bottom of the casement.

This time she had knocked quietly, then loudly, against the back door.

But there had been no reply to her reiterated raps; and only then had she noticed that behind the hole in the kitchen window—*immediately* behind it—was a corresponding hole in the thin beige-brown material of the blind. It was at that point that she'd felt the horrid crawl of fear across her skin. Her near-neighbor worked in North Oxford, almost invariably leaving home at about a quarter to eight. And now it was coming up to the hour. Had reached the hour.

Something was wrong.

Something, Mrs. Norris suspected, was seriously wrong; and she'd rung 999 immediately.

It had been ten minutes later when PCs Graham and Swift had finally forced an entry through the front door of the property to discover the grim truth awaiting them in the back kitchen: the body of a young woman lying dead upon her side, the right cheek resting on the cold red tiles, the light brown hair of her ponytail soaked and stiffened in a pool of blood. Indeed it was not only the dreams of the two comparatively inexperienced constables, but also those of the hardened Scenes-of-Crime Officers, that would be haunted by the sight of so much blood; such a copious outpouring of blood.

And now it was Morse's turn.

⇥⇤

"Oh dear," said Lewis very quietly.

Morse said nothing, holding back (as ever) from any close inspection of a corpse, noting only the bullet wound, somewhere at the bottom of the neck, which clearly had been the cause of death, the cause of all the blood. Yet (as ever, too) Morse, who had never owned a camera in his life, had already taken several mental flashes of his own.

It seemed logical to assume that the murder had occurred toward the end of a fairly conventional breakfast. On the side of a wooden kitchen table— the side nearest the window—a brown plastic-topped stool had been moved slightly askew. On the table itself was a plate, a small heap of salt sprinkled with pepper at its edge, on which lay a brown eggshell beside a wooden eggcup; and alongside, on a second plate, half a round of toasted brown bread, buttered, and amply spread from a jar of Frank Cooper's Oxford Marmalade. And one other item: a white mug bearing the legend GREETINGS FROM GUERNSEY; bearing, too, the remains of some breakfast coffee, long since cold and muddily brown.

That was what Morse saw. And for the present that was enough; he wished to be away from the dreadful scene.

Yet before he left, he forced himself to look once more at the woman who lay there. She was wearing a white nightdress, with a faded-pink floral motif, over which was a light blue dressing gown, reaching about halfway down the shapely, slim, unstockinged legs. It was difficult to be sure about things, of course; but

Morse suspected that the twisted features of the face had been—until so very recently—just as comely as the rest of her. And for a few seconds his own face twisted, too, as if in sympathy with the murdered woman lying at his feet.

The SOCOs had now arrived; and after brief, perfunctory greetings, Morse was glad to escape and leave them to it. Bidding Lewis to initiate some immediate house-to-house inquiries, on both sides of the street, he himself stepped out of the front door into Bloxham Drive, now the scene of considerable police activity, with checkered-capped officers, the flashing blue lights of their cars, and a cordon of blue-and-white tape being thrown round the murder house. A knot of local inhabitants, too, stood whispering there, shivering occasionally in the early morning cold, yet determined to witness the course of events unfolding.

And the media.

Recognizing the Chief Inspector, two pressmen (how so early there?) pleaded for just the briefest interview—a sentence even; a TV crew from Abingdon had already covered Morse's exit from the house; and a Radio Oxford reporter waved a bulbous microphone in front of his face.

But Morse ignored them all with a look of vacuous incomprehension worthy of some deaf-mute, and proceeded to walk slowly to the end of the street (observing, all the time *observing*), where he turned left down one side of the terraced row, then left again, retracing his earlier steps along the uneven paving slabs behind the houses, stopping briefly where he and Lewis had stopped before; then completing the circuit and again curtly dismissing the converging reporters with a wave of his right hand as he walked back along the front of the terrace.

It would be untrue to say that Morse's mind had been particularly acute on this peripatetic reconnaissance. Indeed, only one single feature of the neighborhood had made much of an impression upon him.

A political impression.

Very soon (the evidence was all around him) there was to be an election for one of the local council seats—death of an incumbent, perhaps?—and clearly, if unusually, there appeared to be considerable interest in the matter. Stickers were to be observed in all but two of the front windows of the north-side terrace: green stickers with the red lettering of the Labor candidate's name; white stickers with the royal blue lettering of the Conservative's. With little as yet upon which his mind could fix itself, Morse had taken a straw poll of the support shown, from Number 1 to Number 21. And hardly surprisingly, perhaps, in this marginally depressed and predominantly working-class district, the advantage was significantly with the Labor man, with six stickers to the Tory's two.

One of the stickers favoring the latter cause was displayed in the ground-floor window of Number 15. And for some reason Morse had found himself standing and wondering for a while outside the only other window in the Drive parading its confidence in the Conservative Party—and in a candidate with the splendidly patriotic name of Jonathan Bull; standing and wondering outside Number 1, at the main entrance to Bloxham Drive.

Chapter Eight

Oft have we seen him at the peep of dawn
Brushing with hasty steps the dews away.

—Thomas Gray, *Elegy Written
in a Country Churchyard*

IN HIS EARLIER years Geoffrey Owens had been an owl, preferring to pursue whatever tasks lay before him into the late hours of the night, often through into the still, small hours. But now, in his mid-forties, he had metamorphosed into a lark, his brain seeming perceptibly clearer and fresher in the morning. It had been no hardship, therefore, when he was invited, under the new flexitime philosophy of his employers, to start work early and finish work early—thereby receiving a small bonus into the bargain. And, since the previous September, Owens had made it his regular practice to leave his home in Bloxham Drive just before 7 A.M., incidentally thus avoiding the traffic jams which began to build up in the upper reaches of the Banbury Road an hour or so later; and, on his return journey, missing the corresponding jams the other way, as thousands of motorists left the busy heart of Oxford for the comparative peace of the northern outskirts, and the neighboring villages—such as Kidlington.

It was, all in all, a happy enough arrangement. And one which had applied on Monday, February 19.

Owens had left his house at about ten minutes to seven that morning, when he had, of course, passed the house on the corner, Number 1, where a woman had watched him go. But if he in turn had spotted her, this was in no way apparent, for he had passed without a wave of recognition, and driven up to the junction, where he had turned right, on his way down into Oxford. But if he had not seen her, quite definitely she had seen him.

Traffic had been unusually light for a Monday (more often than not the busiest morning of the week) even at such a comparatively early hour; and without any appreciable holdup Owens soon reached the entrance barrier of the large car park which serves the Oxfordshire Newspapers complex down in Osney Mead, just past the railway station along the Botley Road.

Owens had come to Oxford three years previously with an impressive-looking CV, in which the applicant asserted his "all-round experience in the fields of reporting, copyediting, advertising, and personnel management." And he had been the unanimous choice of the four members of the interviewing panel. Nor had there been the slightest reason since for them to rue their decision. In fact, Owens had proved a profitable investment. With his knowledge of English grammar way above average, his job description had quickly been modified, with an appropriate increase in salary, to include responsibility for recasting the frequently ill-constructed paragraphs of his junior colleagues, and for correcting the heinous errors in orthography which blighted not a few of their offerings; and, in addition to these new tasks, to stand in as required when the Personnel Manager was called away on conferences.

As a result of these changes, Owens himself, nominally the group's senior reporter, had become more and more deskbound, venturing out only for the big stories. Like now. For as he stood in Bloxham Drive that morning, he was never in doubt that this would be one of those "big stories"—not just for himself but also for the steadily increasing number of media colleagues who were already joining him.

All of them waiting . . .

Waiting, in fact, until 11:30 A.M.—well before which time, as if by some sort of collective instinct, each was aware that something grotesque and gruesome had occurred in the house there numbered 17.

Chapter Nine

Instead of being arrested, as we stated, for kicking his wife down a flight of stairs and hurling a lighted kerosene lamp after her, the Revd. James P. Wellman died unmarried four years ago.

—Correction in a U.S. journal, quoted by Burne-Jones in a letter to Lady Horner

AT 11:15 A.M. Lewis suggested that someone perhaps ought to say something.

For the past hour and a half a group of police officers had been knocking on neighborhood doors, speaking to residents, taking brief preliminary statements. But as yet nothing official had been released to the representatives of the media assembled in a street now increasingly crowded with curious onlookers.

"Go ahead!" said Morse.

"Shall I tell them all we know?"

"That won't take you long, will it?"

"No need to keep anything back?"

"For Chrissake, Lewis! You sound as if we've *got* something to hide. If we have, why don't you tell *me*?"

"Just wondered."

Morse's tone softened. "It won't matter much what you tell 'em, will it?"

"All right."

"Just one thing, though. You can remind 'em that we'd all welcome a bit of accuracy for a change. Tell 'em to stick an 'h' in the middle of Bloxham Close —that sort of thing."

"Bloxham *Drive*, sir."

"Thank you, Lewis."

With which, a morose-looking Morse eased himself back in the armchair in the front sitting room, and continued his cursory examination of the papers, letters, documents, photographs, taken from the drawers of a Queen Anne–style escritoire—a rather tasteful piece, thought Morse. Family heirloom, perhaps.

Family . . .

Oh dear!

That was always one of the worst aspects of suicides and murders: the family. This time with Mom and Dad and younger sister already on their way up from Torquay. Still, Lewis was wonderfully good at that sort of thing. Come to think of it, Lewis was quite good at several things, really—including dealing with the Press. And as Morse flicked his way somewhat fecklessly through a few more papers, he firmly resolved (although in fact he forgot) to tell his faithful sergeant exactly that before the day was through.

❧

Immediately on confronting his interlocutors, Lewis was invited by the TV crew to go some way along the street so that he could be filmed walking before appearing in front of the camera talking. Normal TV routine, it was explained: always see a man striding along somewhere before seeing his face on the screen. So, would Sergeant Lewis please oblige with a short perambulation?

No, Sergeant Lewis wouldn't.

What he would do, though, was try to tell them what they wanted to know. Which, for the next few minutes, he did.

A murder had occurred in the kitchen of Number 17 Bloxham Drive: B-L-O-X-H-A-M—

One of the neighbors (unspecified) had earlier alerted the police to suspicious circumstances at that address—

A patrol car had been on the scene promptly; forced open the front door; discovered the body of a young woman—

The woman had been shot dead through the rear kitchen window—

The body had not as yet been officially identified—

The property appeared to show no sign—no *other* sign—of any break in—

That was about it, really.

Amid the subsequent chorus of questions, Lewis picked out the raucous notes of the formidable female reporter from the *Oxford Star*:

"What time was all this, Sergeant?"

As it happened, Lewis knew the answer to that question very well. But he decided to be economical

with the details of the surprisingly firm evidence
already gleaned . . .

>‹

The Jacobs family lived immediately opposite Number 17, where the lady of the house, in dressing gown
and curlers, had opened her front door a few minutes
after 7 A.M. in order to pick up her two pints of Co-op
milk from the doorstep. Contemporaneously, exactly
so, her actions had been mirrored across the street
where another woman, also in a dressing gown
(though without curlers), had been picking up her
own single pint. Each had looked across at the other;
each had nodded a matutinal greeting.

"You're quite *sure*?" Lewis had insisted. "It was
still a bit dark, you know."

"We've got some streetlamps, haven't we,
Sergeant?"

"You *are* sure, then."

"Unless she's got—unless she had a twin sister."

"Sure about the *time*, too? That's very important."

She nodded. "I'd just watched the news headlines
on BBC1—I like to do that. Then I turned the telly
off. I might have filled the kettle again . . . but, like I
say, it was only a few minutes past seven. Five past,
at the outside."

It therefore seemed virtually certain that there was
a time span of no more than half an hour during
which the murder had occurred: between 7:05 A.M.,
when Mrs. Jacobs had seen her neighbor opposite,

and 7:35 A.M. or so, when Mrs. Norris had first noticed the hole in the window. It was unusual—*very* unusual—for such exactitude to be established at so early a stage in a murder inquiry; and there would be little need in this case for the police to be dependent upon (what Morse always called) those prevaricating pathologists . . .

><

"About quarter past seven," answered the prevaricating Lewis.

"You're quite *sure?*" It was exactly the same question Lewis himself had asked.

"No, not sure at all. Next question?"

"Why didn't everybody hear the shot?" (The same young, ginger-headed reporter.)

"Silencer, perhaps?"

"There'd be the sound of breaking glass surely?" (A logically minded man from the *Oxford Star*.)

A series of hand gestures and silent lip movements from the TV crew urged Lewis to look directly into the camera.

Lewis nodded. "Yes. In fact several of the neighbors think they heard something—two of them certainly did. But it could have been lots of things, couldn't it?"

"Such as?" (The importunate ginger-knob again.)

Lewis shrugged. "Could have been the milkman dropping a bottle—?"

"No broken glass here, though, Sergeant."

"Car backfiring? We don't know."

"Does what the neighbors heard fit in with the time all right?" (The TV interviewer with his fluffy cylindrical microphone.)

"Pretty well, yes."

The senior reporter from the *Oxford Mail* had hitherto held his peace. But now he asked a curious question, if it was a question:

"Not the two *immediate* neighbors, were they?"

Lewis looked at the man with some interest.

"Why do you say that?"

"Well, the woman who lives there," a finger pointed to Number 19, "she was probably still asleep at the time, and she's stone-deaf without her hearing aid."

"Really?"

"And the man who lives there," a finger pointed to Number 15, "he'd already left for work."

Lewis frowned. "Can you tell me how you happen to know all this, sir?"

"No problem," replied Geoffrey Owens. "You see, Sergeant, *I* live at Number 15."

Chapter Ten

> Where lovers lie with ardent glow,
> Where fondly each forever hears
> The creaking of the bed below—
> Above, the music of the spheres.
>
> —Viscount Mumbles, 1797–1821

WHEN LEWIS RETURNED from his encounter with the media, Morse was almost ready to leave the murder house. The morning had moved toward noon, and he knew that he might be thinking a little more clearly if he were drinking a little—or at least be starting to think when he started to drink.

"Is there a real-ale pub somewhere near?"

Lewis, pleasantly gratified with his handling of the Press and TV, was emboldened to sound a note of caution.

"Doesn't do your liver much good—all this drinking."

Surprisingly Morse appeared to accept the reminder with modest grace.

"I'm sure you're right; but my medical advisers have warned me it may well be unwise to give up alcohol at my age."

Lewis was not impressed, for he had heard the

same words—exactly the same words—on several previous occasions.

"You've had a good look around, sir?"

"Not really. I know I always find the important things. But I want *you* to have a look around. You usually manage to find the *un*important things—and often they're the things that really matter in the end."

Lewis made little attempt to disguise his pleasure, and straightway relented.

"We could go up to the Boat at Thrupp?"

"Excellent."

"You don't want to stay here any longer?"

"No. The SOCOs'll be another couple of hours yet."

"You don't want to see . . . *her* again?"

Morse shook his head. "I know what she looks like —*looked* like." He picked up two colored photographs and one postcard, and made toward the front door, handing over the keys of the maroon Jaguar to Lewis. "You'd better drive—if you promise to stick to the orange juice."

➤<

Once on their way, Lewis reported the extraordinarily strange coincidence of the pressman, Owens, living next door to the murdered woman. But Morse, who always looked upon any coincidence in life as the norm rather than the exception, was more anxious to set forth the firm details he had himself now gleaned about Ms. Rachel James, for there could now be no real doubt of her identity.

"Twenty-nine. Single. No offspring. Worked as a freelance physiotherapist at a place in the Banbury Road. CV says she went to school at Torquay Comprehensive; left there in 1984 with a clutch of competent O-levels, three A-levels—two Bs, in Biology and Geography, and an E in Media Studies."

"Must have been fairly bright."

"What do you mean? You need to be a moron to get an E in Media Studies," asserted Morse, who had never seen so much as a page of any Media Studies syllabus, let alone a question paper.

He continued:

"Parents, as you know, still alive, on their way here—"

"You'll want me to see them?"

"Well, you *are* good at that sort of thing, aren't you? And if the mother's like most women she'll probably smell the beer as soon as I open the door."

"Good reason for you to join me on the orange juice."

Morse ignored the suggestion. "She bought the property there just over four years ago for £65,000 and the value's been falling ever since by the look of things, so the poor lass is one of those figuring in the negative equity statistics; took out a mortgage of £55,000—probably Mom and Dad gave her the other £10,000; and the saleable value of Number 17 is now £40,000, at the most."

"Bought at the wrong time, sir. But some people *were* a bit irresponsible, don't you think?"

"I'm not an economist, as you know, Lewis. But I'll tell you what would have helped her. Helped so many in her boots."

"A win on the National Lottery?"

"Wouldn't help *many*, that, would it? No. What she could have done with is a healthy dose of inflation. It's a good thing—inflation—you know. Especially for people who've got nothing to start with. One of the best things that happened to some of us. One year I remember I had three jumps in salary."

"Not many would agree with you on that, though, would they? Conservative and Labor both agree about inflation."

"Ah! Messrs. Bull and Thomas, you mean?"

"You noticed the stickers?"

"I notice most things. It's just that some of them don't register—not immediately."

✧

"What'll you have, sir?"

"Lew-is! We've known each other long enough, surely."

As Morse tasted the hostelry's Best Bitter, he passed over a photograph of Rachel James.

"Best one of her I could find."

Lewis looked down at the young woman.

"Real good-looker," he said softly.

Morse nodded. "I bet she'd have set a few hearts all aflutter."

"Including yours, sir?"

Morse drank deeply on his beer before replying. "She'd probably have a good few boyfriends, that's all I'm suggesting. As for my own potential susceptibility, that's beside the point."

"Of course." Lewis smiled good-naturedly. "What else have we got?"

"What do you make of this? One of the few interesting things there, as far as I could see."

Lewis now considered the postcard handed to him. First, the picture on the front: a photograph of a woodland ride, with a sunlit path on the left, and a pool of azured bluebells to the right. Then turning over the card, he read the cramped lines amateurishly typed on the left-hand side:

> *Ten Times I beg, dear Heart, let's Wed!*
> *(Thereafter long may Cupid reigne)*
> *Let's tread the Aisle, where thou hast led*
> *The fifteen Bridesmaides in thy Traine.*
> *Then spend our honeyed Moon a-bed,*
> *With Springs that creake againe—againe!*
> —John Wilmot, 1672

That was all.

No salutation.

No valediction.

And on the right-hand side of the postcard—nothing: no address, with the four dotted, parallel lines devoid of any writing, the top right-hand rectangle devoid of any stamp.

Lewis, a man not familiar with seventeenth-century

love lyrics, read the lines, then read them again, with only semicomprehension.

"Pity she didn't get round to filling in the address, sir. Looks as if she might be proposing to somebody."

"Aren't you making an assumption?"

"Pardon?"

"Did you see a typewriter in the house?"

"She could have typed it at work."

"Yes. You must get along there soon."

"You're the boss."

"Nice drop o' beer, this. In good nick." Morse drained the glass and set it down in the middle of the slightly rickety table, while Lewis took a gentle sip of his orange juice; and continued to sit firmly fixed to his seat.

Morse continued:

"No! You're making a false assumption—I *think* you are. You're assuming she'd just written this to somebody and then forgotten the fellow's address, right? Pretty unlikely, isn't it? If she was proposing to him."

"Perhaps she couldn't find a stamp."

"Perhaps . . ."

Reluctantly Morse got to his feet and pushed his glass across the bar. "You don't want anything more yourself, do you, Lewis?"

"No thanks."

"You've nothing less?" asked the landlady, as Morse tendered a twenty-pound note. "You're the first ones in today and I'm a bit short of change."

Morse turned round. "Any change on you, by any chance, Lewis?"

><

"You see," continued Morse, "you're still assuming she wrote it, aren't you?"

"And she didn't?"

"I think someone wrote the card to *her*, put it in an envelope, and then addressed the envelope—not the card."

"Why not just address the card?"

"Because whoever wrote it didn't want anyone else to read it."

"Why not just phone her up?"

"Difficult—if he was married and his wife was always around."

"He could ring her from a phone box."

"Risky—if anyone saw him."

Lewis nodded without any conviction: "And it's only a bit of poetry."

"Is it?" asked Morse quietly.

Lewis picked up the card again. "Perhaps it's this chap called 'Wilmot,' sir—the date's just there to mislead us."

"Mislead *you*, perhaps. John Wilmot, Earl of Rochester, was a court poet to Charles II. He wrote some delightfully pornographic lyrics."

"So it's—it's all genuine?"

"I didn't say that, did I? The name's genuine, but

not the poem. Any English scholar would know that's not seventeenth-century verse."

"I'm sure you're right, sir."

"And if I'm right about the card coming in an envelope—fairly recently—we might be able to find the envelope, agreed? Find a postmark, perhaps? Even a bit of handwriting?"

Lewis looked dubious. "I'd better get something organized, then."

"All taken care of! I've got a couple of the DCs looking through the wastepaper baskets and the dustbin."

"You reckon this is important, then?"

"Top priority! You can see that. She's been meeting some man—meeting him secretly. Which means he's probably married, probably fairly well-known, probably got a prominent job, probably a local man—"

"Probably lives in Peterborough," mumbled Lewis.

"That's exactly why the postmark's so vital!" countered an unamused Morse. "But if he's an Oxford man . . ."

"Do you know what the population of Oxford *is*?"

"I know it to the nearest *thousand*!" snapped Morse.

Then, of a sudden, the Chief Inspector's mood completely changed. He tapped the postcard.

"Don't be despondent, Lewis. You see, we know just a little about this fellow already, don't we?"

He smiled benignly after draining his second pint; and since no other customers had as yet entered the lounge, Lewis resignedly got to his feet and stepped over to the bar once more.

⤸⤹

Lewis picked up the postcard again.

"Give me a clue, sir."

"You know the difference between nouns and verbs, of course?"

"How could I forget something like that?"

"Well, at certain periods in English literature, all the nouns were spelled with capital letters. Now, as you can see, there are *eight* nouns in those six lines —each of them spelled with a capital letter. But there are *nine* capitals—forgetting the first word of each line. Now which is the odd one out?"

Lewis pretended to study the lines once more. He'd played this game before, and he trusted he could get away with it again, as his eyes suddenly lit up a little.

"Ah . . . I think—I *think* I see what you mean."

"Hits you in the eye, doesn't it, that 'Wed' in the first line? And that's what it was *intended* to do."

"Obviously."

"What's it mean?"

"What, 'Wed'? Well, it means 'marry'—you know, get hitched, get spliced, tie the knot—"

"What else?"

"Isn't that enough?"

"What *else*?"

"I suppose you're going to tell me it's Anglo-Saxon or something."

"Not exactly. Not far off, though. Old English, in fact. And what's it short for?"

" 'Wednesday?' " suggested Lewis tentatively.

Morse beamed at his sergeant. "Woden's day—the fourth day of the week. So we've got a *day*, Lewis. And what else do you need, if you're going to arrange a date with a woman?"

Lewis studied the lines yet again. "Time? Time, yes! I see what you mean, sir. 'Ten Times' . . . 'fifteen Bridesmaides' . . . Well, well, well! Ten-fifteen!"

Morse nodded. "With A.M. likelier than P.M. Doesn't say where though, does it?"

Lewis studied the lines for the fifth time.

" 'Traine,' perhaps?"

"Well done! 'Meet me at the station to catch the ten-fifteen A.M. train'—that's what it says. And we know where that train goes, don't we?"

"Paddington."

"Exactly."

"If only we knew who he was . . ."

Morse now produced his second photograph—a small passport-sized photograph of two people: the woman, Rachel James (no doubt of that), turning partially round and slightly upward in order to kiss the cheek of a considerably older man with a pair of smiling eyes beneath a distinguished head of graying hair.

"Who's he, sir?"

"Dunno. We could find out pretty quickly, though, if we put his photo in the local papers."

"*If* he's local."

"Even if he's not local, I should think."

"Bit dodgy, sir."

"Too dodgy at this stage, I agree. But we can try another angle, can't we? Tomorrow's Tuesday, and the day after that's Wednesday—Woden's day . . ."

"You mean he may turn up at the station?"

"If the card's fairly recent, yes."

"Unless he's heard she's been murdered."

"Or unless he murdered her himself."

"Worth a try, sir. And if he *does* turn up, it'll probably mean he didn't murder her . . ."

Morse made no comment.

"Or, come to think of it, it might be a fairly clever thing to do if he *did* murder her."

Morse drained his glass and stood up.

"You know something? I reckon orange juice occasionally germinates your brain cells."

><

As he drove his chief down to Kidlington, Lewis returned the conversation to where it had begun.

"You haven't told me what you think about this fellow Owens—the dead woman's next-door neighbor."

"Death is always the next-door neighbor," said Morse somberly. "But don't let it affect your driving, Lewis!"

Chapter Eleven

Wednesday, February 21

> *Orandum est ut sit mens sana in corpore sano*
> (Our aim? Just a brain that's not addled with pox,
> And a guaranteed clean bill-of-health from the
>   docs).
>
> —Juvenal, *Satires X*

THE NEXT MEETING of the Lonsdale Fellows had been convened for 10 A.M.

In the Stamper Room.

William Leslie Stamper, b. 1880, had graduated from Oxford University in 1903 with the highest marks (it is said) ever recorded in Classical Moderations. The bracketed caveat in the previous sentence would be unnecessary were it not that the claim for such distinction was perpetuated, in later years, by one person only—by W. L. Stamper himself. And it is pointless to dwell upon the matter since no independent verification is available: the relevant records had been removed from Oxford to a safe place, thereafter never to be seen again, during the First World War—a war in which Stamper had not been an active participant, owing to an illness which was unlikely to prolong his eminently promising career as a don for more than a couple of years or so. Such nonparticipation in the great events of 1914–18 was a major sadness (it is said) to Stamper himself, who was frequently heard to lament his own failure to figure among the casualty lists from the fields of Flanders or Passchendaele.

Now, the reader may readily be forgiven for assuming from the preceding paragraph that Stamper had been a timeserver; a dissembling self-seeker. Yet such an assumption is highly questionable, though not necessarily untrue. When, for example, in 1925, the Mastership of Lonsdale fell vacant, and nominations were sought amid the groves of Academe, Stamper had refused to let his name go forward, on the grounds that if ten years earlier he had been declared unfit to fight in defense of his country he could hardly be considered fit to undertake the governance of the College; specifically so, since the Statutes stipulated a candidate whose body was no less healthy than his brain.

Thereafter, in his gentle, scholarly, pedantic manner, Stamper had passed his years teaching the esoteric skills of Greek Prose and Verse Composition— until retiring at the age of sixty-five, two years before the statutory limit, on the grounds of ill health. No one, certainly not Stamper himself (it is said), anticipated any significant continuation of his life, and the College Fellows unanimously backed a proposal that the dear old boy should have the privilege, during the few remaining years of his life, of living in the finest set of rooms that the College had to offer.

Thus it was that the legendary Stamper had stayed on in Lonsdale as an honorary Emeritus Fellow, with full dining rights, from the year of his retirement, 1945, to 1955; and then to 1965 . . . and 1975; and almost indeed until 1985, when he had finally died at the age of 104—and then not through any dysfunction of the bodily organs, but from a fall beside his rooms in the front quad after a heavy bout of drinking at a Gaudy, his last words (it is said) being a whispered request for the Madeira to be passed round once again.

>‹

The agenda which lay before Sir Clixby Bream and his colleagues that morning was short and fairly straightforward:

(i)   To receive apologies for absence
(ii) To approve the minutes of the previous meeting (already circulated)
(iii) To consider the Auditors' statement on College expenditure, Michaelmas 1995
(iv) To recommend appropriate procedures for the election of a new Master
(v)   AOB

Items (i)–(iii) took only three minutes, and would have taken only one, had not the Tutor for Admissions sought an explanation of why the "Stationery etc." bill for the College Office had risen by four times the current rate of inflation. For which increase the Domestic Bursar admitted full responsibility, since instead of ordering 250 Biros he had inadvertently ordered 250 *boxes* of Biros.

This confession put the meeting into good humor, as it passed on to item (iv).

The Master briefly restated the criteria to be met by potential applicants: first, that he be not in Holy Orders; second, that he be mentally competent, and particularly so in the "Skills of the Arithmetick" (as the original Statute had it); third, that he be free from serious bodily infirmity. On the second criterion, the Master suggested that since it was now virtually impossible (a gentle glance here at the innumerate Professor of Arabic) to fail GCSE Mathematics, there could be little problem for anyone. As far as the third criterion was concerned however (the Master grew more solemn now) there was a sad announcement he had to make. One name previously put forward had been withdrawn—that of Dr. Ridgeway, the brilliant microbiologist from Balliol, who had developed serious heart trouble at the comparatively youthful age of forty-three.

Amid murmurs of commiseration round the table, the Master continued:

"Therefore, gentlemen, we are left with two nominations only . . . unless we . . . unless anyone . . . ? No?"

No.

Well, that was pleasing, the Master declared: he had always wished his successor to be appointed from within the College. And so it would be. Voting would take place in the time-honored way: A single sheet of paper bearing the handwritten name of the preferred candidate, with the signature of the Voting Fellow beneath it, must be delivered to the Master's Lodge before noon on the nineteenth of March, one month away.

The Master proceeded to wish the two candidates well; and Julian Storrs and Denis Cornford, by chance seated next to each other, shook hands smilingly, like a couple of boxers before the weigh-in for a bruising fight.

That was not quite all.

Under AOB, the Tutor for Admissions was moved to make his second contribution of the morning.

"Perhaps it may be possible, Master, in view of the current plethora of pens in the College Office, for the Domestic Bursar to send us each a free Biro with which we can write down our considered choices for Master?"

It was a nice touch, typical of an Oxford SCR; and when at 10:20 A.M. they left the Stamper Room and moved outside into the front quad, most of the Fellows were grinning happily.

But not the Domestic Bursar.

Nor Julian Storrs.

Nor Denis Cornford.

Chapter Twelve

The virtue of the camera is not the power it has to transform the photographer into an artist, but the impulse it gives him to keep on looking—and looking.

—Brooks Atkinson, *Once Around the Sun*

EARLIER THAT SAME morning Morse and Lewis had been sitting together drinking coffee in the canteen at Kidlington Police HQ.

"Well, that's them!" said an unwontedly ungrammatical Morse as he pointed to the photograph which some darkroom boy had managed to enlarge and enhance. "Our one big clue, that; one *small* clue, anyway."

As Lewis saw things, the enlargement appeared to have been reasonably effective as far as the clothing was concerned; yet, to be truthful, the promised "enhancement" of the two faces, those of the murdered woman and of the man so close beside her, seemed to have blurred rather than focused any physiognomical detail.

"Well?" asked Morse.

"Worse than the original."

"Nonsense! Look at that." Morse pointed to the

tight triangular knot of the man's tie, which appeared —just—above a high-necked gray sweater.

Yes. Lewis acknowledged that the color and pattern of the tie were perhaps a little clearer.

"I think I almost recognize that tie," continued Morse slowly. "That deepish maroon color. And that," he pointed again, "that narrow white stripe . . ."

"We never had ties at school," ventured Lewis.

But Morse was too deeply engrossed to bother about his sergeant's former school uniform, or lack of it, as with a magnifying glass he sought further to enhance the texture of the small relevant area of the photograph.

"Bit o' taste there, Lewis. Little bit o' class. I wouldn't be surprised if it's the tie of the Old Wyke-hamists' Classical Association."

Lewis said nothing.

And Morse looked at him almost accusingly. "You don't seem very interested in what I'm telling you."

"Not too much, perhaps."

"All right! Perhaps it's not a public-school tie. So what tie do *you* think it is?"

Again Lewis said nothing.

After a while, a semi-mollified Morse picked up the photograph, returned it to its buff-colored Do-Not-Bend envelope, and sat back in his seat.

He looked tired.

And, as Lewis knew, he was frustrated too, since necessarily the whole of the previous day had been spent on precisely those aspects of detective work that Morse disliked the most: admin., organization, procedures—with as yet little opportunity for him to indulge in the things he told himself he did the best: hypotheses, imaginings, the occasional leap into the semidarkness.

It was now 9 A.M.

"You'd better get off to the station, Lewis. And good luck!"

"What are *you* planning to do?"

"Going down into Oxford for a haircut."

"We've got a couple of new barbers' shops opened here. No need to—"

"I—am—going—down—into—Oxford, all right? A bit later, I'm going to meet a fellow who's an expert on ties, all right?"

"I'll give you a lift, if you like."

"No. It only takes one of those shapely lasses in Shepherd and Woodward's about ten minutes to trim my locks—and I'm not meeting this fellow till eleven."

"King's Arms, is it?"

"Ah! You're prepared to guess about *that*."

"Pardon?"

"So why not have a guess about the tie? Come on!"

"I dunno."

"Nor do *I* bloody know. That's exactly why we've got to guess, man."

Lewis stood by the door now. It was high time he went.

"I haven't got a clue about all those posh ties you see in the posh shops in the High. For all I know he probably got it off the tie rack in Marks and Spencer's."

"No. I don't think so."

"Couldn't we just cut a few corners? Perhaps we ought to put the photo in the *Oxford Mail*. We'd soon find out who he was then."

Morse considered the possibility anew.

"Ye-es . . . and if we find he's got nothing to do with the murder . . ."

"We can eliminate him from inquiries."

"Ye-es. Eliminate his marriage, too—"

"—if he's married—"

"—and ruin his children—"

"—if he's got any."

"You just get off to the railway station, Lewis."

Morse had had enough.

Chapter Thirteen

It is the very temple of discomfort.

—John Ruskin, *The Seven Lamps of Architecture*—
referring to the building of a railway station

AT 9:45 A.M. Lewis was seated strategically at one of the small round tables in the refreshment area adjacent to Platform One. Intermittently an echoing loudspeaker announced arrivals or apologies for delays; and, at 9:58, recited a splendid litany of all the stops on the slow train to Reading: Radley, Culham, Appleford, Didcot Parkway, Cholsey, Goring and Streatley . . .

Cholsey, yes.

Mrs. Lewis was a big fan of Agatha Christie, and he'd often promised to take her to Cholsey churchyard where the great crime novelist was buried. But one way or another he'd never got round to it.

The complex was busy, with passengers constantly leaving the station through the two automatic doors to Lewis's right, to walk down the steps outside to the taxi rank and buses for the city center; passengers constantly entering through those same doors, making for the ticket windows, the telephones, the Rail Information office; passengers turning left, past

Lewis, in order to buy newspapers, sweets, paper-backs, from the Menzies shop—or sandwiches, cakes, coffee, from the Quick Snack counter alongside.

From where he sat, Lewis could just read one of the display screens: the 10:15 train to Paddington, it appeared, would be leaving on time—no minutes late. But he had seen no one remotely resembling the man whose photograph he'd tucked inside his copy of the *Daily Mirror*.

At 10:10 A.M. the train drew in to Platform One, and passengers were now getting on. But still there was no one to engage Lewis's attention; no one standing around impatiently as if waiting for a part-ner; no one sitting anxiously consulting a wrist-watch every few seconds, or walking back and forth to the exit doors and scanning the occupants of incoming taxis.

No one.

Lewis got to his feet and went out on to the plat-form, walking quickly along the four coaches which comprised the Turbo Express for Paddington, memo-rizing as best he could the face he'd so earnestly been studying that morning. But, again, he could find no one resembling the man who had once sat beside the murdered woman in a photographic booth.

No one.

It was then, at the last minute (quite literally so), that the idea occurred to him.

A young-looking ticket collector was leaning out of one of the rear windows while a clinking refreshment trolley was being lifted awkwardly aboard. Lewis showed him his ID; showed him the photograph.

"Have you ever seen either of these two on the Paddington train? Or any other train?"

The acne-faced youth examined the ID card as if suspecting, perchance, that it might be a faulty ticket; then, equally carefully, looked down at the photograph before looking up at Lewis.

Someone blew a whistle.

"Yes, I have. Seen *him*, anyway. Do you want to know his name, Sergeant? I remember it from his Railcard."

Chapter Fourteen

A well-tied tie is the first serious step in life.

—Oscar Wilde

MORSE CAUGHT a No. 2A bus into the center of Oxford, alighting at Carfax, thence walking down the High and entering Shepherd and Woodward's, where he descended the stairs to Gerrard's hairdressing saloon.

"The usual, sir?"

Morse was glad that he was being attended to by Gerrard himself. It was not that the proprietor was gifted with trichological skills significantly superior to those of his attractive female assistants; it was just that Gerrard had always been an ardent admirer of Thomas Hardy, and during his life had acquired an encyclopedic knowledge of the great man's works.

"Yes, please," answered Morse, looking morosely into the mirror at hair that had thinly drifted these last few years from ironish-gray to purish-white.

✶✶

As Morse stood up to wipe the snippets of hair from his face with a hand towel, he took out the photograph and showed it to Gerrard.

"Has he ever been in here?"

"Don't think so. Shall I ask the girls?"

Morse considered. "No. Leave it for the present."

"Remember the Hardy poem, Mr. Morse? 'The Photograph'?"

Morse did. Yet only vaguely.

"Remind me."

"I used to have it by heart but . . ."

"We all get older," admitted Morse.

Gerrard now scanned the pages of his extraordinary memory.

"You remember Hardy'd just burned a photo of one of his old flames—he didn't know if she was alive or not—she was someone from the back of beyond of his life—but he felt awfully moved—as if he was putting her to death somehow—when he burned the photo . . . Just a minute . . . just a minute, I think I've got it:

> Well—she knew nothing thereof did she survive,
> And suffered nothing if numbered among the dead;
> Yet—yet—if on earth alive
> Did she feel a smart, and with vague strange anguish strive?
> If in heaven, did she smile at me sadly and shake her head?"

Morse felt saddened as he walked out into the High. Hardy always managed to make him feel sad. And particularly so now, since only a few days earlier he'd consigned a precious photograph to the flames: a photograph hitherto pressed between pages 88–89 of his *Collected Poems of A. E. Housman*—the photograph of a dark-haired young woman seated on a broken classical column somewhere in Crete. A woman named Ellie Smith; a woman whom he'd loved—and lost.

Morse pondered the probabilities. Had other photographs been burned or torn to little pieces since the murder of Rachel James—photographs hitherto kept in books or secret drawers?

Perhaps Lewis was right. Why not publish the photo in the *Oxford Mail*? Assuredly, there'd be hundreds of incoming calls: so many of them wrong, of course—but some few of them probably right . . .

Morse turned left into Alfred Street, and walked down the narrow cobbled lane to the junction with Blue Boar Street, where he tried the saloon-bar door of the Bear Inn.

Locked—with the opening hour displayed disappointingly as midday. It was now 11:20 A.M., and Morse felt thirsty. Perhaps he was always thirsty. That morning, though, he felt preternaturally thirsty. In fact he would gladly have swallowed a pint or two of ice-cold lager—a drink which at almost any other time would have been considered a betrayal by a real-ale addict like Morse.

He tapped lightly on the glass of the door. Tapped again. The door was opened.

A few minutes later, after offering identification, after a brief explanation of his purpose, Morse was seated with the landlord, Steven Lowbridge, at a table in the front bar.

"Would you like a coffee or something?" asked Sonya, his wife.

Morse turned round and looked toward the bar, where a row of beers paraded their pedigrees on the hand pumps.

"Is the Burton in good nick?"

The landlord (Morse learned) had been at the Bear Inn for five years, greatly enjoying his time there. A drinking house had been on the site since 1242, and undergraduates and undergraduettes were still coming in to crowd the comparatively small pub: from Oriel and Christ Church mostly; from Lincoln and Univ., too.

And the ties?

The Bear Inn was nationally—internationally—renowned for its ties: about five thousand of them at the last count. Showcases of ties covered the walls, covered the ceilings, in each of the bars: ties from Army regiments, sports clubs, schools and OB associations; ties from anywhere and everywhere. The collection started (Morse learned) in 1954, when the incumbent landlord had invited any customer with an interesting-looking tie to have the last three or four inches of its back end cut off—in exchange for a couple of pints of beer. Thereafter, the snipped-off portions were put on display in cabinets, with a small square of white card affixed to each giving provenance and description.

Morse nodded encouragingly as the landlord told his well-rehearsed tale, occasionally casting a glance at the cabinet on the wall immediately opposite: Yale University Fencing Club; Kenya Police; Welsh Schoolboys' Hockey Association; Women's Land Army . . .

Ye gods!

What a multitude of ties!

Morse's glass was empty; and the landlady tentatively suggested that the Chief Inspector would perhaps enjoy a further pint?

Morse had no objection; and made his way to the Gents where, as he washed his hands, he wondered whether all the washbasin plugs in the world could have disappeared—plugs from every pub, from every hotel, from every public convenience in the land. Somewhere (Morse mused) there must surely be a prodigious pile of basin plugs, as high as some Egyptian pyramid.

Back in the bar, Morse produced his photograph and pointed to the little patch of tie.

"Do you think there's anything like that here?"

Lowbridge looked down at the slimly striped maroon tie, shaking his head dubiously.

"Don't *think* so . . . But make yourself at home—please have a look round—for as long as you like."

Morse experienced disappointment.

If only Lewis were there! Lewis—so wonderfully competent with this sort of thing: checking, checking, checking, the contents of the cabinets.

Help, Lewis!

But Lewis was elsewhere. And for twenty-five minutes or so, Morse moved round the two bars, with increasing fecklessness and irritation.

Nothing was matching . . .

Nothing.

"Find what you're after?" It was the darkly attractive Sonya, just returned from a shopping expedition to the Westgate Centre.

"No, sadly no," admitted Morse. "It's a bit like a farmer looking for a lost contact lens in a plowed field."

"That what you're looking for?"

Sonya Lowbridge pointed to the tie in the photograph that still lay on the table there.

Morse nodded. "That's it."

"But I can tell you where you can find that."

"You can?" Morse's eyes were suddenly wide, his mouth suddenly dry.

"Yep! I was looking for a tie for Steve's birthday. And you'll find one just like that on the tie rack in Marks and Spencer's."

Chapter Fifteen

A Slave has but one Master; yet ambitious folk
have as many masters as there are people who may
be useful in bettering their position.

—La Bruyère, *Characters*

"WELL?"

Julian Storrs closed the front door behind him,
hung up his dripping plastic mac, and took his wife
into his arms.

"No external candidates—just the two of us."

"That's wonderful news!" Angela Storrs moved
away from her husband's brief, perfunctory embrace,
and led the way into the lounge of the splendidly furnished property in Polstead Road, a thoroughfare
linking the Woodstock Road with Aristotle Lane (the
latter, incidentally, Morse's favorite Oxford street
name).

"Certainly not bad news, is it? If the gods just smile
on us a little . . ."

"Drink?"

"I think I may have earned a small brandy."

She poured his drink; poured herself a large dry martini; lit a cigarette; and sat beside him on the brown-
leather settee. She clinked her glass with his, and
momentarily her eyes gleamed with potential triumph.

"To *you*, Sir Julian!"

"Just a minute! We've got to win the bloody thing first. No pushover, old Denis, you know: good College man—fine scholar—first-class brain—"

"Married to a second-class tart!"

Storrs shook his head with an uneasy smile.

"You're being a bit cruel, love."

"Don't call me 'love'—as if you come from Rotherham, or somewhere."

"What's wrong with Rotherham?" He put his left arm around her shoulders, and forced an affectionate smile to his lips as he contemplated the woman he'd married just over twenty years previously—then pencil-slim, fresh-faced, and wrinkle-free.

Truth to tell, she was aging rather more quickly than most women of her years. Networks of varicose veins marred the long, still-shapely legs; and her stomach was a little distended around the waistband of the elegant trouser-suits which recently she almost invariably wore. The neck had grown rather gaunt, and there were lines and creases round her eyes. Yet the face itself was firmly featured still; and to many a man she remained an attractive woman—as she had appeared to Julian Storrs when first he had encountered her . . . in those extraordinary circumstances. And few there were who even now could easily resist the invitation of those almond eyes when after some dinner party or drinks reception she removed the dark glasses she had begun to wear so regularly.

Having swiftly swallowed her martini, Angela

Storrs got to her feet and poured herself another—her husband making no demur. In fact, he was quite happy when she decided to indulge her more than occasional craving for alcohol, since then she would usually go to bed, go to sleep, and reawaken in a far more pleasant frame of mind.

"What are your chances—honestly?"

"Hope is a Christian virtue, you know that."

"Christ! Can't you think of anything better to say than that?"

He was silent awhile. "It means a lot to you, Angela, doesn't it?"

"It means a lot to you, too," she replied, allowing her slow words to take their full effect. "It *does*, doesn't it?"

"Yes," he replied softly, "it means almost everything to me."

Angela got up and poured herself another martini.

"I'm glad you said that. You know why? Because it doesn't just mean *almost* everything to me—it means *literally* everything. I want to be the Master's Wife, Julian. I want to be Lady Angela! Do you understand how much I want that?"

"Yes . . . yes, I think I do."

"So . . . so if we have to engage in any 'dirty tricks' business . . ."

"What d'you mean?"

"Nothing specific."

"What d'you mean?" he repeated.

"As I say . . ."

"Come on! Tell me!"

"Well, let's say if it became known in the College that Shelly Cornford was an insatiable nymphomaniac . . . ?"

"That just isn't *fair*!"

Angela Storrs got to her feet and drained the last drop of her third drink:

"Who said it *was*?"

"Where are you going?"

"Upstairs, for a lie down, if you don't object. I'd had a few before you got back—hadn't you noticed? But I don't suppose so, no. You haven't really noticed me much at all recently, have you?"

"What's that supposed to mean?"

But she was already leaving the room, and seemed not to hear.

Storrs took another small sip of his brandy, and pulled the copy of the previous evening's *Oxford Mail* from the lower shelf of the coffee table, its front-page headline staring at him again:

MURDER AT KIDLINGTON
Woman Shot Through Kitchen Window

><

"What did you tell Denis?"

"He's got a tutorial, anyway. I just said I'd be out shopping."

"He told you about the College Meeting?"

She nodded.

"You pleased?"

"Uh, uh!"

"It'll be a bit of a nerve-racking time for you."

"You should know!"

"Only a month of it, though."

"What d'you think his chances are?"

"Difficult to say."

"Will *you* vote for him?"

"I don't have a vote."

"Unless it's a tie."

"Agreed. But that's unlikely, they tell me. Arithmetically quite impossible—if all twenty-three Fellows decide to vote."

"So you won't really have much say in things at all."

"Oh, I wouldn't say that. I'll be a bit surprised if one or two of the Fellows don't ask me for a little advice about, er, about their choice."

"And?"

"And I shall try to be helpful."

"To Denis, you mean?"

"Now I didn't *say* that, did I?"

The great cooling towers of Didcot power station loomed into view on the left, and for a while little more was said as the two of them continued the drive south along the A34, before turning off, just before the Ridgeway, toward the charming little village of West Ilsley.

"I feel I'm letting poor old Denis down a bit," he said, as the dark blue Daimler pulled up in front of the village pub.

"Don't you think *I* do?" she snapped. "But I don't keep on about it."

At the bar, he ordered a dry white wine for Shelly Cornford and a pint of Old Speckled Hen for himself; and the pair of them studied the Egon Ronay menu chalked up on a blackboard before making their choices, and sitting down at a window table overlooking the sodden village green.

"Do you think we should stop meeting?" He asked it quietly.

She appeared to consider the question more as an exercise in logical evaluation than as any emotional dilemma.

"I don't want that to happen."

She brushed the back of her right wrist down the front of his dark gray suit.

"Pity we've ordered lunch," he said quietly.

"We can always give it a miss."

"Where shall we go?"

"Before we go anywhere, I shall want *you* to do something for *me*."

"You mean something for Denis?"

She nodded decisively.

"I can't really promise you too much, you know that."

She looked swiftly around the tables there, before moving her lips to his ear. "*I* can, though. I can promise you everything, Clixby," she whispered.

✢

From his room in College, Denis Cornford had rung Shelly briefly just before 11 A.M. She'd be out later, as she'd mentioned, but he wanted to tell her about the College Meeting as soon as possible.

He told her.

He was pleased—she could sense that.

She was pleased—he could sense that.

Cornford had half an hour to spare before his next tutorial with a very bright first-year undergraduette from Nottingham who possessed one of the most astonishingly retentive memories he had ever encountered, and a pair of the loveliest legs that had ever folded themselves opposite him. Yet he experienced not even the mildest of erotic daydreams as now, briefly, he thought about her.

He walked over to the White Horse, the narrow pub between the two Blackwell's shops just opposite the Sheldonian; and soon he was sipping a large Glenmorangie, and slowly coming to terms with the prospect that in a month's time he might well be the Master of Lonsdale College. By nature a diffident man, he was for some curious reason beginning to feel a little more confident about his chances. Life was a funny business—and the favorite often failed to win the Derby, did it not?

Yes, odd things were likely to happen in life.

Against all the odds, as it were.

His black-stockinged student was sitting cross-legged on the wooden steps outside his room, getting

to her feet as soon as she saw him. Being with Cornford, talking with him for an hour every week—that
had become the highlight of her time at Oxford. But
History was the great fascination in his life—not her.

She knew that.

Chapter Sixteen

Prosōpagnoia (n.): the failure of any person to recognize the face of any other person, howsoever recently the aforementioned persons may have mingled in each other's company.

> —*Small's Enlarged English Dictionary*,
> 13th Edition, 1806

FROM OXFORD RAILWAY station, at 10:20 A.M., Lewis had tried to ring Morse at HQ. But to no avail. The dramatic news would have to wait awhile, and at least Lewis now had ample time to execute his second order of the day.

There had been just the two of them at the Oxford Physiotherapy Center—although "Center" seemed a rather grandiloquent description of the ground-floor premises of the large, detached redbrick house halfway down the Woodstock Road ("1901" showing on the black drainpipe): the small office, off the spacious foyer; the single treatment room, to the right, its two beds separated by mobile wooden screens; and an inappropriately luxurious loo, to the left.

Rachel James's distressed partner, a plain-featured, muscular divorcée in her mid-forties, could apparently throw little or no light on the recent tragedy. Each of them a fully qualified physiotherapist, they had gone freelance after a difference of opinion with the Hospital Trust, and two years earlier had decided to join forces and form their own private practice: women for the most part, troubled with ankles and knees and elbows and shoulders. The venture had been fairly successful, although they would have welcomed a few more clients—especially Rachel, perhaps, who (as Lewis learned for a second time) had been wading deeper and deeper into negative equity.

Boyfriends?—Lewis had ventured.

Well, she was attractive—face, figure—and doubtless there had been a good many admirers. But no specific beau; no one that Rachel spoke of as anyone special; no incoming calls on the office phone, for example.

"That hers?" Lewis had asked.

"Yes."

Lewis took down a white coat from its hook behind the door and looked at the oval badge: CHARTERED SOCIETY OF PHYSIOTHERAPY printed round a yellow crest. He felt inside the stiffly starched pockets.

Nothing.

Not even Morse (Lewis allowed the thought) could have made much of *that*.

Each of the two women had a personal drawer in the office desk, and Lewis looked carefully through the items which Rachel had kept at hand during her own working hours: lipstick; lip salve; powder compact; deodorant stick; a small packet of tissues; two

Biros, blue and red; a yellow pencil; a pocket English dictionary (OUP); and a library book. Nothing else. No personal diary; no letters.

Again Lewis felt (though wrongly this time) that Morse would have shared his disappointment.

><

As for Morse, he had called in at his bachelor flat in North Oxford before returning to Police HQ. Always, after a haircut, he went through the ritual of washing his hair—and changing his shirt, upon which even a few stray hairs left clinging seemed able to effect an intense irritation on what, as he told himself (and others), was a particularly sensitive skin.

When he finally returned to HQ he found Lewis already back from his missions.

"You're looking younger, sir."

"No, you're wrong. I reckon this case has put years on me already."

"I meant the haircut."

"Ah, yes. Rather nicely done, isn't it?"

"You had a good morning, sir—apart from the haircut?"

"Well, you know—er—satisfactory. What about you?"

Lewis smiled happily.

"Do you want the good news first or the bad news?"

"The bad news."

"Well, not 'bad'—just not 'news' at all, really. I

don't think we're going to get many leads from her workplace. In fact I don't think we're going to get any." And Lewis proceeded to give an account of his visit to the Oxford Physiotherapy Centre.

"What time did she get there every morning?"

Lewis consulted his notes. "Five past, ten past eight —about then. Bit early. But if she left it much later she'd hit the heavy Kidlington traffic down into Oxford, wouldn't she?"

"Mm . . . The first treatments don't begin till quarter to nine, you say."

"Or nine o'clock."

"What did she do before the place opened?"

"Dunno."

"*Read*, Lewis!"

"Well, like I said, there was a library book in her drawer."

"What was it?"

"I didn't make a note."

"Can't you remember?"

Ye-es, Lewis thought he could. Yes!

"Book called *The Masters*, sir—by P. C. Snow."

Morse laughed and shook his head.

"He wasn't a bloody police constable, Lewis! You mean *C. P.* Snow."

"Sorry, sir."

"Interesting, though."

"In what way?"

But Morse ignored the question.

"*When* did she get it from the library?"

"How do I know?"

"You just," said Morse slowly, sarcastically, "take fourteen days from the date printed for the book's return, which you could have found, if you'd looked, by gently opening the front cover."

"Perhaps they let you have three weeks—at the library she borrowed it from."

"And which library was that?"

Somehow Lewis managed to maintain his good humor.

"Well, at least I can give you a very straight answer to that: I haven't the faintest idea."

"And what's the good news?"

This time, it was Lewis's turn to make a slow, impressive pronouncement:

"I know who the fellow is—the fellow in the photo."

"You do?" Morse looked surprised. "You mean he turned up at the station?"

"In a way, I suppose he did, yes. There was no one like him standing around waiting for his girlfriend. But I had a word with this ticket collector—young chap who's only been on the job for a few weeks. And he recognized him straightaway. He'd asked to look at his rail pass and he remembered him because he got a bit shirty with him—and probably because of that he remembered his name as well."

"A veritable plethora of pronouns, Lewis! Do you know how many *he*'s and *him*'s and *his*'s you've just used?"

"No. But I know *one* thing—he told me his name!" replied Lewis, happily adding a further couple of potentially confusing pronouns to his earlier tally. "His name's *Julian Storrs*."

For many seconds Morse sat completely motionless, feeling the familiar tingling across his shoulders. He picked up his silver Parker pen and wrote some letters on the blotting pad in front of him. Then, in a whispered voice, he spoke:

"*I know him, Lewis.*"

"You didn't recognize him, though—?"

"Most people," interrupted Morse, "as they get older, can't remember names. For them 'A name is troublesome'—anagram—seven letters—what's that?"

" 'Amnesia'?"

"Well done! I'm all right on names, usually. But as I get older it's *faces* I can't recall. And there's a splendid word for this business of not being able to recognize familiar faces—"

" 'Pro-sop-a-something,' isn't it?"

Morse appeared almost shell-shocked as he looked across at his sergeant. "How in heaven's name . . . ?"

"Well, as you know, sir, I didn't do all that marvelously at school—as I told you, we didn't even have a school tie—but I was ever so good at one thing," a glance at the blotting pad, "I was best in the class at reading things upside down."

Chapter Seventeen

Facing the media is more difficult than bathing a leper.

—Mother Teresa of Calcutta

THERE HAD BEEN little difficulty in finding out information on Julian Charles Storrs—a man to whom Morse (as he now remembered) had been introduced only a few months previously at an exhibition of Thesiger's desert photography in the Pitt Rivers Museum. But Morse said nothing of this to Lewis as the pair of them sat together that same evening in Kidlington HQ; said nothing either of his discovery that the tie whose provenance he had so earnestly sought was readily available from any Marks & Spencer's store, priced £6.99.

"We shall have to see this fellow Storrs soon, sir."

"I'm sure we shall, yes. But we've got nothing against him, have we? It's not a criminal offense to get photographed with some attractive woman. . . . Interesting, though, that she was reading *The Masters.*"

"I've never read it, sir."

"It's about the internal shenanigans in a Cambridge College when the Master dies. And recently I read in the *University Gazette* that the present Master of

Lonsdale is about to hang up his mortarboard—see what I mean?"

"I think I do," lied Lewis.

"Storrs is a Fellow at Lonsdale—the Senior Fellow, I think. So if he suggested she might be interested in reading that book . . ."

"Doesn't add up to much, though, does it? It's *motive* we've got to look for. Bottom of everything —motive is."

Morse nodded. "But perhaps it does add up a bit," he added quietly. "If he wants the top job badly enough—and if she reminded him she could go and queer his pitch . . ."

"Kiss-and-tell sort of thing?"

"Kiss-and-*not*-tell, if the price was right."

"Blackmail?" suggested Lewis.

"She'd have letters."

"The postcard."

"Photographs."

"*One* photograph."

"Hotel records. Somebody would use a credit card, and it wouldn't be *her*."

"He'd probably pay by cash."

"You're not trying to *help* me by any chance, are you, Lewis?"

"All I'm trying to do is be honest about what we've got—which isn't much. I agree with you, though: it wouldn't have been *her* money. Not exactly rolling in it, that's for sure. Must have been a biggish layout

—setting up the practice, equipment, rent, and everything. And she'd got a mortgage on her own place, and a car to run."

Yes, a car. Morse, who never took the slightest interest in any car except his own, visualized again the white Mini which had been parked outside Number 17.

"Perhaps you ought to look a bit more carefully at that car, Lewis."

"Already have. Logbook in the glove compartment, road atlas under the passenger seat, fire extinguisher under the back seat—"

"No drugs or pornography in the boot?"

"No. Just a wheel brace and a Labor party poster."

Lewis looked at his watch: 8:35 P.M. It had been a long day, and he felt very tired. And so, by the look of him, did his chief. He got to his feet.

"Oh, and two cassettes: Ella Fitzgerald and a Mozart thing."

"*Thing?*"

"Clarinet thing, yes."

"Concerto or Quintet, was it?"

Blessedly, before Lewis could answer (for he had no answer), the phone rang.

Chief Superintendent Strange.

"Morse? In your office? I almost rang the Red Lion."

"How can I help, sir?" asked Morse wearily.

"TV—that's how you can help. BBC wants you for

the *Nine O'clock News* and ITV for *News at Ten*. One of the crews is here now."

"I've already told 'em all we know."

"Well, you'd better think of something else, hadn't you? This isn't just a murder, Morse. This is a *PR exercise*."

Chapter Eighteen

Thursday, February 22

> For example, in such enumerations as "French,
> German, Italian, and Spanish," the two commas
> take the place of "ands"; there is no comma after
> "Italian," because, with "and," it would be otiose.
> There are, however, some who favor putting one
> there, arguing that, since it may sometimes be
> needed to avoid any ambiguity, it may as well be
> used always for the sake of uniformity.
>
> —Fowler, *Modern English Usage*

JUST AFTER LUNCHTIME on Thursday, Morse found himself once again wandering aimlessly around Number 17 Bloxham Drive, a vague, niggling instinct suggesting to him that earlier he'd missed something of importance there.

But he was beginning to doubt it.

In the now-cleared kitchen, he switched on the wireless, finding it attuned to Radio 4. Had it been *on* when the police had first arrived? Had she been listening to the *Today* program when just for a second, perhaps, she'd looked down at the gush of blood that had spurted over the front of her nightclothes?

So what if she had been? Morse asked himself, conscious that he was getting nowhere.

In the front living room, he looked again along the single shelf of paperbacks. Women novelists, mostly: Jackie Collins, Jilly Cooper, Danielle Steel, Sue Townsend. . . . He read four or five of the authors' opening sentences, without once being instantly hooked, and was about to leave when he noticed Craig Raine's *A Choice of Kipling's Prose*—its white spine completely uncreased, as if it had been a very recent purchase. Or a gift? Morse withdrew the book and flicked through some of the short stories that once had meant—still meant—so very much to him. "They" was there, although Morse confessed to himself that he had never really understood its meaning. But genius? Christ, ah! And "On Greenhow Hill"; and "Love-o'-Women" —the latter (Morse was adamant about it) the greatest short story in the English language. He looked at the title page: no words *to* anyone; *from* anyone. Then, remembering a book he'd once received from a lovely, lost girl, he turned to the inside of the back cover: and there, in the bottom right-hand corner, he saw the penciled capitals: FOR R FROM J — RML.

"Remember My Love."

It could have been anyone though—so many names beginning with "J": Jack, James, Jason, Jasper, Jeremy, John, Joseph, Julian . . .

So what?

Anyway, these days, Morse, it could have been a woman, could it not?

><

Upstairs, in the front bedroom, he looked down at the double bed that almost monopolized the room, and noted again the two indented pillows, one atop the other, in their Oxford blue pillowcases, whereon for the very last time Rachel James had laid her pretty head. The winter duvet, in matching blue, was still turned back as she had left it, the under sheet only lightly creased. Nor was it a bed (of this Morse felt certain) wherein the murdered woman had spent the last night of her life in passionate lovemaking. Better, perhaps, if she had . . .

Standing on the bedside table was a glass of stale-looking water, beside which lay a pair of bluish earrings whose stones (Morse suspected) had never been fashioned from earth's more precious store.

But the Chief Inspector was forming something of a picture, so he thought.

Picture . . . Pictures . . .

Two framed pictures only on the bedroom walls: the statutory Monet; and one of Gustav Klimt's gold-patterned compositions. Plenty of posters and stickers, though: anti deer hunting; anti export of live animals; anti French nuclear tests; pro the NHS; pro the whales; pro legalized abortion. About par for the course at her age, thought Morse. Or at *his* age, come to think of it.

He pulled the side of the curtains slightly away from the wall, and briefly surveyed the scene below. An almost reverent hush now seemed to have settled upon Rachel's side of the street. One uniformed policeman stood at the front gate—but only the one—talking to a representative of the Press—but only the one: the one who had lived next door to the murdered woman, at Number 15; the one with the ponytail; the one whom Morse would have to interview so very soon; the one he ought already to have interviewed.

Then, from the window, he saw his colleague, Sergeant Lewis, getting out of a marked police car; and thoughtfully he walked down the stairs. Odd—very odd, really—that with all those stickers around the bedroom, the one for the party the more likely (surely?) to further those advertised causes had been left in the boot of her car, where earlier Lewis had found it. Why hadn't she put it up, as so many other householders in the terrace had done, in one of her upper or lower windows?

Aware that whatever had been worrying him had still not been identified, Morse turned the Yale lock to admit Lewis, the latter carrying the lunchtime edition of the *Oxford Mail*.

"I reckon it's about time we interviewed *him*," began Lewis, pointing through the closed door.

"All in good time," agreed Morse, taking the newspaper where, as on the previous two days, the murder still figured on page one, although no longer as the lead story.

POLICE PUZZLED BY
KIDLINGTON KILLING

The brutal murder of the physiotherapist Rachel James, which has caused such a stir in the local community, has left the police baffled, according to Inspector Morse of the Thames Valley CID.

The murdered woman was seen as a quietly unobtrusive member of the community with no obvious enemies, and as yet the police have been unable to find any plausible motive for her murder.

Neighbors have been swift to pay their tributes. Mrs. Emily Jacobs, who waved a greeting just before Rachel was murdered, said she was a friendly, pleasant resident who would be sadly missed.

Similar tributes were paid by other local inhabitants who are finding it difficult to come to terms with their neighborhood being the scene of such a terrible murder and a center of interest for the national media.

For the present, however, Bloxham Drive has been sealed off to everyone except local residents, official reporters and a team of police officers carefully searching the environs of No. 17.

But it seems inevitable that the street will soon be a magnet for sightseers, drawn by a ghoulish if natural curiosity, once police activity is scaled down and restrictions are lifted.

A grim-faced Sergeant Lewis, after once again examining the white Mini still parked outside the property, would make no comment other than confirming that various leads were being followed.

Rachel's parents, who live in Devon, have identified

the body as that of their daughter, and a bouquet of white lilies bearing the simple inscription "To our darling daughter" lies in cellophaned wrapping beside the front gate of No. 17.

The tragedy has cast a dark cloud over the voting taking place today for the election of a councillor to replace Terry Burgess who died late last year following a heart attack.

"Nicely written," conceded Morse. "Bit pretentious, perhaps . . . and I do wish they'd all stop *demoting* me!"

"No mistakes?"

Morse eyed his sergeant sharply. "Have I missed something?"

Lewis said nothing, smiling inexplicably, as Morse read through the article again.

"Well, I'd've put a comma after 'reporters' myself. Incidentally, do you know what such a comma's called?"

"Remind me."

"The 'Oxford Comma.' "

"Of course."

"Why are you grinning?"

"That's just it, sir. It's that 'grim-faced.' Should be 'grin-faced,' shouldn't it? You see, the missus rang me up half an hour ago: she's won fifty pounds on the Premium Bonds. Bond, really. She's only got one of 'em."

"Congratulations!"

"Thank you, sir."

For a final time Morse looked through the article, wondering whether the seventeenth word from the beginning and the seventeenth word from the end had anything to do with the number of the house in which Rachel James had been murdered. Probably not. Morse's life was bestrewn with coincidences.

"Is that ponytailed ponce still out there?" he asked suddenly.

Lewis looked out of the front window.

"No, sir. He's gone."

"Let's hope he's gone to one of those new barbers' shops you were telling me about?" Morse's views were beset with prejudices.

Chapter Nineteen

She is disturbed
When the phone rings at 5 A.M.
And with such urgency
Aware that one of these calls
Will summon her to witness another death
Commanding more words than she
The outside observer can provide—and yet
Notepad poised and ready
She picks up the receiver.

—Helen Peacocke, *Ace Reporter*

AT 2:25 P.M. THAT same day, Morse got into the maroon Jaguar and after looking at his wristwatch drove off. First, down to the Cutteslowe Roundabout, then straight over and along the Banbury Road to the Martyrs' Memorial, where he turned right into Beaumont Street, along Park End Street, and out under the railway bridge into Botley Road, where just beyond the river bridge he turned left into the Osney Industrial Estate.

There was, in fact, one vacant space in the limited parking lots beside the main reception area to Oxford City and County Newspapers; but Morse pretended not to notice it. Instead he asked the girl at the reception desk for the open sesame to the large staff car park, and was soon watching the black-and-white barrier lift as he inserted a white plastic card into some electronic contraption there. Back in reception, the same young girl retrieved the precious ticket before giving Morse a VISITOR badge, and directing him down a corridor alongside, on his left, a vast open-plan complex, where hundreds of newspaper personnel appeared too preoccupied to notice the "Visitor."

Owens, as Morse discovered, was one of the few employees granted some independent square-footage there, his small office hived off by wood-and-glass partitions.

"You live, er, she lived next door, I'm told," began Morse awkwardly.

Owens nodded.

"Bit of luck, I suppose, in a way—for a reporter, I mean?"

"For me, yes. Not much luck for her, though, was it?"

"How did you first hear about it? You seem to have been on the scene pretty quickly, sir."

"Della rang me. She lives in the Drive—Number 1. She'd seen me leave for work."

"What time was that?"

"Must have been . . . ten to seven, five to seven?"

"You usually leave about then?"

"I do now, yes. For the past year or so we've been working a fair amount of flexitime and, well, the earlier I leave home the quicker I'm here. Especially in term time when—" Owens looked shrewdly across his desk at Morse. "But you know as much as I do about the morning traffic from Kidlington to Oxford."

"Not really. I'm normally going the other way—North Oxford to Kidlington."

"Much more sensible."

"Yes . . ."

Clearly Owens was going to be more of a heavy-weight than he'd expected, and Morse paused awhile to take his bearings. He'd made a note only a few minutes since of exactly how long the same distance had taken him, from Bloxham Drive to Osney Mead. And even with quite a lot of early afternoon traffic about—even with a couple of lights against him—he'd done the journey in fourteen and a half minutes.

"So you'd get here at about . . . about *when*, Mr. Owens?"

The reporter shrugged his shoulders. "Quarter past? Twenty past? Usually about then."

A nucleus of suspicion was beginning to form in Morse's brain as he sensed that Owens was perhaps exaggerating the length of time it had taken him to reach work that Monday morning. If he *had* left at, say, ten minutes to seven, he could well have been in the car park at—what?—seven o'clock? With a bit of luck? So why . . . why had Owens suggested quarter past—even twenty past?

"You can't be more precise?"

Again Morse felt the man's shrewd eyes upon him.

"You mean the later I got here the less likely I am to be a suspect?"

"You realize how important times are, Mr. Owens —a sequence of times—in any murder inquiry like this?"

"Oh yes, I know it as well as you do, Inspector. I've covered quite a few murders in my time. . . . So . . . so why don't you ask Della what time she saw me leave? Della Cecil, that is, at Number 1. She'll probably remember better than me. And as for getting here . . . well, that'll be fairly easy to check. Did you know that?"

Owens took a small white rectangular card from his wallet, with a number printed across the top—008 14922—and continued: "I push that in the thing there and the whatsit goes up and something somewhere records the time I get into the car park."

Clearly the broad-faced, heavy-jowled reporter had about as much specialist knowledge of voodoo technology as Morse, and the latter switched the thrust of his questions.

"This woman who saw you leave, I shall have to see her—you realize that?"

"You wouldn't be doing your job if you didn't. Cigarette, Inspector?"

"Er, no, no thanks. Well, er, perhaps I will, yes. Thank you. This woman, as I say, do you know her well?"

"Only twenty houses in the Drive, Inspector. You get to know most people, after a while."

"You never became, you know, more friendly? Took her out? Drink? Meal?"

"Why do you ask that?"

"I've just got to find out as much as I can about everybody there, that's all. Otherwise, as you say, I wouldn't be doing my job, would I, Mr. Owens?"

"We've had a few dates, yes—usually at the local."

"Which is?"

"The Bull and Swan."

"Ah, 'Brakspear,' 'Bass,' 'Bishop's Finger' . . ."

"I wouldn't know. I'm a lager man myself."

"I see," said a sour-faced Morse. Then, after a pause, "What about Rachel James? Did you know her well?"

"She lived next *door*, dammit! Course I knew her fairly well."

"Did you ever go inside her house?"

Owens appeared to consider the question carefully. "Just the twice, if I've got it right. Once when I had a few people in for a meal and I couldn't find a corkscrew and I knocked on her back door and she asked me in, because it was pissing the proverbials, while she looked around for hers. The other time was one hot day last summer when I was mowing the grass at the back and she was hanging out her smalls and I asked her if she wanted me to do her patch and she said she'd be grateful, and when I'd done it she asked me if I'd like a glass of something and we had a drink together in the kitchen there."

"Lager, I suppose."

"Orangeade."

Orangeade, like water, had never played any significant role in Morse's dietary, but he suddenly realized that at that moment he would have willingly drunk a pint of anything, so long as it was ice-cold.

Even lager.

"It was a hot day, you say?"

"Boiling."

"What was she wearing?"

"Not much."

"She was an attractive girl, wasn't she?"

"To me? I'm always going to be attracted to a woman with not much on. And, as I remember, most of what she'd got on that day was mostly off, if you follow me."

"So she'd have a lot of boyfriends?"

"She was the sort of woman men would lust after, yes."

"Did you?"

"Let's put it this way, Inspector. If she'd invited me to bed that afternoon, I'd've sprinted up the stairs."

"But she didn't invite you?"

"No."

"Did she invite other men?"

"I doubt it. Not in Bloxham Drive, anyway. We don't just have Neighborhood Watch here; we've got a continuous Nosey-Parker Surveillance Scheme."

"Even in the early morning?"

"As I told you, somebody saw me go to work on Monday morning."

"You think others may have done?"

"Bloody sure they did!"

Morse switched tack again. "You wouldn't remember—recognize—any of her occasional boyfriends?"

"No."

"Have you heard of a man called Julian Storrs?"

"Yes."

"You know him?"

"Not really, no. But he's from Lonsdale, and I interviewed him for the *Oxford Mail* last year—December, I think it was—when he gave the annual Pitt Rivers Lecture. On Captain Cook, as I recall. I'd never realized how much the natives hated that fellow's guts—you know, in the Sandwich Islands or somewhere."

"I forget," said Morse, as if at some point in his life he *had* known . . .

At his local grammar school, the young Morse had been presented with a choice of the 3 Gs: Greek, Geography, or German. And since Morse had joined the Greek option, his knowledge of geography had ever been fatally flawed. Indeed, it was only in his late twenties that he had discovered that the Balkan States and the Baltic States were not synonymous. Yet about Captain Cook's voyages Morse should (as we shall see) have known at least a little—*did* know a little—since his father had adopted that renowned British navigator, explorer, and cartographer as his greatest hero in life—unlike (it seemed) the natives of those "Sandwich Islands or somewhere. . . ."

"You never saw Mr. Storrs in Bloxham Drive?"

In their sockets, Owens' eyes shot from bottom left to top right, like those of a deer that has suddenly sniffed a predator.

"Never. Why?"

"Because," Morse leaned forward a few inches as he summoned up all his powers of creative ingenuity, "because someone in the Drive—this is absolutely confidential, sir!—says that he was seen, fairly recently, going into, er, another house there."

"*Which* house?" Owens' voice was suddenly sharp.

Morse held up his right hand and got to his feet. "Just a piece of gossip, like as not. But we've got to check out every lead, you know that."

Owens remained silent.

"You've always been a journalist?"

"Yes."

"Which papers . . . ?"

"I started in London."

"Whereabouts?"

"Soho—around there."

"When was that?"

"Mid-seventies."

"Wasn't that when Soho was full of sex clubs and striptease joints?"

"*And* more. Gets a bit boring, all that stuff though, after a time."

"Yes. So they tell me."

⇥⇤

"I read your piece today in the *Oxford Mail*," said Morse as the two men walked toward reception. "You write well."

"Thank you."

"I can't help remembering you said 'comparatively' crime-free area."

"That was in yesterday's."

"Oh."

"Well . . . we've only had one burglary this last year, and we've had no joyriders around since the council put the sleeping policemen in. We still get a bit of mindless vandalism, of course—you'll have seen the young trees we tried to plant round the back. And litter—litter's always a problem—and graffiti . . . And someone recently unscrewed most of the latches on the back gates—you know, the things that click as the gates shut."

"I didn't know there was a market for those," muttered Morse.

"And you're wasting your time if you put up a name for your house, or something like that. I put a little notice on my front gate. Lasted exactly eight days. Know what it was?"

Morse glanced back at the corporate workforce seated in front of VDU screens at desks cluttered with in trays, out trays, file cases, handbooks, and copy being corrected and cosseted before inclusion in forthcoming editions of Oxford's own *Times, Mail, Journal, Star* . . .

" 'No Free Newspapers?' " he suggested *sotto voce*.

❧

Morse handed in his Visitor badge at reception.

"You'll need to give me another thing to get out with."

"No. The barrier lifts automatically when you leave."

"So once you're in . . ."

She smiled. "You're in! It's just that we used to get quite a few cars from the Industrial Estate trying it on."

❧

Morse turned left into the Botley Road and drove along to the Ring Road junction where he took the northbound A34, coming off at the Pear Tree Round-about, and then driving rather too quickly up the last stretch to Kidlington HQ—where he looked at his wristwatch again.

Nine and a half minutes.

Only nine and a half minutes.

Chapter Twenty

It is a capital mistake to theorize before one has data.
—Conan Doyle, *Scandal in Bohemia*

AS MORSE CLIMBED the stairs to Lewis's office he was experiencing a deep ache in each of his calves.

"Hardest work I've done today, that!" he admitted as, panting slightly, he flopped into a chair.

"Interview go okay, sir?"

"Owens? I wouldn't trust that fellow as far as I could kick him."

"Which wouldn't be too far, in your present state of health."

"Genuine journalist he may be—but he's a phony witness, take it from me!"

"Before you go on, sir, we've got the preliminary postmortem report here."

"You've read it through?"

"Tried to. Bullet entry in the left submandibular—"

"Lew-is! Spare me the details! She was shot through the window, through the blind, in the morning twilight. You mustn't expect much accuracy about the thing! You've been watching too many old cowboy films where they mow down the baddies at hundreds of yards."

"Distance of about eighteen inches to two feet, that's what it says, judging from—"

"What's it say about the *time*?"

"She's not quite so specific there."

"Why the hell not? We told her *exactly* when the woman was shot!"

"Dr. Hobson says the temperature in the kitchen that morning wasn't much above zero."

"Economizing everywhere, our Rachel," said Morse rather sadly.

"And it seems you get this sort of 'refrigeration factor'—"

"In which we are not particularly interested, Lewis, because we *know*—" Morse suddenly stopped. "Unless . . . unless our distinguished pathologist is suggesting that Rachel may have been murdered just a *little* earlier than we've been assuming."

"I don't think she's trying to suggest anything, sir. Just giving us the facts as far as she sees them."

"I suppose so."

"Do you want to read the report?"

"I shall have to, shan't I, if *you* can't understand it?"

"I didn't say that—"

But again Morse interrupted him, almost eagerly now recounting his interview with Owens . . .

>‹

". . . So don't you see, Lewis? *He* could have done it. Quarter of an hour it took me, to the newspaper offices via Banbury Road; ten minutes back via the Ring Road. So if he left home about ten to seven—clocked into the car park at seven, say—hardly anything on the roads—then drove straight *out* of the car park—there's no clocking out there—that's the system they have—drove hell for leather back to Bloxham Close—"

"*Drive*, sir."

"—parks his car up on the road behind the houses," Morse switched now to the vivid present tense, "—goes through the vandalized fence there —down the grass slope—taps on her window—the thin blinds still drawn," Morse's eyes seemed almost mesmerized, "—sees her profile more clearly as she gets nearer—for a second or two scrutinizes the dark outline at the gas-lit window—"

"It's electric there."

"—then he fires through the window into her face —and hits her just below the jaw."

Lewis nodded this time. "The submandibular bit, you're right about that."

"Then he goes up the bank again—gets in his car —back to Osney Mead. But he daren't go into the car park again—of course not! So he leaves his car somewhere near, and goes into the office from the rear of the car park. Nobody much there to observe his comings and goings—most of the people get in there about eightish, so I learn. *Quod erat demonstrandum!* I know you're going to ask me what his motive was, and I don't know. But this time we've

found the murderer before we've found the motive.
Not grumbling too much about that, are you?"

"Yes! It just won't hold water."

"And why's that?"

"There's this woman from Number 1, for a start.
Miss Cecil—"

"Della—Owens called her Della."

"She saw him leave, didn't she? About seven
o'clock? That's why she knew he'd be at his desk
when she rang him as soon as she saw the police
arrive—just after eight."

"One hour—one whole hour! You can do a lot in
an hour."

"You still can't put a quart into a pint pot."

"We've now gone metric, by the way, Lewis. Look,
what if they're in it *together*—have you thought of
that? Owens is carrying a torch for that Miss Cecil,
believe me! When I happened to mention Julian
Storrs—"

"You didn't do that, surely?"

"—and when I said he'd been seen knocking at one
of the other doors there—"

"But nobody—"

"—he was jealous, Lewis! And there are only two
houses in the Close," Lewis gave up the struggle,
"occupied by nubile young women: Number 17 and
Number 1, Miss James and Miss Cecil, agreed?"

"I thought you just said they were in it *together*."

"I said they might be, that's all. I'm just thinking
aloud, for Christ's sake! One of us has got to think.

And I'm a bit weary and I'm much underbeered. So give me a chance!"

Lewis waited a few seconds. Then:

"Is it my turn to speak, sir?"

Morse nodded weakly, contemplating the thread-bare state of Lewis's carpet.

"I don't know whether you've been down the Botley Road in the morning recently—even in the fairly early morning—but it's one of the worst bottlenecks in Oxford. You drove there and back in midafternoon, didn't you? But you want Owens to do three journeys between Kidlington and Osney Mead. First he drives to work—perhaps fairly quickly, agreed. Twenty minutes, say? He drives back—a bit quicker? Quarter of an hour, say. He parks his car somewhere—it's not going to be in Bloxham Drive, though. He murders his next-door neighbor. Drives back into Oxford after that—another twenty, twenty-five minutes *at least* now. Finds a parking space—and this time it's not going to be in the car park, as you say. Walks or runs to his office, not going in the front door, either—for obvious reasons. Gets into his office and is sitting there at his desk when his girlfriend—if you're right about that—rings him up and tells him he'll be in for a bit of a scoop if he gets out again to Bloxham Drive. It's just about possible, sir, if *all* the lights are with him *every* time, if almost everybody's decided to walk to work that morning. But it's very improbable even then. And remember it's *Monday* morning —the busiest morning of the week in Oxford."

Morse looked hurt.

"You still think it's just *about* possible?"

Lewis considered the question again.

"No, sir. I know you always like to think that most murders are committed by next-door neighbors or husbands or wives—"

"But what if this woman at Number 1 isn't telling us the truth?" queried Morse. "What if she never made that phone call at all? What if she's in it with him? What if she's more than willing to provide him with a nice little alibi? You see, you're probably right about the timescale of things. He probably *wouldn't* have had time to get back here to Kidlington, commit the murder, and then return to the office and be sitting quietly at his desk when she rang him."

"So?"

"So she's lying. Just like *he* is! He got back here—easy!—murdered Rachel James—and *stayed* here, duly putting in an appearance as the very first reporter on the scene!"

"I'm sorry, sir, but she *isn't* lying, not about this. I don't know what you think the rest of us have been doing since Monday morning but we've done quite a bit of checking up already. And she's *not* lying about the phone call to Owens' office. One of the lads went along to BT and confirmed it. The call was monitored and it'll be listed on the itemized telephone bill of the subscriber—Number 1 Bloxham Drive!"

"Does it give the *time*?"

Lewis appeared slightly uneasy. "I'm not quite sure about that."

"And if our ace reporter Owens is privileged enough to have an answerphone in his office—which he *is* . . ."

Ye-es. Perhaps Morse was on to something after all. Because if the two of them *had*, for some reason, been working together . . . Lewis put his thoughts into words:

"You mean he needn't have gone in to work at all. . . . Ye-es. You say that electronic gadget records the number on your card, and the time—but it doesn't record the car itself, right?"

Morse nodded encouragement. And Lewis, duly encouraged, continued:

"So if somebody *else* had taken his card—and if *he* stayed in the Drive all the time . . ."

Morse finished it off for him: "He's got a key to Number 1—he's in there when she drives off—he walks along the back of the terrace—shoots Rachel James—goes back to Number 1—rings up his own office number—waits for the answerphone pips— probably doesn't say anything—just keeps the line open for a minute or two—and Bob's your father's brother."

Lewis sighed. "I'd better get on with a bit of fourth-grade clerical checking, sir—this parking business, the phone call, any of his colleagues who might have seen him—"

"Or her."

"It's worth checking, I can see that."

"Tomorrow, Lewis. We're doing nothing more today."

"And this woman at Number 1?"

"Is she a nice-looking lass?"

"Very much so."

"You leave that side of things to me, then."

Morse got to his feet and went to the door. But then returned, and sat down again.

"That 'refrigeration factor' you mentioned, Lewis —time of death and all that. Interesting, isn't it? So far, we've been assuming that the bullet went through the window and ended up in the corpse, haven't we? But if—just *if*—Rachel James had been murdered a bit *earlier*, inside Number 17, and then someone had fired through the window *at some later stage* . . . You see what I mean? Everybody's alibi is up the pole, isn't it?"

"There'd be another bullet, though, wouldn't there? We've got the one from Rachel's neck; but there'd be another one somewhere in the kitchen if someone fired—"

"Not necessarily the murderer, remember!"

"But if *someone* fired just through the window, without aiming at anything . . ."

"Did the SOCOs have a good look at the ceiling, the walls—the floorboards?"

"They did, yes."

"Somebody might have picked it up and pocketed it."

"Who on earth—"

"I've not the faintest idea."

"Talking of bullets, sir, we've got another little report—from ballistics. Do you want to read it?"

"Not tonight."

"Very short, sir."

He handed Morse the single, neatly typed paragraph:

Ballistics Report: Prelim.
17 Bloxham Drive, Kidlington, Oxon

.577 heavy-caliber revolver. One of the Howdah pistols probably—perhaps the Lancaster Patent four-barrel. An old firing piece but if reasonably well cared for could be in good working nick like as not in 1996.
  Acc. to recent catalogues readily available in USA: $370 to $700. Tests progressing.

ASH
2-22-96

Morse handed the report back. "I'm not at all sure I know what 'caliber' means. Is it the diameter of the bullet or the diameter of the barrel?"

"Wouldn't they be the same, sir?"

Morse got up and walked wearily to the door once more.

"Perhaps so, Lewis. Perhaps so."

Chapter Twenty-One

A Conservative is one who is enamored of existing
evils, as distinguished from the Liberal, who
wishes to replace them with others.

—Ambrose Bierce, *The Devil's Dictionary*

MORSE DID NOT go straight home to his North Oxford
flat that evening; nor, *mirabile dictu*, did he make for
the nearest hostelry—at least not immediately. Instead,
he drove to Bloxham Drive, pulling in behind the single police car parked outside Number 17, in which a
uniformed officer sat reading the *Oxford Mail*.

"Constable Brogan, sir," was the reply in answer to
Morse's question.

"Happen to know if Number 1's at home?"

"The one with the N-reg Rover, you mean?"

Morse nodded.

"No. But she keeps coming backward and forward
all the time. She seems a very busy woman, that one."

"Anything to report?"

"Not really, sir. We keep getting a few gawpers, but
I just ask them to move along."

"Gently, I trust."

"Very gently, sir."

"How long are you on duty for?"

"Finish at midnight."

Morse pointed to the front window. "Why don't you nip in and watch the telly?"

"Bit cold in there."

"You can put the gas-fire on."

"It's electric, sir."

"Please yourself!"

"Would that be official, sir?"

"*Anything* I say's official, lad."

"My lucky night, then."

Mine, too, thought Morse as he looked over his shoulder to see an ash-blonde alighting from her car outside Number 1.

He hastened along the pavement in what could be described as an arrested jog, or perhaps more accurately as an animated walk.

"Good *evening*."

She turned toward him as she inserted her latchkey. "Yes?"

"A brief word—if it's possible . . . er . . ."

Morse fumbled for his ID card. But she forestalled the need.

"Another police sergeant, are you?"

"Police, yes."

"I can't spare much time—not tonight. I've got a busy few hours ahead."

"I shan't keep you long."

She led the way through into a tastefully furbished and furnished front room, taking off her ankle-length white mackintosh, placing it over the back of the red-leather settee, and bidding Morse sit opposite her as she smoothed the pale blue dress over her hips and crossed her elegant, nylon-clad legs.

"Do you mind?" she asked, lifting a cigarette in the air.

"No, no," muttered Morse, wishing only that she'd offered one to him.

"What can I do for you?" She had a slightly husky, upper-class voice, and Morse guessed she'd probably attended one of the nation's more prestigious public schools.

"Just one or two questions."

She smiled attractively: "Go ahead."

"I understand that my colleague, Sergeant Lewis, has spoken to you already."

"Nice man—in a gentle, shy sort of way."

"Really? I'd never quite thought of him . . ."

"Well, you're a bit older, aren't you?"

"What job do you do?"

She opened her handbag and gave Morse her card.

"I'm the local agent for the Conservative party."

"Oh dear! I *am* sorry," said Morse, looking down at the small oblong card:

Adèle Beatrice Cecil
Conservative Party Agent
1 Bloxham Drive
Kidlington, Oxon, OX5 2NY
For information please ring
01865 794768

"Was that supposed to be a sick joke?" There was an edge to her voice now.

"Not really. It's just that I've never had a friend who's a Tory, that's all."

"You mean you didn't vote for us today?"

"I don't live in this ward."

"If you give me your address, I'll make sure you get some literature, Sergeant."

"Chief Inspector, actually," corrected Morse, oblivious of the redundant adverb.

She tugged her dress a centimeter down her thighs. "How can I help?"

"Do you know Mr. Owens well?"

"Well enough."

"Well enough to hand him a newspaper scoop?"

"Yes."

"Have you ever slept with him?"

"Not much finesse about you, is there?"

"Just a minute," said Morse softly. "I've got a terrible job to do—just up the street here. And part of it's to ask some awkward questions about what's going on in the Close—"

"*Drive.*"

"To find out who knows who—*whom*, if you prefer it."

"They did teach us English grammar at Roedean, yes."

"You haven't answered my question."

Adèle breathed deeply, and her gray eyes stared across almost fiercely.

"Once, yes."

"But you didn't repeat the experience?"

"I said 'once'—didn't you hear me?"

"You still see him?"

"Occasionally. He's all right: intelligent, pretty well read, quite good fun, sometimes—and he promised he'd vote Conservative today."

"He sounds quite compatible."

"Are you married, Inspector?"

"*Chief* Inspector."

"Are you?"

"No."

"Do you wish you were?"

Perhaps Morse didn't hear the question.

"Did you know Rachel James fairly well?"

"We had a heart-to-heart once in a while."

"You weren't aware of any one particular boy-friend?"

She shook her head.

"Would you say she was attractive to men?"

"Wouldn't you?"

"I only saw her the once."

"I'm sorry." She said it quietly. "Please, forgive me."

"Do you know a man called Storrs? Julian Storrs?"

"Good gracious, yes! Julian? He's one of our Vice Presidents. We often meet at do's. In fact, I'm seeing him next week at a fund-raising dinner at The Randolph. Would you like a complimentary ticket?"

"No, perhaps not."

"Shouldn't have asked, should I? Anyway," she got to her feet, "I'll have to be off. They'll be starting the count fairly soon."

They walked to the front door.

"Er . . . when you rang Mr. Owens on Monday morning, just after eight o'clock you say, you did *speak* to him, didn't you?"

"Of course."

Morse nodded. "And one final thing, please. My sergeant found some French letters—"

"French letters? How old *are* you, Chief Inspector? Condoms, for heaven's sake."

"As I say, we found two packets of, er, condoms in one of her bedroom drawers."

"Big deal!"

"You don't know if she ever invited anyone home to sleep with her?"

"No, I don't."

"I thought," said Morse hesitantly, "most women were on the pill these days?"

"A lot of them *off* it, too—after that thrombosis scare."

"I suppose so, yes. I'm . . . I'm not really an expert in that sort of thing."

"And don't forget safe sex."

"No. I'll . . . I'll try not to."

"Did she keep them under her nighties?"

Morse nodded sadly, and bade goodnight to Adèle Beatrice Cecil.

ABC.

As he walked slowly along to the Jaguar, he felt a slight tingling behind the eyes at the thought of Rachel James, and the nightdress she'd been wearing when she was murdered; and the condoms so carefully concealed in her lingerie drawer—along with the hopes and fears she'd had, like everyone. And he thought of Auden's immortal line on A. E. Housman:

Kept tears like dirty postcards in a drawer.

As he started the Jaguar, Morse noticed the semi-stroboscopic light inside the lounge; and trusted that PC Brogan had managed to activate the heating system in Number 17 Bloxham Drive.

Chapter Twenty-Two

O Beer! O Hodgson, Guinness, Allsopp, Bass!
Names that should be on every infant's tongue!

—Charles Stuart Calverly

MORSE HEADED SOUTH along the Banbury Road, turning left just after the Cutteslowe Roundabout, and through the adjoining Carlton and Wolsey Roads (why hadn't the former been christened "Cardinal"?); then, at the bottom of the Cutteslowe Estate, down the steeply sloping entry to the Cherwell, a quietly civilized public house where the quietly civilized landlord kept an ever watchful eye on the Brakspear and the Bass. The car phone rang as he unfastened his safety belt.

Lewis.

Speaking from HQ.

"I thought I'd told you to go home! The eggs and chips are getting cold."

Lewis, as Morse earlier, showed himself perfectly competent at ignoring a question.

"I've had a session on the phone with Ox and Cow Newspapers, sir—still at work there, quite a few of them. Owens' car park card is number 14922 and it was registered by the barrier contraption there at 7:04

on Monday morning. Seems he's been in fairly early these last couple of months. Last week, for example, Monday to Friday, 7:37, 7:06, 7:11, 7:00, 7:18."

"So what? Shows he can't get up that early on Monday mornings."

"That's not all, though."

"It *is*, Lewis! It's still the *card* you're on about—not the *car*! Can't you see that?"

"Please listen to me for a change, sir. The personnel fellow who looked out the car park things for me, he just happened to be in earlyish last Monday morning himself: 7:22. There weren't many others around then, but one of the ones who was . . . Guess who, sir?"

"Oh dear!" said Morse for the second time that evening.

"Yep. Owens! Ponytail 'n all."

"Oh."

In that quiet monosyllable Lewis caught the depth of Morse's disappointment. Yet he felt far from dismayed himself, knowing full well as he did, after so many murder investigations with the pair of them in harness, that Morse's mind was almost invariably at its imaginative peak when one of his ill-considered, top-of-the-head hypotheses had been razed to the ground—in this case by some lumbering bulldozer like himself. And so he understood the silence at the other end of the line: a long silence, like that at the Cenotaph in commemoration of the fallen.

Lewis seldom expected (seldom received) any thanks. And in truth such lack of recognition concerned him little, since only rarely did Morse show the slightest sign of graciousness or gratitude to anyone.

Yet he did so now.

"Thank you, my old friend."

><

At the bar Morse ordered a pint of Bass and proceeded to drink it speedily.

At the bar Morse ordered a second pint of Bass and proceeded to drink it even more speedily—before leaving and driving out once more to Bloxham Drive, where no one was abroad and where the evening's TV programs appeared to be absorbing the majority of the households.

Including Number 17.

The Jaguar door closed behind him with its accustomed aristocratic click, and he walked slowly through the drizzle along the street. Still the same count: six for Labor; two for the Tories; and two apparently unprepared to parade their political allegiances.

Yes! YES!

Almost everything (he saw it now so clearly) had been pushing his mind toward that crucial clue—toward the breakthrough in the case.

It had not been Owens who had murdered Rachel James—almost certainly he *couldn't* have done it, anyway.

And that late evening, as if matching his slow-paced walk, a slow and almost beatific smile had settled round the mouth of Chief Inspector Morse.

Chapter Twenty-Three

Friday, February 23

> **Thirteen Unlucky:** The Turks so dislike the num-
> ber that the word is almost expunged from their
> vocabulary. The Italians never use it in making up
> the numbers of their lotteries. In Paris, no house
> bears that number.
>
> *—Brewer's Dictionary of Phrase and Fable*

As LEWIS PULLED into Bloxham Drive, he was faced
with an unfamiliar sight: a smiling, expansive-looking
Morse was leaning against the front gate of Number
17, engaged in a relaxed, impromptu press conference
with one camera crew (ITV), four reporters (two from
national, two from local newspapers—but no Owens),
and three photographers. Compared with previous
mornings, the turnout was disappointing.

It was 9:05 A.M.

Lewis just caught the tail end of things. "So it'll be
a waste of time—staying on here much longer. You
won't expect me to go into details, of course, but I
can tell you that we've finished our investigations in
this house."

If the "this" were spoken with a hint of some audial

semi-italicization, it was of no moment, for no one appeared to notice it.

"Any leads? Any new leads?"

"To the murder of Rachel James, you mean?"

"Who else?"

"No. No new leads at all, really . . . Well, perhaps one."

On which cryptic note, Morse raised his right hand to forestall the universal pleas for clarification, and with a genial—perhaps genuine?—smile, he turned away.

"Drive me round the block a couple of times, Lewis. I'd rather all these people buggered off, and I don't think they're going to stay much longer if they see us go."

Nor did they.

Ten minutes later the detectives returned to find the Drive virtually deserted.

"How many houses are there here, Lewis?"

"Not sure." From Number 17 Lewis looked along to the end of the row. Two other houses—presumably Numbers 19 and 21, although the figures from the front gate of the latter had been removed. Then he looked across to the other side of the street where the last even-numbered house was 20. The answer, therefore, appeared to be reasonably obvious.

"Twenty-one."

"That's an *odd* number, isn't it?"

Lewis frowned. "Did you think I thought it was an *even* number?"

Morse smiled. "I didn't mean 'odd' as opposed to 'even'; I meant 'odd' as opposed to 'normal.'"

"Oh!"

"Lew-is! You don't build a street of terraced houses with one side having ten and the other side having eleven, now do you? You get a bit of symmetry into things; a bit of regularity."

"If you say so."

"And I *do* say so!" snapped Morse, with the conviction of a fundamentalist preacher asserting the divine authority of Holy Writ.

"No need to be so sharp, sir."

"I should have spotted it from day one! From those political stickers, Lewis! Let's count, okay?"

The two men walked along the odd-numbered side of Bloxham Drive. And Lewis nodded: six Labor; two Tory; two don't-knows.

Ten.

"You see, Lewis, we've perhaps been a little misled by these minor acts of vandalism here. We've got several houses minus the numbers originally screwed into their front gates—*and their back gates.* So we were understandably confused."

Lewis agreed. "I still am, sir."

"How many odd numbers are there between one and twenty-one—inclusive?"

"I reckon it's ten, sir. So I suppose there must be eleven."

Morse grinned. "Write 'em down!"

So Lewis did, in his notebook: 1, 3, 5, 7, 9, 11, 13, 15, 17, 19, 21. Then counted them.

"I was right, sir. Eleven."

"But only ten houses, Lewis."

"I don't quite follow."

"Of course you do. It happens quite often in hotel floors and hotel room numbers . . . and street numbers. They miss one of them out."

Enlightenment dawned on Lewis's honest features.

"Number thirteen!"

"Exactly! Do you know there used to be people in France called 'fourteeners' who made a living by going along to dinner parties where the number of guests was thirteen?"

"Where do you find all these bits and pieces?"

"Do you know, I think I saw that on the back of a matchbox in a pub in Grimsby. I've learned quite a lot in life from the back of matchboxes."

"What's it all got to do with the case, though?"

Morse reached for Lewis's notebook, and put brackets round the seventh number. Then, underneath the first few numbers, he wrote in an arrow, →, pointing from left to right.

"Lewis! If you were walking along the back of the houses, starting from Number 1—she must be feeling a bit sore about the election, by the way . . . Well, let's just go along there."

The two men walked to the rear of the terrace, where (as we have seen) several of the back gates had been sadly, if not too seriously, vandalized.

"Get your list, Lewis, and as we go along, just put a ring round those gates where we *haven't* got a number, all right?"

At the end of the row, Lewis's original list, with its successive emendations, appeared as follows:

$$1, \ 3, \ 5, \ \textcircled{7,} \ 9, \ 11, \ (13), \ \textcircled{15,} \ \textcircled{17,} \ 19, \ \textcircled{21}$$

$\longrightarrow$

"You see," said Morse, "the vandalism gets worse the further you get into the Close, doesn't it? As it gets further from the main road."

"Yes."

"So just picture things. You've got a revolver and you walk along the back here in the half-light. *You know the number you want.* You know the morning routine, too: breakfast at about seven. All you've got to do is knock on the kitchen window, wait till you see the silhouette behind the thin blind, the silhouette of a face with one distinctive feature—a ponytail. You walk along the back; you see Number 11; you move along to the next house—Number 13—*you think*! And so the house after that *must* be Number 15. And to confirm things, there's the ponytailed silhouette. You press the trigger—and there you have it, Lewis! The Horseman passes by. But you've got it wrong, haven't you? Your intended victim is living at Number 15, not Number 17!"

"So," said Lewis slowly, "whoever stood at the kitchen window thought he—or she—was firing . . ."

Morse nodded somberly. "Yes. Not at Rachel James, but *Geoffrey Owens.*"

Chapter Twenty-Four

Men entitled to bleat BA after their names.
—D. S. MacColl

THE SENIOR COMMON Room at Lonsdale is comparatively small, and for this reason has a rather more
intimate air about it than some of the spacious SCRs
in the larger Oxford Colleges. Light-colored, beautifully grained oak-paneling encloses the room on all
sides, its coloring complemented by the light-brown
leather sofas and armchairs there. Copies of almost
all the national dailies, including the *Sun* and the *Mirror*, are to be found on the glass-topped coffee tables;
and indeed it is usually these tabloids which are
flipped through first—sometimes intently studied—
by the majority of the dons.

Forgathered here on the evening of Friday, February 23 (7:00 for 7:30) was a rather overcrowded
throng of dons, accompanied by wives, partners,
friends, to enjoy a Guest Night—an occasion cele-
brated by the College four times per term. A white-
coated scout stood by the door with a silver tray
holding thinly fluted glasses of sherry: either the pale
amber "dry" variety or the darker brown "medium,"
for it was a basic assumption in such a setting that no

one could ever wish for the deeply umbered "sweet."

A gowned Jasper Bradley took a glass of dry, drained it at a swallow, put the glass back onto the tray, and took another. He was particularly pleased with himself that day; *and* with the *Classical Quarterly*, whose review of *Greek Moods and Tenses* (J. J. Bradley, 204 pp., £45.50, Classical Press) contained the wonderful lines that Bradley had known by heart:

> *A small volume, but one which plumbs the unfathomed mysteries of the aorist subjunctive with imaginative insights into the very origins of language.*

Yes. He felt decidedly chuffed.

"How's tricks?" he asked, looking up at Donald Franks, a very tall astrophysicist, recently head-hunted from Cambridge, whose dark, lugubrious features suggested that for his part he'd managed few imaginative insights that week into the origins of the universe.

"So-so."

"Who d'you fancy then?"

"What—of the women here?"

"For the Master's job."

"Dunno."

"Who'll you vote for?"

"Secret ballot, innit?"

Mr. and Mrs. Denis Cornford now came in, each

taking a glass of the medium sherry. Shelly looked extremely attractive and perhaps a little skimpily dressed for such a chilly evening. She wore a light-weight white two-piece suit; and as she bent down to pick up a cheese nibble her low-cut, bottle green blouse gaped open to reveal a splendid glimpse of her beautiful breasts.

"Je-sus!" muttered Bradley.

"She certainly flouts her tits a bit," mumbled the melancholy Franks.

"You mean 'flaunts' 'em, I think."

"If you say so," said Franks, slightly wounded.

Bradley moved to the far end of the room where Angela Storrs stood talking to a small priest, clothed all in black, with buckled shoes and leggings.

"Ah, Jasper! Come and meet Father Dooley from Sligo."

Clearly Angela Storrs had decided she had now done her duty; for soon she drifted away—tall, long-legged, wearing a dark gray trouser-suit with a white high-necked jumper. There was about her an almost patrician mien, her face high-cheekboned and pale, with the hair swept back above her ears and fastened in a bun behind. It was obvious to all that she had been a very attractive woman. But she was aging a little too quickly perhaps; and the fact that over the last two or three years she had almost invariably worn trousers did little to discourage the belief that her legs had succumbed to an unsightly cordage of varicose veins. If she were on sale in an Arab wife market (in the cruel words of one of the younger dons) she would have passed her "best before" date several years earlier.

"I knew the Master many years ago—and his poor wife. Yes . . . that was long ago," mused the little priest.

Bradley was ready with the appropriate response of scholarly compassion.

"Times change, yes. *Tempora mutantur: et nos mutamur in illis.*"

"I think," said the priest, "that the line should read: *Tempora mutantur:* nos et *mutamur in illis.* Otherwise the hexameter won't scan, will it?"

"Of course it won't, sorry."

The scout now politely requested dons—wives—partners—guests—to proceed to the Hall. And Jasper Bradley, eminent authority on the aorist subjunctive in Classical Greek, walked out of the SCR more than slightly wounded.

> ✵

Sir Clixby Bream brought up the rear as the room emptied, and lightly touched the bottom of Angela Storrs standing just in front of him.

Sotto voce he lied into her ear: "You're looking ravishing tonight. And I'll tell you something else—I'd far rather be in bed with you now than face another bloody Guest Night."

"So would I!" she lied, in a whisper. "And I've got a big favor to ask of *you,* too."

"We'll have a word about it after the port."

"*Before* the port, Clixby! You're usually blotto after it."

＊

Sir Clixby banged his gavel, mumbled *Benedictus benedicat*, and the assembled company seated themselves, the table plan having positioned Julian Storrs and Denis Cornford at diagonally opposite ends of the thick oak table, with their wives virtually opposite each other in the middle.

"I love your suit!" lied Shelly Cornford, in a not unpleasing Yankee twang.

"You look very nice, too," lied Angela Storrs, smiling widely and showing such white and well-aligned teeth that no one could be in much doubt that her upper plate had been disproportionately expensive.

After which preliminary skirmish, each side observed a dignified truce, with neither a further word nor a further glance between them during the rest of the dinner.

At the head of the table, the little priest sat on the Master's right.

"Just the two candidates, I hear?" he said quietly.

"Just the two: Julian Storrs and Denis Cornford."

"The usual shenanigans, I assume? The usual horse-trading? Clandestine cabals?"

"Oh no, nothing like that. We're all very civilized here."

"How do you know that?"

"Well, you've only got to hear what people say—the way they say it."

The little priest pushed away his half-eaten guinea fowl.

"You know, Clixby, I once read that speech often gets in the way of genuine communication."

Chapter Twenty-Five

Saturday, February 24

There never was a scandalous tale without
some foundation.

—Richard Brinsley Sheridan,
The School for Scandal

WHILE THE GUEST NIGHT was still in progress,
while still the port and Madeira were circulating in
their time-honored directions, an overwearied Morse
had decided to retire comparatively early to bed,
where almost unprecedentedly he enjoyed a deep,
unbroken slumber until 7:15 the following morning,
when gladly would he have turned over and gone
back to sleep. But he had much to do that day. He
drank two cups of instant coffee (which he preferred
to the genuine article); then another cup, this time
with one slice of brown toast heavily spread with butter and Frank Cooper's Oxford Marmalade.

By 8:45 he was in his office at Kidlington HQ,
where he found a note on his desk:

Please see Chief Sup. Strange A S A P

The meeting, almost until the end, was an amiable

enough affair, and Morse received a virtually unin-terrupted hearing as he explained his latest thinking on the murder of Rachel James.

"Mm!" grunted Strange, resting his great jowls on his palms when Morse had finished. "So it *could* be a contract killing that went cockeyed, you think? The victim gets pinpointed a bit too vaguely, and the killer shoots at the wrong pigtail—"

"Ponytail, sir."

"Yes—through the wrong window. Right?"

"Yes."

"What about the motive? The key to this sort of mess is almost always the *motive*, you know that."

"You sound just like Sergeant Lewis, sir."

Strange looked dubiously across the desk, as if a little uncertain as to whether he *wanted* to sound just like Sergeant Lewis.

"Well?"

"I agree with you. That's one of the reasons it could have been a case of misidentity. We couldn't really find any satisfactory motive for Rachel's murder any-where. But if somebody wanted *Owens* out of the way—well, I can think of a dozen possible motives."

"Because he's a newshound, you mean?"

Morse nodded. "Plenty of people in highish places who've got some sort of skeleton in the sideboard—"

"Cupboard."

"Who'd go quite a long way to keep the, er, cup-board firmly locked."

"Observed openly masturbating on the M40, you

mean? Weekend away with the PA? By the way, *you've* got a pretty little lass for a secretary, I see. Don't you ever lust after her?"

"I seem to have lost most of my lust recently, sir."

"We all do. It's called getting old."

Strange lifted his large head, and eyed Morse over his half lenses.

"Now about the case. It won't be easy, will it? You've no reason to think he's got a lot of stuff stashed under his mattress?"

"No . . . no, I haven't."

"You'd no real reason for thinking he'd killed Rachel?"

"No . . . no, I hadn't."

"So he's definitely out of the frame?"

Morse considered the question awhile. " 'Fraid so, yes. I wish he weren't."

"So?"

"So I'll—*we'll* think of some way of approaching things."

"Nothing irregular! You promise me that! We're just about getting over one or two unsavory incidents in the Force, aren't we? And we're not going to start anything here. Is that clear, Morse?"

"To be fair, sir, I usually do go by the book."

Strange pointed a thick finger.

"Well, *usually*'s not bloody good enough for me! You—go—by—the book, matey! Understood?"

⇥⇤

Morse walked heavily back to his office, where a refreshed-looking Lewis awaited him.

"Everything all right with the Super?"

"Oh, yes. I just told him about our latest think-ing—"

"*Your* latest thinking."

"He understands the difficulties. He just doesn't want us to bend the rules of engagement too far, that's all."

"So what's the plan?"

"Just nip and get me a drink first, will you?"

"Coffee?"

Morse pondered. "I think I'll have a pint of natural, lead-free orange juice. Iced."

><

"So what's the plan?" repeated Lewis, five minutes later.

"Not quite sure, really. But if I'm right, if it *was* something like a contract killing, it must have been arranged because Owens was threatening to expose somebody. And if he was—"

"Lot of 'if's,' sir."

"*If* he was, Lewis, he must have some evidence tucked away somewhere: vital evidence, damning evidence. It could be in the form of newspaper cut-tings or letters or photographs—anything. *And* he must have been pretty sure about his facts if he's been trying to extort some money or some favors or whatever from any disclosures. Now, as I see it, he must have come across most of his evidence in the course of his career as a journalist. Wouldn't you think so? Sex scandals, that sort of thing."

"Like as not, I suppose."

"So the plan's this. I want you, once you get the chance, to go and see the big white chief at the newspaper offices and get a look at all the confidential stuff on Owens. They're sure to have it in his appointment file or somewhere: previous jobs, references, testimonials, CV, internal appraisals, comments—"

"Gossip?"

"Anything!"

"Is that what you mean by not bending the rules too much?"

"We're *not* bending the rules—not too much. We're on a *murder* case, Lewis, remember that! Every member of the public's got a duty to help us in our inquiries."

"I just hope the editor agrees with you, that's all."

"He does," said Morse, a little shamefacedly. "I rang him while you went to the canteen. He just wants us to do it privately, that's all, and confidentially. Owens only works alternate Saturdays, and this is one of his days off."

"You don't want to do it yourself?"

"It's not that I don't *want* to. But you're so much better at that sort of thing than I am."

A semimollified Lewis elaborated: "Then, if anything sticks out as important . . . just follow it up . . . and let you know?"

"Except for one thing, Lewis. Owens told me he worked for quite a while in Soho when he started. And if there's anything suspicious or interesting about that period of his life . . ."

"You'd like to do that bit of research yourself."

"Exactly. I'm better at that sort of thing than you are."

"What's your program for today, then?"

"Quite a few things, really."

"Such as?" Lewis looked up quizzically.

"Well, there's one helluva lot of paperwork, for a start. *And* filing. So you'd better stay and give me a hand for a while—after you've fetched me another orange juice. And please tell the girl not to dilute it quite so much this time. And just a cube or two more ice perhaps."

"And then?" persisted Lewis.

"And then I'm repairing to the local in Cutteslowe, where I shall be trying to thread a few further thoughts together over a pint, perhaps. And where I've arranged to meet an old friend of mine who may possibly be able to help us a little."

"Who's that, sir?"

"It doesn't matter."

"Not—?"

"Where's my orange juice, Lewis?"

Chapter Twenty-Six

MARIA: No, I've just got the two O-levels—and
the tortoise, of course. But I'm fairly well known
for some other accomplishments.
JUDGE: Known to whom, may I ask?
MARIA: Well, to the police for a start.

—Diana Doherty, *The Re-trial of Maria Macmillan*

AT TEN MINUTES to noon Morse was enjoying his pint of Brakspear's bitter. The Chief Inspector had many faults, but unpunctuality had never been one of them. He was ten minutes early.

JJ, a sparely built, nondescript-looking man in his mid-forties, walked into the Cherwell five minutes later.

✦

When Morse had rung at 8:30 A.M., Malcolm "JJ" Johnson had been seated on the floor, on a black cushion, only two feet away from the television screen, watching a hard-core porn video and drinking his regular breakfast of two cans of Beamish stout—just after the lady of the household had left for her job (mornings only) in one of the fruiterers' shops in Summertown.

Accepted wisdom has it that in such enlightened

times as these most self-respecting burglars pursue their trade by day; but JJ had always been a night man, relying firmly on local knowledge and reconnaissance. And often in the daylight hours, as now, he wondered why he didn't spend his leisure time in some more purposeful pursuits. But in truth he just couldn't think of any. At the same time, he did realize, yes, that sometimes he was getting a bit bored. Over the past two years or so, the snooker table had lost its former magnetism; infidelities and fornication were posing too many practical problems, as he grew older; and even darts and dominoes were beginning to pall. Only gambling, usually in Ladbrokes' premises in Summertown, had managed to retain his undivided attention over the years: for the one thing that never bored him was acquiring money.

Yet JJ had never been a miser. It was just that the acquisition of money was a necessary prerequisite to the *spending* of money; and the spending of money had always been, and still was, the greatest purpose of his life.

Educated (if that be the word) in a run-down comprehensive school, he had avoided the three Bs peculiar to many public school establishments: beating, bullying, and buggery. Instead, he had left school at the age of sixteen with a delight in a different triad: betting, boozing, and bonking—strictly in that order. And to fund such expensive hobbies he had come to rely on one source of income, one line of business only: burglary.

He now lived with his long-suffering, faithful, strangely influential, common-law wife in a council house on the Cutteslowe Estate that was crowded with crates of lager and vodka and gin, with all the latest computer games, and with row upon row of tasteless seaside souvenirs. And home, after two years in jail, was where he wanted to stay.

No! JJ didn't want to go back inside. And that's why Morse's call had worried him so. So much, indeed, that he had turned the video to "Pause" even as the eager young stud was slipping between the sheets.

What did Morse want?

>‹

"Hello, Malcolm!"

Johnson had been "Malcolm" until the age of ten, when the wayward, ill-disciplined young lad had drunk from a bottle of Jeyes Fluid under the misapprehension that the lavatory cleaner was lemonade. Two stomach pumpings and a week in hospital later, he had emerged to face the world once more; but now with the sobriquet "Jeyes"—an embarrassment which he sought to deflect, five years on, by the rather subtle expedient of having the legend "JJ—all the Js" tattooed longitudinally on each of his lower arms.

Morse drained his glass and pushed it over the table.

"Coke, is it, Mr. Morse?"

"Bit early for the hard stuff, Malcolm."

"Half a pint, was it?"

"Just tell the landlord 'same again.'"

A Brakspear it was—and a still mineral water for JJ.

"One or two of those gormless idiots you call your pals seem anxious to upset the police," began Morse.

"Look. I didn't 'ave nothin' to do with that—'onest! You know me." Looking deeply unhappy, JJ dragged deeply on a king-size cigarette.

"I'm not really interested in that. I'm interested in your doing me a favor."

JJ visibly relaxed, becoming almost his regular, perky self once more. He leaned over the table, and spoke quietly:

"I'll tell you what. I got a red-'ot video on up at the country mansion, if you, er . . ."

"Not this morning," said Morse reluctantly, conscious of a considerable sacrifice. And it was now *his* turn to lean over the table and speak the quiet words:

"I want you to break into a property for me."

"Ah!"

The balance of power had shifted, and JJ grinned broadly to reveal two rows of irregular and blackened teeth. He pushed his empty glass across the table.

"Double vodka and lime for me, Mr. Morse. I suddenly feel a bit thirsty, like."

※

For the next few minutes Morse explained the mission; and JJ listened carefully, nodding occasionally, and once making a penciled note of an address on the back of a pink betting slip.

"Okay," he said finally, "so long as you promise, you know, to see me okay if . . ."

"I can't promise anything."

"But you will?"

"Yes."

"Okay, then. Gimme a chance to do a bit o' recce, okay? Then gimme another buzz on the ol' blower, like, okay? When had you got in mind?"

"I'm not quite sure."

"Okay—that's it then."

Morse drained his glass and stood up, wondering whether communication in the English language could ever again cope without the word "okay."

"Before you go . . ." JJ looked down at his empty glass.

"Mineral water, was it?" asked Morse.

"Just tell the landlord 'same again.'"

>‹

Almost contented with life once more, JJ sat back and relaxed after Morse had gone. Huh! Just the one bleedin' door, by the sound of it. Easy. Piece o' cake!

>‹

Morse, too, was pleased with the way the morning had gone. Johnson, as the police were well aware, was one of the finest locksmen in the Midlands. As a teenager he'd held the reputation of being the quickest car thief in the county. But his incredible skills had only really begun to burgeon in the eighties, when all manner of house locks, burglar alarms, and safety devices had surrendered meekly to his unparalleled knowledge of locks and keys and electrical circuits.

In fact "JJ" Johnson knew almost as much about burglary as J. J. Bradley knew about the aorist subjunctive.

Perhaps more.

Chapter Twenty-Seven

The faults of the burglar are the qualities of the financier.

—Bernard Shaw, *Major Barbara*

IN FACT, MORSE'S campaign was destined to be launched that very day.

Lewis had called back at HQ at 2 P.M. with a slim folder of photocopied documents—in which Morse seemed little interested; and with the news that Geoffrey Owens had left his home the previous evening to attend a weekend conference on Personnel Management, in Bournemouth, not in all likelihood to be back until late P.M. the following day, Sunday. In this latter news Morse seemed more interested.

"Well done, Lewis! But you've done quite enough for one day. You look weary and I want you to go home. Nobody can keep up the hours you've been setting yourself."

As it happened, Lewis was feeling wonderfully fresh; but he *had* promised that weekend to accompany his wife (if he could) on her quest for the right sort of dishwasher. They could well afford the luxury now, and Lewis himself would welcome some alleviation of his domestic duties at the sink.

"I'll accept your offer—on one condition, sir. You go off home, too."

"Agreed. I was just going anyway. I'll take the folder with me. Anything interesting?"

"A few little things, I suppose. For instance—"

"Not now!"

"Aren't you going to tell me how *your* meeting went?"

"*Not now!* Let's call it a day."

As the two detectives walked out of the HQ block, Morse asked his question casually:

"By the way, did you discover which swish hotel they're at in Bournemouth?"

⇥⇤

Back in his flat, Morse made two phone calls: the first to Bournemouth; the second to the Cutteslowe Estate. Yes, a Mr. Geoffrey Owens was present at the conference there. No, Mr. Malcolm Johnson had not yet had a chance to make his recce—of course he hadn't! But, yes, he would repair the omission forthwith in view of the providential opportunity now afforded (although Johnson's own words were considerably less pretentious).

"And no more booze today, Malcolm!"

"What me—drink? On business? Never! And you better not drink, neither."

"Two sober men—that's what the job needs," agreed Morse.

"What time you pickin' me up then?"

"No. You're picking *me* up. Half past seven at my place."

"Okay. And just remember you got more to lose than I 'ave, Mr. Morse."

Yes, far more to lose, Morse knew that; and he felt a shudder of apprehension about the risky escapade he was undertaking. His nerves needed some steadying.

He poured himself a good measure of Glenfiddich; and shortly thereafter fell deeply asleep in the chair for more than two hours.

Bliss.

><

Johnson parked his filthy F-reg Vauxhaull in a fairly convenient lay-by on the Deddington Road, the main thoroughfare which runs at the rear of the odd-numbered houses in Bloxham Drive. As instructed, Morse stayed behind, in the murky shadow of the embankment, as Johnson eased himself through a gap in the perimeter fence, where vandals had smashed and wrenched away several of the vertical slats, and then, with surprising agility, descended the steep stretch of slippery grass that led down to the rear of the terrace.

The coast seemed clear.

Morse looked on nervously as the locksman stood in his trainers at the back of Number 15, patiently and methodically doing what he did so well. Once, he snapped to taut attention hard beside the wall as a light was switched on in one of the nearby houses, throwing a yellow rectangle over the glistening grass —and then switched off.

Six minutes.

By Morse's watch, six minutes before Johnson turned the knob, carefully eased the door open, and disappeared within—before reappearing and beckoning a tense and jumpy Morse to join him.

"Do you want the lights on?" asked Johnson as he played the thin beam of his large torch around the kitchen.

"What do *you* think?"

"Yes. Let's 'ave 'em on. Lemme just go and pull the curtains through 'ere." He moved into the front living room, where Morse heard a twin swish, before the room burst suddenly into light.

An ordinary, somewhat spartan room: settee; two rather tatty armchairs; dining table and chairs; TV set; electric fire installed in the old fireplace; and above the fireplace, on a mantelpiece patinated deep with dust, the only object perhaps which any self-respecting burglar would have wished to take—a small, beautifully fashioned ormolu clock.

Upstairs, the double bed in the front room was unmade, an orange bath towel thrown carelessly across the duvet; no sign of pajamas. On the bedside table two items only: Wilbur Smith's *The Seventh Scroll* in paperback, and a packet of BiSoDoL Extra indigestion tablets. An old-fashioned mahogany wardrobe monopolized much of the remaining space, with coats/suits/trousers on their hangers, and six pairs of shoes neatly laid in parallels at the bottom; and on the shelves, to the left, piles of jumpers, shirts, pants, socks, and handkerchiefs.

The second bedroom was locked.

"Malcolm!" whispered Morse down the stairwell.

Two and a half minutes later, Morse was taking stock of a smaller but clearly more promising room: a large bookcase containing a best-seller selection from over the years; one armchair; one office chair; the latter set beneath a veneered desk with an imitation leather top, four drawers on either side, and between them a longer drawer with two handles—locked.

"Malcolm!" whispered Morse down the stairwell.

Ninety seconds only this time, and clearly the locksman was running into form.

The eight side drawers contained few items of interest: stationery, insurance documents, car documents, bank statements, pens and pencils—but in the bottom left-hand drawer a couple of pornographic paperbacks. Morse opened *Topless in Torremolinos* at random and read a short paragraph.

In its openly titillating way, it seemed to him surprisingly well written. And there was that one striking simile where the heroine's bosom was compared to a pair of fairy cakes—although Morse wasn't at all sure what a fairy cake looked like. He made a mental note of the author, Ann Berkeley Cox, and read the brief dedication on the title page, "For Geoff From

ABC," before slipping the book into the pocket of his mackintosh.

✦

Johnson was seated in an armchair, in the living room, in the dark, when Morse came down the stairs holding a manila file.

"Got what you wanted, Mr. Morse?"

"Perhaps so. Ready?"

With the house now in total darkness, the two men felt their way to the kitchen, when Morse stopped suddenly.

"The torch! Give me the torch."

Retracing his steps to the living room, he shone the beam along an empty mantelpiece.

"Put it back!" he said.

Johnson took the ormolu clock from his overcoat pocket and replaced it carefully on its little dust-free rectangle.

"I'm glad you made me do that," confided Johnson quietly. "I shouldn't 'a done it in the first place. Anyway, me conscience'll be clear now."

There was a streak of calculating cruelty in the man, Morse knew that. But in several respects he was a lovable rogue; even sometimes, as now perhaps, a reasonably honest one. And oddly it was Morse who was beginning to worry—about his own conscience.

He went quickly up to the second bedroom once more and slipped the book back in its drawer.

At last, as quietly as it had opened, the back door closed behind them and the pair now made their way up the grassy gradient to the gap in the slatted perimeter fence.

"You've not lost your old skills," volunteered Morse.

"Nah! Know what they say, Mr. Morse? Old burglars never die—they simply steal away."

⇥⇤

In the darkened house behind them, on the mantelpiece in the front living room, a little dust-free rectangle still betrayed the spot where the beautifully fashioned ormolu clock had so recently stood.

Chapter Twenty-Eight

When you have assembled what you call your
"facts" in logical order, it is like an oil lamp you
have fashioned, filled, and trimmed; but which will
shed no illumination unless first you light it.

—Saint-Exupéry, *The Wisdom of the Sands*

BACK IN HIS flat, Morse closed the door and shot the
bolts, both top and bottom. It was an oddly needless
precaution, yet an explicable one, perhaps. As a
twelve-year-old boy, he remembered so vividly
returning from school with a magazine, and locking
all the doors in spite of his certain knowledge that no
other member of the family would be home for several hours. And then, even then, he had waited
awhile, relishing the anticipatory thrill before daring
to open the pages.

It was just that sensation he felt now as he switched
on the electric fire, poured a glass of Glenfiddich, lit
a cigarette, and settled back in his favorite armchair
—not this time, however, with the *Naturist Journal*
which (all those years ago now) had been doing the
rounds in Lower IVA, but with the manila file just
burgled from the house in Bloxham Drive.

The cover was well worn, with tears and creases

along its edges; and maroon rings where once a wine glass had rested, amid many doodles of quite intricate design. Inside the file was a sheaf of papers and cuttings, several of them clipped or stapled together, though not arranged in any chronological or purposeful sequence.

Nine separate items.

• Two newspaper cuttings, snipped from one of the less inhibited of the Sunday tabloids, concerning a Lord Hardiman, together with a photograph of the aforesaid peer fishing in his wallet (presumably for Deutschmarks) outside a readily identifiable sex establishment in Hamburg's Reeperbahn. Clipped to this material was a further photograph of Lord Hardiman arm-in-arm with Lady Hardiman at a polo match in Great Windsor Park (September 1984).

• A letter (August 1979) addressed to Owens from a firm of solicitors in Cheltenham informing the addressee that it was in possession of letters sent by him (Owens) to one of their clients (unspecified); and that some arrangement beneficial to each of the parties might possibly be considered.

• A glossy, highly defined photograph showing a paunchy elderly man fondling a frightened-looking prepubescent girl, both of them naked. Penciled on the back was an address in St. Albans.

- A stapled sheaf of papers showing the expenses of a director in a Surrey company manufacturing surgical appliances, with double exclamation points against several of the mammoth amounts claimed for foreign business trips.

- A brief, no-nonsense letter (from a woman, perhaps?) in large, curly handwriting, leaning italic-fashion to the right: "If you contact me again I shall take your letters to the police—I've kept them all. You'll get no more money from me. You're a despicable human being. I've got nothing more to lose, not even my money." No signature but (again) a penciled address, this time in the margin, in Wimbledon.

- Four sets of initials written on a small page probably torn from the back of a diary:

AM✓   DC✓   JS✓   CB

Nothing more—except a small tick in red Biro against the first three.

- Two further newspaper cuttings, paper-clipped together. The first (*The Times* Diary, 2-2-96) reporting as follows:

After a nine-year tenure Sir Clixby Bream is retiring as Master of Lonsdale College, Oxford. Sir Clixby would, indeed should, have retired earlier. It is only

182 • *Colin Dexter*

the inability of anyone in the College (including the classicists) to understand the Latin of the original Statutes that has prolonged Sir Clixby's term. The present Master has refused to speculate whether such an extension of his tenure has been the result of some obscurity in the language of the Statutes themselves; or the incompetence of his classical colleagues, none of whom appears to have been nominated as a possible successor.

The second, a cutting from the *Oxford Mail* (November 1995) of an article written by Geoffrey Owens; with a photograph alongside, the caption reading, "Mr. Julian Storrs and his wife Angela at the opening of the Polynesian Art Exhibition at the Pitt Rivers Museum."

- A smudgy photocopy of a typed medical report, marked "Strictly Private and Confidential," on the notepaper of a private health clinic in the Banbury Road:

Ref.:	Mr. J. C. Storrs
Diagnosis:	Inoperable liver cancer confirmed. For second opn. see letter Dr. O. V. Maxim (Churchill)
Prognosis:	Seven/eight months, or less. Possibly (??) a year. No longer.
Patient Notes:	Honesty best in this case. Strong personality.
Next Appt.:	See book, but A S A P.
	RHT

Clipped to this was a cutting from the obituary columns of one of the national dailies—*The Independent*, by the look of it—announcing the death of the distinguished cancer specialist Robert H. Turnbull.

- Finally, three photographs, paper-clipped together:

    (i)   A newspaper photograph of a strip club, showing in turn (though indistinguishably) individual photographs of the establishment's principal performers, posted on each side of the narrow entrance; showing also (with complete clarity) the inviting legend: SEXIEST RAUNCHIEST SHOW IN SOHO.

    (ii) A full-length, black-and-white photograph of a tallish bottle-blonde in a dark figure-hugging gown, the thigh-slit on the left revealing a length of shapely leg. About the woman there seemed little that was less than genuinely attractive—except the smile perhaps.

    (iii) A color photograph of the same woman seated completely naked, apart from a pair of extraordinarily thin stiletto heels, on a bar stool somewhere—her overfirm breasts suggesting that the smile in the former photograph was not the only thing about her that might be semi-artificial. The legs, now happily revealed in all their lengthy glory, were those of a young dancer—the legs of a Cyd Charisse or a Betty Grable, much better than those in the *Naturist Journal* . . .

Morse closed the file, and knew what he had read: an agenda for blackmail—and possibly for murder.

Chapter Twenty-Nine

Sunday, February 25

He was advised by a friend, with whom he afterward lost touch, to stay at the Wilberforce Temperance Hotel.

—Geoffrey Madan, *Notebooks*

I hate those who intemperately denounce beer—and call it Temperance.

—G. K. Chesterton

SOCRATES, ON HIS last day on earth, avowed that death, if it be but one long and dreamless sleep, was a blessing most devoutly to be wished. Morse, on the morning of Sunday, February 25—without going quite so far as Socrates—could certainly look back on his own long and dreamless sleep with a rare gratitude, since the commonest features of his nights were regular visits to the loo, frequent draughts of water, occasional doses of Nurofen and Paracetamol, an intake of indigestion tablets, and finally (after rising once more from his crumpled bed linen) a tumbler of Alka-Seltzer.

The Observer was already poking thickly through the letter-box as he hurriedly prepared himself a sub-continental breakfast.

10:30 A.M.

><

It was 11:15 A.M. when he arrived at HQ, where Lewis had already been at work for three hours, and where he was soon regaling the chief about his visit to the newspaper offices.

A complete picture of Owens—built up from testimonials, references, records, impressions, gossip—showed a competent, hardworking, well-respected employee. That was the good news. And the bad? Well, it seemed the man was aloof, humorless, unsympathetic. In view of the latter shortcomings (Lewis had suggested) it was perhaps puzzling to understand why Owens had been sent off on a personnel management course. Yet (as the editor had suggested) some degree of aloofness, humorlessness, lack of sympathy, was perhaps precisely what was required in such a role.

Lewis pointed to the cellophane folder in which his carefully paginated photocopies were assembled.

"And one more thing. He's obviously a bit of a hit with some of the girls there—especially the younger ones."

"In spite of his ponytail?"

"Because of it, more likely."

"You're not serious?"

"And you're never going to catch up with the twentieth century, are you?"

"One or two possible leads?"

"Could be."

"Such as?"

"Well, for a start, the Personnel Manager who saw Owens on Monday. I'll get a statement from him as soon as he gets back from holiday—earlier, if you'd like."

Morse looked dubious. "Ye-es. But if somebody intended to murder Owens, not Rachel James . . . well, Owens' alibi is neither here nor there really, is it? You're right, though. Let's stick to official procedure. I've always been in favor of rules and regulations."

As Lewis eyed his superior officer with scarce disguised incredulity, he accepted the manila file handed to him across the desk; and began to read.

Morse himself now opened the "Life" section of *The Observer* and turned to the crossword set by Azed (for Morse, the Kasparov of cruciverbalists) and considered 1 across: "Elephant-man has a mouth that's deformed (6)." He immediately wrote in MAHOUT, but then put the crossword aside, trusting that the remaining clues might pose a more demanding challenge, and deciding to postpone his hebdomadal treat until later in the day. Otherwise, he might well have completed the puzzle before Lewis had finished with the file.

>*<

"How did you come by this?" asked Lewis finally.

"Yours not to reason how."

"He's a blackmailer!"

Morse nodded. "We've found no evidential motive for Rachel's murder, but . . ."

". . . dozens of 'em for his."

"About *nine*, Lewis—if we're going to be accurate."

Morse opened the file, and considered the contents once more. Unlike that of the obscenely fat child fondler, neither photograph of the leggy blonde stripper was genuinely pornographic—certainly not the wholly nude one, which seemed to Morse strangely unerotic; perhaps the one of her in the white dress, though . . . "Unbuttoning" had always appealed to Morse more than "unbuttoned"; "undressing" than "undressed"; "almost naked" to completely so. It was something to do with Plato's idea of process; and as a young classical scholar Morse had spent so many hours with that philosopher.

"Quite a bit of legwork there, sir."

"Yes. Lovely legs, aren't they?"

"No! I meant there's a lot of work to do there—research, going around."

"You'll need a bit of help, yes."

"Sergeant Dixon—couple of his lads, too—that'd help."

"Is Dixon still eating the canteen out of jam doughnuts?"

Lewis nodded. "*And* he's still got his pet tortoise—"

"—always a step or two in front of him, I know."

⤭

For half an hour the detectives discussed the file's explosive material. Until just after noon, in fact.

"Coffee, sir?"

"Not for me. Let's nip down to the King's Arms in Summertown."

"Not for me," echoed Lewis. "I can't afford the time."

"As you wish." Morse got to his feet.

"Do you think you should be going out quite so much—on the booze, I mean, sir?" Lewis took a deep breath and prepared for an approaching gale, force ten. "You're getting worse, not better."

Morse sat down again.

"Let me just tell you something, Lewis. I care quite a bit about what you think of me as a boss, as a colleague, as a detective—as a *friend*, yes! But I don't give two bloody monkeys about what you think of me as a boozer, all right?"

"No, it's not all right," said Lewis quietly. "As a professional copper, as far as solving murders are concerned—"

"*Is* concerned!"

"—it doesn't matter. Doesn't matter to me at all." Lewis's voice grew sharper now. "You do your job—you spend all your time sorting things out—I'm not worried about that. And if the Chief Constable told me you *weren't* doing your job, I'd resign myself. But he *wouldn't* say that—never. What he'd say—

what others would say—what others *are* saying—is that you're ruining yourself. Not the Force, not the department, not the murder inquiries—nothing!—*except yourself.*"

"Just hold on a second, will you?" Morse's eyes were blazing.

"No! No, I won't. You talked about me as a friend, didn't you, just now? Well, as a friend I'm telling you that you're buggering up your health, your retirement, your life—everything!"

"Listen!" hissed Morse. "I've never myself tried to tell any other man how to live his life. And I will *not* be told, at my age, how I'm supposed to live mine. Even by you."

After a prolonged silence, Lewis spoke again.

"Can I say something else?"

Morse shrugged indifferently.

"Perhaps it doesn't matter much to most people whether you kill yourself or not. You've got no wife, no family, no relatives, except that aunt of yours in Alnwick—"

"She's dead, too."

"So, what the hell? What's it matter? Who cares? Well, *I* care, sir. And the missus cares. And for all I know that girl Ellie Smith, *she* cares."

Morse looked down at his desk. "Not any longer, no."

"And *you* ought to care—care for yourself—just a bit."

For some considerable while Morse refrained from

making any answer, for he was affected by his sergeant's words more deeply than he would ever be prepared to admit.

Then, finally:

"What about that coffee, Lewis?"

"And a sandwich?"

"And a sandwich."

><

By early afternoon Morse had put most of his cards on the table, and he and Lewis had reached an agreed conclusion. No longer could either of them accept that Rachel James had been the intended victim: each of them now looked toward Geoffrey Owens as by far the likelier target. Pursuance of the abundant clues provided by the Owens file would necessarily involve a great deal of extra work; and fairly soon a strategy was devised, with Lewis and Dixon allocated virtually everything except the Soho slot.

"You know, I could probably fit that in fairly easily with the Wimbledon visit," Lewis had volunteered.

But Morse was clearly unconvinced:

"The Soho angle's the most important of the lot."

"Do you honestly believe that?"

"Certainly. That's why—"

The phone rang, answered by Morse.

Owens (he learned) had phoned HQ ten minutes earlier, just after 3 P.M., to report that his property had been burgled over the weekend, while he was away.

"And you're dealing with it? . . . Good . . . Just the one item you say, as far as he knows? . . . I see . . . Thank you."

Morse put down the phone; and Lewis picked up the file, looking quizzically across the desk.

But Morse shook his head. "Not the file, no."

"What, then?"

"A valuable little ormolu clock from his living room."

"Probably a professional, sir—one who knows his clocks."

"Don't ask me. I know nothing about clocks."

Lewis grinned. "We both know somebody who does though, don't we, sir?"

Chapter Thirty

This world and the next—and after that *all* our troubles will be over.

> —Attributed to General Gordon's aunt

NO KNOCK. THE door opened. Strange entered.

"Haven't they mentioned it yet, Morse? The pubs are open all day on Sundays now."

As Strange carefully balanced his bulk on the chair opposite, Morse lauded his luck that Lewis had taken the Owens material down the corridor for photocopying.

"Just catching up on a bit of routine stuff, sir."

"Really?"

"Why are *you* here?"

"It's the wife," confided Strange. "Sunday afternoons she always goes round the house dusting everything. Including me!"

Morse was smiling dutifully as Strange continued: "Making progress?"

"Following up a few things, yes."

"Mm . . . Is your brain as bright as it used to be?"

"I'm sure it's not."

"Mm . . . You don't *look* quite so bright, either."

"We're all getting older."

"Worse luck!"

"Not really, surely? 'No wise man ever wished to be younger.'"

"Bloody nonsense!"

"Not my nonsense—Jonathan Swift's."

Elbows on the desk, Strange rested his large head on his large hands.

"I'm probably finishing in September, I suppose you'd heard."

Morse nodded. "I'm glad they're letting you go."

"What the 'ell's *that* supposed to mean?"

"Well, I should think Mrs. Strange'll be pleased to have you around, won't she? Retirement, you know. . . . Getting up late and watching all the other poor sods go off to work, especially on Monday mornings. That sort of thing. It's what we all work for, I suppose. What we all wait for."

"You mean," muttered Strange, "*that's* what I've been flogging me guts out all this time for—thirty-two years of it? I used to do your sort of job, you know. Caught nearly as many murderers as you in me day. It's just that I used to do it a bit different, that's all. Mostly used to wait till they came to *me*. No problem, often as not: jealousy, booze, sex, next-door neighbor between the sheets with the missus. *Motive*—that's what it's all about."

"Not always quite so easy, though, is it?" ventured Morse, who had heard the sermon several times before.

"Certainly not when *you're* around, matey!"

"This case needs some very careful handling, sir. Lots of sensitive inquiries—"

"Such as?"

"About Owens, for a start."

"You've got some new evidence?"

"One or two vague rumors, yes."

"Mm . . . I heard a vague rumor myself this afternoon. I heard Owens' place got burgled. I suppose you've heard that, too?" He peered at Morse over his half-lenses.

"Yes."

"Only one thing pinched. Hm! A clock, Morse."

"Yes."

"We've only got one or two clock specialists on the patch, as far as I remember. Or is it just the one?"

"The one?"

"You've not seen him—since they let him out again?"

"Ah, Johnson! Yes. I shall have to call round to see him pretty soon, I suppose."

"What about tomorrow? He's probably your man, isn't he?"

"I'm away tomorrow."

"Oh?"

"London. Soho, as a matter of fact. Few things to check out."

"I don't know why you don't let Sergeant Lewis do all that sort of tedious legwork."

Morse felt the Chief Superintendent's small, shrewd eyes upon him.

"Division of labor. Someone's got to do it."

"You know," said Strange, "if I hadn't got a Supers' meeting in the morning, I'd join you. See the sights . . . and everything."

"I don't think Mrs. Strange'd approve."

"What makes you think I'd tell her?"

"She's—she's not been all that well, has she?"

Strange slowly shook his head, and looked down at the carpet.

"What about you, sir?"

"Me? I'm fine, apart from going deaf and going bald and hemorrhoids and blood pressure. Bit overweight, too, perhaps. What about you?"

"I'm fine."

"How's the drinking going?"

"Going? It's going, er . . ."

"'Quickly?' Is that the word you're looking for?"

"That's the word."

Strange appeared about to leave. And—blessedly! —Lewis, Morse realized, must have been aware of the situation, since he had put in no appearance.

But Strange was not quite finished: "Do you ever worry how your liver's coping with all this booze?"

"We've all got to die of something, they say."

"Do you ever think about that—about dying?"

"Occasionally."

"Do you believe in life after death?"

Morse smiled. "There was a sign once that Slough Borough Council put up near one of the churches there: NO ROAD BEYOND THE CEMETERY."

"You don't think there is, then?"

"No," answered Morse simply.

"Perhaps it's just as well if there isn't—you know, rewards and punishments and all that sort of thing."

"I don't want much reward, anyway."

"Depends on your ambition. You never had much o' that, did you?"

"Early on, I did."

"You could've got to the top, you know that."

"Not doing a job I enjoyed, I couldn't. I'm not a form filler, am I? Or a committeeman. Or a clipboard man."

"Or a *procedure* man," added Strange slowly, as he struggled to his feet.

"Pardon?"

"Bloody piles!"

Morse persisted. "What did you mean, sir?"

"Extraordinary, you know, the sort of high-tech stuff we've got in the Force these days. We've got a machine here that even copies color photos. You know, like the one— Oh! Didn't I mention it, Morse? I had a very pleasant little chat with Sergeant Lewis in the photocopying room just before I came in here. By the look of things, you've got quite a few alternatives to go on there."

"Quite a lot of 'choices,' sir. Strictly speaking, you only have 'alternatives' if you've just got the two options."

"Fuck off, Morse!"

⊹

That evening Morse was in bed by 9:45 P.M., slowly reading but a few more pages of Juliet Barker's *The Brontës*, before stopping at one sentence, and reading it again:

> *Charlotte remarked, "I am sorry you have changed your residence as I shall now again lose my way in going up and down stairs, and stand in great tribulation, contemplating several doors, and not knowing which to open."*

It seemed as good a place to stop as any; and Morse was soon nodding off, in a semi-upright posture, the thick book dropping on to the duvet, the whiskey on his bedside table (unprecedentedly) unfinished.

Chapter Thirty-One

A time
Older than the time of chronometers, older
Than time counted by anxious worried women
Lying awake, calculating the future,
Trying to unweave, unwind, unravel
And piece together the past and the future.

—T. S. Eliot, *The Dry Salvages*

THE RESULT OF one election had already been declared, with Mr. Ivan Thomas, the Labor candidate, former unsuccessful aspirant to municipal honors, now preparing to assume his duties as councillor for the Gosforth ward at Kidlington, near Oxford.

At Lonsdale College, five miles further south, in the golden heart of Oxford, the likely outcome of another election was still very much in the balance, with the wives of the two nominees very much—and not too discreetly, perhaps—to the fore in the continued canvasing. As it happened, each of them (like Morse) was in bed—or in *a* bed—comparatively early that Sunday evening.

><

Shelly Cornford was always a long time in the bathroom, manipulating her waxed flossing-ribbon in between and up and down her beautifully healthy teeth. When finally she came into the bedroom, her husband was sitting up against the pillows reading the *Sunday Times* Books Section. He watched her as she took off her purple Jaeger dress, and then unfastened her black bra, her breasts bursting free. So very nearly he said something at that point; but the back of his mouth was suddenly dry, and he decided not to. Anyway, it had been only a small incident, and his wife was probably completely unaware of how she could affect some other men—with a touch, a look, a movement of her body. But he'd never been a jealous man.

Not if he could help it.

She got into bed in her Oxford blue pajamas and briefly turned toward him.

"Why wasn't Julian at dinner tonight?"

"Up in Durham—some conference he was speaking at. He's back tonight—Angela's picking him up from the station, so she said."

"Oh."

"Why do you ask?"

"No reason, darling. Night-night! Sweet dreams, my sweetie!"

She blew a kiss across the narrow space between their beds, turned her back toward him, and snuggled her head into the green pillows.

"Don't be too long with the light, please."

A few minutes later she was lying still, breathing quite rhythmically, and he thought she was asleep.

As quietly as he could, he maneuvered himself down beneath the bedclothes, and straightway turned off the light. And tried, tried far too hard, to go to sleep himself . . .

><

. . . After evensong earlier that same evening in the College Chapel, the Fellows and their guests had been invited (as was the custom) to the Master's Lodge, where they partook of a glass of sherry before dining at 7:30 P.M. at the top table in the main hall, the students seated on the long rows of benches below them. It was just before leaving the Master's Lodge that Denis had looked round for his wife and found her by the fireplace speaking to David Mackenzie, one of the younger dons, a brilliant mathematician, of considerable corpulence, who hastily folded the letter he had been showing to Shelly and put it away.

Nothing in that, perhaps? Not in itself, no. But he, Denis Cornford, knew what was in the letter. And that, for the simplest of all reasons, since Mackenzie had shown him the same scented purple sheets in the SCR the previous week; and Cornford could recall pretty accurately, though naturally not verbatim, the passage he'd been invited to consider. Clearly the letter had been, thus far, the highlight of Mackenzie's term:

Remember what you scribbled on my menu that night? Your handwriting was a bit wobbly(!) and I couldn't quite make out just that one word: "I'd love

*to take you out and make a f— of you." I think it was
"fuss" and it certainly begins with an "f." Could be
naughty; could be perfectly innocent. Please
enlighten me!*

Surely it was ridiculous to worry about such a thing.
But there was something else. The two of them had
been giggling together like a pair of adolescents, and
looking at each other, and she had put a hand on his
arm. And it was almost as if they had established a
curious kind of intimacy from which he, Denis Cornford, was temporarily excluded.

Could be naughty.

Could be perfectly innocent . . .

※

"Would you still love me if I'd got a spot on my
nose?"

"Depends how big it was, my love."

"But you still want my body, don't you," she whispered, "in spite of my varicose veins?"

Metaphorically, as he lay beside her, Sir Clixby
sidestepped her full-frontal assault as she turned herself toward him.

"You're a very desirable woman, and what's more
you know it!" He moved his hands down her naked
shoulders and fondled the curves of her bosom.

"I *hope* I can still do something for you," she whispered. "After all, you've promised to do something
for me, haven't you?"

Perhaps Sir Clixby should have been a diplomat:

"Do you know something? I thought the Bishop was never going to finish tonight, didn't you? I shall have to have a word with the Chaplain. God knows where he found *him*?"

She moved even closer to the Master. "Come on! We haven't got all night. Julian's train gets in at ten past ten."

➤❖

Two of the College dons stood speaking together on the cobblestones outside Lonsdale as the clock on Great Saint Mary's struck ten o'clock; and a sole undergraduate passing through the main gate thought he heard a brief snatch of their conversation:

"Having a woman like *her* in the Lodge? The idea's unthinkable!"

But who the woman was, the passerby was not to know.

Chapter Thirty-Two

Monday, February 26

How shall I give thee up, O Ephraim? How shall I cast thee off, O Israel?

—Hosea, ch. 2, v. 8

AT 8:45 A.M. THERE were just the two of them, Morse and Lewis, exchanging somewhat random thoughts about the case, when the young blonde girl (whom Strange had already noticed) came in with the morning post. She was a very recent addition to the typing pool, strongly recommended by the prestigious Marlborough College in the High, her secretarial skills corroborated by considerable evidence, including a Pitman Shorthand Certificate for 120 wpm.

"Your mail, sir. I'm . . ." (she looked frightened) "I'm terribly sorry about the one on top. I just didn't notice."

But Morse had already taken the letter from its white envelope, the latter marked, in the top left-hand corner, "Strictly Private and Personal."

Hullo Morse

Tried you on the blower at Christmas but they said you were otherwise engaged probably in the boozer. I'm getting spliced. No, don't worry! I'm not asking you for anything this time!! He's nice and he's got a decent job and he says he loves me and he's okay in bed so what the hell. I don't really love him and you bloody well know why that is, don't you, you miserable stupid sod. Because I fell in love with you and I'm just as stupid as you are. St. Anthony told me to tell you something but I'm not going to. I want to put my arms round you and hug you tight. God help me! Why didn't you look for me a bit harder Morse?

Ellie

No address.

Of course, there was no address.

"Did you read this?" Morse spoke in level tones, looking up at his secretary with unblinking eyes.

"Only till . . . you know, I realized . . ."

"You shouldn't have opened it."

"No, sir," she whispered.

"You can type all right?"

She nodded.

"And you can take shorthand?"

She nodded, despairingly.

"But you can't read?"

"As I said, sir . . ." The tears were starting.

"I heard what *you* said. Now just you listen to what *I'm* saying. This sort of thing will never happen again!"

"I promise, sir, it'll—"

"Listen!" Morse's eyes suddenly widened with an almost manic gleam, his nostrils flaring with suppressed fury as he repeated in a slow, soft voice: "It won't happen again—not if you want to work for me any longer. Is that clear? *Never.* Now get out," he hissed, "and leave me, before I get angry with you."

After she had left, Lewis too felt almost afraid to speak.

"What was all that about?" he asked finally.

"Don't you start poking your bloody nose—" But the sentence went no further. Instead, Morse picked up the letter and passed it over, his saddened eyes focused on the wainscoting.

After reading the letter, Lewis said nothing.

"I don't have much luck with the ladies, do I?"

"She's still obviously wearing the pendant."

"I hope so," said Morse; who might have said rather more, but there was a knock on the door, and DC Learoyd was invited into the sanctum.

Morse handed over the newspaper cuttings concerning Lord Hardiman, together with the photograph, and explained Learoyd's assignment:

"Your job's to find out all you can. It doesn't look all that promising, I know. Hardly blackmail stuff these days, is it? But Owens thinks it is. And that's the point. We're not really interested in how many times he's been knocking on the doors of the knocking shops. It's finding the nature of his connection with *Owens*."

Learoyd nodded his understanding, albeit a little unhappily.

"Off you go, then."

But Learoyd delayed. "Whereabouts do you think would be a good place to start, sir?"

Morse's eyeballs turned ceilingward.

"What about looking up His Lordship in *Debrett's Peerage*, mm? It might just tell you where he lives, don't you think?"

"But where can I find a copy?"

"What about that big building in the center of Oxford—in Bonn Square. You've heard of it? It's called the Central Library."

><

Item 2 in the manila file, as Lewis had discovered earlier that morning, was OBE (Overtaken By Events, in Morse's shorthand). The Cheltenham firm of solicitors had been disbanded in 1992, its clientèle dispersed, to all intents and purposes now permanently incommunicado.

><

Item 3 was to be entrusted into the huge hands of DC Elton, who now made his entrance; and almost immediately his exit, since he passed no observations, and asked no questions, as he looked down at the paunchy pedophiliac from St. Albans.

"Leave it to me, sir."

"And while you're at it, see how the land lies *here*." Morse handed over the documentation on Item 4— the accounts sheets from the surgical appliances company in Croydon.

"Good man, that," commented Lewis, as the door closed behind the massive frame of DC Elton.

"Give me Learoyd every time!" confided Morse. "At least he's got the intelligence to ask a few half-witted questions."

"I don't quite follow you."

"Wouldn't *you* need a bit of advice if you called in at some place selling surgical appliances? With Elton's great beer gut they'll probably think he's called in for a temporary truss."

Lewis didn't argue.

He knew better.

><

Also OBE, as Lewis had already discovered, was Item 5. The address Owens had written on the letter was—had been—that of a home for the mentally handicapped in Wimbledon. A Social Services inspection had uncovered gross and negligent mal-practices; and the establishment had been closed down two years previously, its management and nursing staff redeployed or declared redundant. Yet no prosecutions had ensued.

"Forlorn hope," Lewis had ventured.

And Morse had agreed. "Did you know that 'forlorn

hope' has got nothing to do with 'forlorn' or 'hope'?
It's all Dutch: 'Verloren hoop'—'lost troop.'"

"Very useful to know, sir."

Seemingly oblivious to such sarcasm, Morse contemplated once more the four sets of initials that comprised Item 6:

$$\textbf{AM}^{\checkmark} \quad \textbf{DC}^{\checkmark} \quad \textbf{JS}^{\checkmark} \quad \textbf{CB}$$

with those small ticks in red Biro set against the first three of them.

"Any ideas?" asked Lewis.

" 'Jonathan Swift,' obviously, for 'JS.' I was only talking about him to the Super yesterday."

"Julian Storrs?"

Morse grinned. "Perhaps *all* of 'em are dons at Lonsdale."

"I'll check."

"So that leaves Items seven and eight—both of which I leave in your capable hands, Lewis. And lastly my own little assignment in Soho, Item nine."

"Coffee, sir?"

"Glass of iced orange juice!"

❖

After Lewis had gone, Morse re-read Ellie's letter, deeply hurt, and wondering whether people in the ancient past had found it quite so difficult to cope with disappointments deep as his. But at least things were over; and in the long run that might make things much easier. He tore the letter in two, in four, in eight, in sixteen, and then in thirty-two—would have torn it in sixty-four, had his fingers been strong enough—before dropping the little square pieces into his wastepaper basket.

>‹

"No ice in the canteen, sir. Machine's gone kaput."

Morse shrugged indifferently and Lewis, sensing that the time might be opportune, decided to say something which had been on his mind:

"Just one thing I'd like to ask . . ."

Morse looked up sharply. "You're not going to ask me where Lonsdale is, I hope!"

"No. I'd just like to ask you not to be too hard on that new secretary of yours, that's all."

"And what the hell's that got to do with you?"

"Nothing really, sir."

"I *agree*. And when I want your bloody advice on how to handle my secretarial staff, I'll come and ask for it. Clear?"

Morse's eyes were blazing anew. And Lewis, his own temperature now rising rapidly, left his superior's office without a further word.

>‹

Just before noon, Jane Edwards was finalizing an angry letter, spelling out her resignation, when she heard the message over the intercom: Morse wanted to see her in his office.

"Si' down!"

She sat down, noticing immediately that he seemed tired, the whites of his eyes lightly veined with blood.

"I'm sorry I got so cross, Jane. That's all I wanted to say."

She remained where she was, almost mesmerized.

Very quietly he continued: "You *will* try to forgive me—please?"

She nodded helplessly, for she had no choice.

And Morse smiled at her sadly, almost gratefully, as she left.

Back in the typing pool Ms. Jane Edwards surreptitiously dabbed away the last of the slow-dropping tears, tore up her letter (so carefully composed) into sixty-four pieces; and suddenly felt, as if by some miracle of St. Anthony, most inexplicably happy.

Chapter Thirty-Three

A recent survey has revealed that 80.5 percent of
Oxford dons seek out the likely pornographic
potential on the Internet before making use of that
facility for purposes connected with their own dis-
ciplines or research. The figure for students, in the
same university, is 2 percent lower.

—Terence Benczik, *A Possible Future for
Computer Technology*

UNTIL THE AGE OF twelve, Morse's reading had comprised little beyond a weekly diet of the *Dandy* comic,
and a monthly diet of the *Meccano Magazine*—the
legacy of the latter proving considerably the richer, in
that Morse had retained a lifelong delight in model
train sets and in the railways themselves. Thus it was
that as he stood on Platform One at Oxford Station, he
was much looking forward to his journey. Usually, he
promised himself a decent read of a decent book on a
trip like this. But such potential pleasures seldom
materialized; hadn't materialized that afternoon either,
when the punctual 2:15 P.M. from Oxford arrived fifty-
nine minutes later at Paddington, where Morse immediately took a taxi to New Scotland Yard.

Although matters there had been prearranged, it
was purely by chance that Morse happened to meet

Paul Condon, the Metropolitan Commissioner, in the main entrance foyer.

"They're ready for you, Morse. Can't stay myself, I'm afraid. Press conference. It's not just the ethnic minorities I've upset this time—it's the ethnic majorities, too. All because I've published a few more official crime statistics."

Morse nodded. He wanted to say something to his old friend: something about never climbing in vain when you're going up the Mountain of Truth. But he only recalled the quotation after stepping out of the lift at the fourth floor, where Sergeant Rogers of the Porn Squad was awaiting him.

Once in Rogers' office, Morse produced the photograph of the strip club. And immediately, with the speed of an experienced ornithologist recognizing a picture of a parrot, Rogers had identified the premises.

"Just off Brewer Street." He unfolded a detailed map of Soho. "Here—let me show you."

>←

The early evening was overcast, drizzly and dank, when like some latter-day Orpheus Morse emerged from the depths of Piccadilly Circus Underground; when, after briefly consulting his A–Z, he proceeded by a reasonably direct route to a narrow, seedy-looking thoroughfare, where a succession of establishments promised XXXX videos and magazines (imported), sex shows (live), striptease (continuous)—and a selection of freshly made sandwiches (various).

And there it was! *Le Club Sexy*. Unmistakably so, but prosaically and repetitively now rechristened *Girls Girls Girls*. It made the former proprietors appear comparatively imaginative.

Something—some aspiration to the higher things in life, perhaps—prompted Morse to raise his eyes from the ground-floor level of the gaudily lurid fronts there to the architecture, some of it rather splendid, above.

Yet not for long.

"Come in out of the drizzle, sir! Lovely girls here."

Morse showed his ID card, and moved into the shelter of the tiny entrance foyer.

"Do you know *her*?"

The young woman, black stockings and black miniskirt meeting at the top of her thighs, barely glanced at the photograph thrust under her eyes.

"No."

"Who runs this place? I want to see him."

"*Her*. But she ain't 'ere now, is she? Why don't you call back later, handsome?"

A helmeted policeman was ambling along the opposite pavement, and Morse called him over.

"Okay," the girl said quickly. "You bin 'ere before, right?"

"Er—one of my officers, yes."

"Me mum used to know her, like I told the other fellah. Just a minute."

She disappeared down the dingy stairs.

"How can I help you, sir?"

Morse showed his ID to the constable.

"Just keep your eyes on me for a few minutes."

But there was no need.

Three minutes later, Morse had an address in Praed Street, no more than a hundred yards from Paddington Station where earlier, at the entrance to the Underground, he had admired the bronze statue of one of his heroes, Isambard Kingdom Brunel.

So Morse now took the Tube back. It had been a roundabout sort of journey.

><

She was in.

She asked him in.

And Morse, from a moth-eaten settee, agreed to sample a cup of Nescafé.

"Yeah, Angie Martin! Toffee-nosed little tart, if you know wo' I mean."

"Tell me about her."

"You're the *second* one, encha?"

"Er—one of my officers, yes."

"Nah! He wasn't from the fuzz. Couldna bin! Giv me a couple o' twennies 'e did."

"What did he want to know?"

"Same as you, like as not."

"She was quite a girl, they say."

"Lovely on 'er legs, she was, if you know wo' I mean. Most of 'em, these days, couldn't manage the bleedin' Barn Dance."

"But *she* was good?"

"Yeah. The men used to love 'er. Stick fivers down 'er boobs and up 'er suspenders, if you know wo' I mean."

"She packed 'em in?"

"Yeah."

"And then?"

"Then there was this fellah, see, and he got to know 'er and see 'er after the shows, like, and 'e got starry-eyed, the silly sod. Took 'er away. Posh sort o' fellah, if you know wo' I mean. Dresses, money, 'otels—all that sort o' thing."

"Would you remember *his* name?"

"Yeah. The other fellah—'e showed me his photo, see?"

"His name?"

"Julius Caesar, I fink it was."

Morse showed her the photograph of Mr. and Mrs. Julian Storrs.

"Yeah. That's 'im an' 'er. That's Angie."

"Do you know why I'm asking about her?"

She looked at him shrewdly, an inch or so of gray roots merging into a yellow mop of wiry hair.

"Yeah, I got a good idea."

"My, er, colleague told you?"

"Nah! Worked it out for meself, dint I? She was tryin' to forget wo' she was, see? She dint want to say she were a cheap tart who'd open 'er legs for a fiver, if you know wo' I mean. Bi' o' class, tho', Angie. Yeah. Real bi' o' class."

"Will you be prepared to come up to Oxford—

we'll pay your expenses, of course—to sign a statement?"

"Oxford? Yeah. Why not? Bi' o' class, Oxford, innit?"

"I suppose so, yes."

"Wo' she done? Wo' sort of inquiry you workin' on?"

"Murder," said Morse softly.

❋

Mission accomplished, Morse walked across Praed Street and into the complex of Paddington Station, where he stood under the high Departures Board and noted the time of the next train: Slough, Maidenhead, Reading, Didcot, Oxford.

Due to leave in forty minutes.

He retraced his steps to the top of the Underground entrance, crushed a cigarette stub under his heel, and walked slowly down toward the ticket office, debating the wisdom of purchasing a second Bakerloo line ticket to Piccadilly Circus—from which station he might take the opportunity of concentrating his attention on the ground-floor attractions of London's Soho.

Chapter Thirty-Four

The average, healthy, well-adjusted adult gets up at seven-thirty in the morning feeling just plain terrible.

—Jean Kerr, *Where Did You Put the Aspirin?*

WITH A LECTURE A.M. and a Faculty Meeting early P.M., Julian Storrs had not been able to give Lewis much time until late P.M.; but he was ready and waiting when, at 4 o'clock precisely, the front doorbell rang at his home, a large redbricked property in Polstead Road, part of the Victorian suburb that stretches north from St. Giles' to Summertown.

Lewis accepted the offer of real coffee, and the two of them were soon seated in armchairs opposite each other in the high-ceilinged living room, its furniture exuding a polished mahogany elegance, where Lewis immediately explained the purpose of his call.

As a result of police investigations into the murder of Rachel James, Storrs' name had moved into the frame; well, at least his photograph had moved into the frame.

Storrs himself said nothing as he glanced down at the twin passport photograph that Lewis handed to him.

"That *is* you, sir? You and Ms. James?"

Storrs took a deep breath, then exhaled. "Yes."

"You were having an affair with her?"

"We . . . yes, I suppose we were."

"Did anybody know about it?"

"I'd hoped not."

"Do you want to talk about it?"

Storrs talked. Though not for long . . .

❧❧

He'd first met her just over a year earlier when he'd pulled a muscle in his right calf following an ill-judged decision to take up jogging. She was a physiotherapist, masseuse, manipulator—whatever they called such people now; and after the first two or three sessions they had met together *outside* the treatment room. He'd fallen in love with her a bit—a lot; must have done, when he considered the risks he'd taken. About once a month, six weeks, they'd managed to be together when he had some lecture to give or meeting to attend. Usually in London, where they'd book a double room, latish morning, in one of the hotels behind Paddington, drink a bottle or two of champagne, make love together most of the afternoon and—well, that was it.

"Expensive sort of day, sir? Rail fares, hotel, champagne, something to eat . . ."

"Not really expensive, no. Off-peak day returns, one of the cheaper hotels, middle-range champagne, and we'd go to a pub for a sandwich at lunchtime.

Hundred and twenty, hundred and thirty pounds—that would cover it."

"You didn't give Ms. James anything for her services?"

"It wasn't like that. I think—I hope—she enjoyed being with me. But, yes, I did sometimes give her something. She was pretty short of money—you know, her mortgage, HP commitments, the rent on the clinic."

"How much, sir?"

"A hundred pounds. Little bit more sometimes, perhaps."

"Does Mrs. Storrs know about this?"

"No—and she mustn't!" For the first time Lewis was aware of the sharp, authoritative tone in the Senior Fellow's voice.

"How did you explain spending so much?"

"We have separate accounts. I give my wife a private allowance each month."

Lewis grinned diffidently. "You could always have said they were donations to Oxfam."

Storrs looked down rather sadly at the olive-green carpet. "You're right. That's just the sort of depths I would have sunk to."

"Why didn't you get in touch with us? We made several appeals for anybody who knew Rachel to come forward. We guaranteed every confidence."

"You must understand, surely? I was desperately anxious not to get drawn into things in any way."

"Nothing else?"

"What do you mean?"

"Was someone trying to blackmail you, sir, about your affair with her?"

"Good God, no! What on earth makes you think that?"

Lewis drank the rest of his never-hot now-cold real coffee, before continuing quietly:

"I don't believe you, sir."

And slowly the truth, or some of it, was forthcoming.

✧

Storrs had received a letter about a fortnight earlier from someone—no signature—someone giving a P.O. Box address; someone claiming to have "evidence" about him which would be shouted from the rooftops unless a payment was duly made.

"Of?" asked Lewis.

"Five thousand pounds."

"And you paid it?"

"No. But I was stupid enough to send a thousand, in fifty-pound notes."

"And did you get this 'evidence' back?"

Storrs again looked down at the carpet, and shook his head.

"You didn't act very sensibly, did you, sir?"

"In literary circles, Sergeant, that is what is called 'litotes.'"

"Did you keep the letter?"

"No," lied Storrs.

"Did you keep a note of the P.O. Box number?"

"No," lied Storrs.

"Was it care of one of the local newspapers?"

"Yes."

"*Oxford Mail?*"

"*Oxford Times.*"

The living room door opened, and there entered a darkly elegant woman, incongruously wearing a pair of sunglasses, and dressed in a black trouser-suit— "Legs right up to the armpits," as Lewis was later to report.

Mrs. Angela Storrs briefly introduced herself, and picked up the empty cups.

"Another coffee, Sergeant?"

Her voice was Home Counties, rather deep, rather pleasing.

"No thanks. That was lovely."

Her eyes smiled behind the sunglasses—or Lewis thought they smiled. And as she closed the living room door softly behind her, he wondered where she'd been throughout the interview. Outside the door, perhaps, listening? Had she heard what her husband had said? Or had she known it all along?

Then the door quietly opened again.

"You won't forget you're out this evening, darling? You haven't *all* that much time, you know."

Lewis accepted the cue and hurried on his questioning apace:

"Do you mind telling me exactly what you were doing between seven A.M. and eight A.M. last Monday, sir?"

"Last Monday morning? Ah!" Lewis sensed that Julian Storrs had suddenly relaxed—as if the tricky part of the examination was now over—as if he could safely resume his wonted donnish idiom.

"How I wish every question my students asked were susceptible to such an unequivocal answer! You see, I was in bed with my wife and we were having sex together. And why do I recall this so readily, Sergeant? Because such an occurrence has not been quite so common these past few years; nor, if I'm honest with you, quite so enjoyable as once it was."

"Between, er, between seven and eight?" Lewis's voice was hesitant.

"Sounds a long time, you mean? Huh! You're right. More like twenty past to twenty-five past seven. What I do remember is Angela—Mrs. Storrs—wanting the news on at half past. She's a great *Today* fan, and she likes to know what's going on. We just caught the tail end of the sports news—then the main headlines on the half-hour."

"Oh!"

"Do you believe me?"

"Would Mrs. Storrs remember . . . as clearly as you, sir?"

Storrs gave a slightly bitter-sounding laugh. "Why don't you ask her? Shall I tell her to come through? I'll leave you alone."

"Yes, I think that would be helpful."

Storrs got to his feet and walked toward the door.

"Just one more question, sir." Lewis too rose to his feet. "Don't you think you were awfully naive to send off that money? I think anyone could have told you you weren't going to get anything back—except another blackmail note."

Storrs walked back into the room.

"Are you a married man, Sergeant?"

"Yes."

"How would you explain—well, say a photograph like the one you showed me?"

Lewis took out the passport photo again.

"Not too difficult, surely? You're a well-known man, sir—quite a distinguished-looking man, perhaps? So let's just say one of your admiring under-graduettes sees you at a railway station and says she'd like to have a picture taken with you. You know, one of those 'Four color photos in approximately four minutes' places. Then she could carry the pair of you around with her, like some girls carry pictures of pop stars around."

Storrs nodded. "Clever idea! I wish *I'd* thought of it. Er . . . can I ask *you* a question?"

"Yes?"

"Why are you still only a sergeant?"

Lewis made no comment on the matter, but asked a final question:

"You're standing for the Mastership at Lonsdale, I understand, sir?"

"Ye-es. So you can see, can't you, why all this business, you know . . . ?"

"Of course."

Storrs' face now suddenly cleared.

"There are just the two of us: Dr. Cornford—Denis Cornford—and myself. And may the better man win!"

He said it lightly, as if the pair of them were destined to cross swords in a mighty game of Scrabble —and called through to Angela, his wife.

Chapter Thirty-Five

Keep your eyes wide open before marriage, half
shut afterward.

—Benjamin Franklin, *Poor Richard's Almanack*

IN OXFORD THAT same early evening the clouds were
inkily black, the forecast set for heavy rain, with
most of those walking along Broad Street or around
Radcliffe Square wearing raincoats and carrying
umbrellas. The majority of these people were students making their way to College Halls for their
evening meals, much as their predecessors had done
in earlier times, passing through the same streets, past
the same familiar buildings, and later returning to the
same sort of accommodation, and in most cases
doing some work for the morrow, when they would
be listening to the same sort of lectures. Unless, perhaps, they were students of Physics or some similar
discipline where breakthroughs ("Breaksthrough, if
we are to be accurate, dear boy") were as regular as
inaccuracies in the daily weather forecasts.

But that evening the forecast was surprisingly accurate; and at 6:45 P.M. the rains came.

Denis Cornford looked out through the window
onto Holywell Street where the rain bounced off the

surface of the road like arrowheads. St. Peter's (Dinner, 7:00 for 7:30 P.M.) was only ten minutes' walk away but he was going to get soaked in such a downpour.

"What do you think, darling?"

"Give it five minutes. If it keeps on like this, I should get a cab. You've got plenty of time."

"What'll you be doing?" he asked.

"Well, I don't think I'll be venturing out too far, do you?" She said it in a gentle way, and there seemed no sarcasm in her voice. She came up behind him and placed her hands on his shoulders as he stood indecisively staring out through the sheeted panes.

"Denis?"

"Mm?"

"Do you really want to be Master all *that* much?"

He turned toward her and looked directly into her dazzlingly attractive dark eyes, with that small circular white light in the center of their irises—eyes which had always held men, and tempted them, and occasioned innumerable capitulations.

"Yes, Shelly. Yes, I do! Not quite so badly as Julian, perhaps. But badly enough."

"What would you give—to be Master?"

"Most things, I suppose."

"Give up your work?"

"A good deal of that would go anyway. It would be different work, that's all."

"Would you give *me* up?"

He took her in his arms. "Of course, I would!"

"You don't really mean—?"

He kissed her mouth with a strangely passionate tenderness.

A few minutes later they stood arm-in-arm at the window looking out at the ceaselessly teeming rain.

"I'll ring for a cab," said Shelly Cornford.

✦

On Mondays the dons' attendance at Lonsdale Dinner was usually fairly small, but Roy Porter would be there, Angela Storrs knew that: Roy Porter was almost always there. She rang him in his rooms at 6:55 P.M.

"Roy?"

"Angela! Good to hear your beautiful voice."

"Flattery will get you exactly halfway between nowhere and everywhere."

"I'll settle for that."

"You're dining tonight?"

"Yep."

"Would you like to come along afterward and cheer up a lonely old lady."

"Julian away?"

"Some Brains Trust at Reading University."

"Shall I bring a bottle?"

"Plenty of bottles here."

"Marvelous."

"Nine-ish?"

"About then. Er . . . Angela? Is it something you want to talk about or is it just . . . ?"

"Why not both?"

"You want to know how things seem to be going with the election?"

"I'm making no secret of that."

"You do realize I don't know anything definite at all?"

"I don't expect you to. But I'd like to talk. You can understand how I feel, can't you?"

"Of course."

"And I've been speaking to Julian. There *are* one or two little preferments perhaps in the offing, if he's elected."

"Really?"

"But like you, Roy, I don't know anything definite."

"I understand. But it'll be good to be together again."

"Oh, yes. Have a drink or two together."

"Or three?"

"Or four?" suggested Angela Storrs, her voice growing huskier still.

⇥⇤

The phone rang at 7:05 P.M.

"Shelly?"

"Yes."

"You're on your own?"

"You know I am."

"Denis gone?"

"Left fifteen minutes ago."

"One or two things to tell you, if we could meet?"

"What sort of things?"

"Nothing definite. But there's talk about a potential benefaction from the States, and one of the trustees met Denis—met *you*, I gather, too—and, well, I can tell you all about it when we meet."

"*All* about it?"

"It's a biggish thing, and I think we may be slightly more likely to pull it off, perhaps, if Denis . . ."

"And you'll be doing your best?"

"I can't promise anything."

"I know that."

"So?"

"So?"

"So you're free and I'm free."

"On a night like this? Far too dangerous. Me coming to the Master's Lodge? No chance."

"I agree. But, you see, one of my old colleagues is off to Greece—he's left me his key—just up the Banbury Road—lovely comfy double bed—crisp clean sheets—central heating—*en suite* facilities—mini bar. Tariff? No pounds, no shillings, no pence."

"You remember pre-decimalization?"

"I'm not *too* old, though, am I? And I'd just love to be with you now, at this minute. More than anything in the world."

"You ought to find a new variation on the theme, you know! It's getting a bit of a cliché."

"Cleesháy," she'd said; but however she'd pronounced it, the barb had found its mark; and Sir Clixby's voice was softer, more serious as he answered her.

"I need you, Shelly. Please come out with me. I'll get a taxi round to you in ten minutes' time, if that's all right?"

There was silence on the other end of the line.

"Shelly?"

"Yes?"

"Will that be all right?"

"No," she replied quietly. "No it won't. I'm sorry."

The line was dead.

><

Just before nine o'clock, Cornford rang home from St. Peter's:

"Shelly? Denis. Look, darling, I've just noticed in my diary . . . You've not had a call tonight, have you?"

Shelly's heart registered a sudden, sharp stab of panic.

"No, why?"

"It's just that the New York publishers said they might be ringing. So, if they do, please make a note of the number and tell 'em I'll ring them back. All right?"

"Fine. Yes."

"You having a nice evening?"

"Mm. It's lovely to sit and watch TV for a change. No engagements. No problems."

"See you soon."

"I hope so."

Shelly put down the phone slowly. "I've just noticed in my diary," he'd said. But he hadn't, she knew that. She'd looked in his diary earlier that day, to make sure of the time of the St. Peter's do. That had been the only entry on the page for 2-26-96.

➤◄

Just before ten o'clock, Julian Storrs rang his wife from Reading; rang three times.

The number was engaged.

He rang five minutes later.

The number was still engaged.

He rang again, after a further five minutes.

She answered.

"Angie? I've been trying to get you these last twenty minutes."

"I've only been talking to Mom, for Christ's sake!"

"It's just that I shan't be home till after midnight, that's all. So I'll get a taxi. Don't worry about meeting me."

"Okay."

After she had hung up, Angela Storrs took a Thames Trains timetable from her handbag and saw that Julian could easily be catching an earlier train: the 22:40 from Reading, arriving Oxford 23:20. Not that it mattered. Perhaps he was having a few drinks with his hosts? Or perhaps—the chilling thought struck her—he was checking up on her?

Hurriedly she rang her mother in South Kensington. And kept on talking. The call would be duly registered on the itemized BT lists and suddenly she felt considerably easier in her mind.

><

Morse had caught the 23:48 from Paddington that night, and at 01:00 sat unhearing as the Senior Conductor made his lugubrious pronouncement: "Oxford, Oxford. This train has now terminated. Please be sure to take all your personal possessions with you. Thank you."

From a deeply delicious cataleptic state, Morse was finally prodded into consciousness by no less a personage than the Senior Conductor himself.

"All right, sir?"

"Thank you, yes."

But in truth things were not all right, since Morse had been deeply disappointed by his evening's sojourn in London. And as he walked down the station steps to the taxi rank, he reminded himself of what he'd always known—that life was full of disappointments: of which the most immediate was that not a single taxi was in sight.

Chapter Thirty-Six

Tuesday, February 27

> Initium est dimidium facti (Once you've started,
> you're halfway there).
>
> —Latin proverb

AN UNSHAVEN MORSE was still dressed in his mauve
and Cambridge blue pajamas when Lewis arrived at
10 o'clock the following morning. Over the phone
half an hour earlier he had learned that Morse was
feeling "rough as a bear's arse"—whatever that was
supposed to mean.

For some time the two detectives exchanged information about their previous day's activities; and fairly
soon the obvious truth could be simply stated: Owens
was a blackmailer. Specifically, as far as investigations had thus far progressed, with the Storrs' household being the principal victims: he, for his current
infidelity; she, for her past as a shop-soiled Soho tart.
One thing seemed certain: that *any* disclosure was
likely to be damaging, probably fatally damaging, to
Julian Storrs' chances of election to the Mastership of
Lonsdale.

Morse considered for a while.

"It still gives us a wonderful motive for one of them murdering Owens—not much of a one for murdering Rachel."

"Unless Mrs. Storrs was just plain jealous, sir?"

"Doubt it."

"Or perhaps Rachel got to know something, and was doing a bit of blackmailing herself? She needed the money all right."

"Yes." Morse stroked his bristly jaw and sighed wearily. "There's such a lot we've still got to check on, isn't there? Perhaps you ought to get round to Rachel's bank manager this morning."

"Not this morning, sir—or this afternoon. I'm seeing his lordship, Sir Clixby Bream, at a quarter to twelve; then I'm going to find out who's got access to the photocopier and whatever at the Harvey Clinic."

"Waste o' time," mumbled Morse.

"I dunno, sir. I've got a feeling it may all tie in together somehow."

"What with?"

"I'll know more after I've been to Lonsdale. You see, I've already learned one or two things about the situation there. The present Master's going to retire soon, as you know, and the new man's going to be taking up the reins at the start of the summer term—"

"*Trinity* term."

"—and they've narrowed it down to two candidates: Julian Storrs and a fellow called Cornford, Denis Cornford—he's a Lonsdale man himself, too. And they say the odds are fairly even."

"Who's this 'they' you keep talking about?"

"One of the porters there. We used to play cricket together."

"Ridiculous game!"

"What's *your* program today, sir?"

But Morse appeared not to hear his sergeant's question.

"Cup o' tea, Lewis?"

"Wouldn't say no."

Morse returned a couple of minutes later, with a cup of tea for Lewis and a pint glass of iced water for himself. He sat down and looked at his wristwatch: twenty-five past ten.

"What's your program today?" repeated Lewis.

"I've got a meeting at eleven-thirty this morning. Nothing else much. Perhaps I'll do a bit of thinking —it's high time I caught up with you."

As Lewis drank his tea, talking of this and that, he was aware that Morse seemed distanced—seemed almost in a world of his own. Was he listening at all?

"Am I boring you, sir?"

"What? No, no! Keep talking! That's always the secret, you know, if you want to start anything—start *thinking*, say. All you've got to do is listen to somebody talking a load of nonsense, and somehow, suddenly, something emerges."

"I wasn't talking nonsense, sir. And if I was, *you* wouldn't have known. You weren't listening."

Nor did it appear that Morse was listening even now —as he continued: "I wonder what time the postman comes to Polstead Road. Storrs usually caught the ten-fifteen train from Oxford, you say . . . So he'd leave the house about a quarter to ten—bit earlier, perhaps? He's got to get to the station, park his car, buy a ticket—buy *two* tickets . . . So if the postman called about then . . . perhaps Storrs met him as he left the house and took his letters with him, and read them as he waited for Rachel, then stuffed 'em in his jacket pocket."

"So?"

"So if . . . What do most couples do after they've had sex together?"

"Depends, I suppose." Lewis looked uneasily at his superior. "Go to sleep?"

Morse smiled waywardly. "It's as tiring as that, is it?"

"Well, if they did it more than once."

"Then she—*she*, Lewis—stays awake and goes quietly through his pockets and finds the blackmail letter. By the way, did you ask him *when* he received it?"

"No, sir."

"Well, find out! She sees the letter and she knows she can blackmail *him*. Not about the affair they're having, perhaps—they're both in that together—but about something else she discovered from the letter. . . . You know, I suspect that our Ms. James was getting a bit of a handful for our Mr. Storrs. What do *you* think?" (But Lewis was given no time at all to think.) "What were the last couple of dates they went to London together?"

"That's something else I shall have to check, sir."

"Well, check it! You see, we've been coming round to the idea that somebody was trying to murder Owens, haven't we? And murdered Rachel by mistake. But perhaps we're wrong, Lewis. Perhaps we're wrong."

Morse looked flushed and excited as he drained his iced water and got to his feet.

"I'd better have a quick shave."

"What else have you got on your program—?"

"As I say, you see what happens when you start talking nonsense! You're indispensable, old friend. Absolutely *indispensable!*"

Lewis, who had begun to feel considerable irritation at Morse's earlier brusque demands, was now completely mollified.

"I'll be off then, sir."

"No you won't! I shan't be more than a few minutes. You can run me down to Summertown."

(*Almost* completely mollified.)

⋇

"You still haven't told me what—" began Lewis as he waited at the traffic lights by South Parade.

But a clean-shaven Morse had suddenly stiffened in his safety belt beside him.

"What did you say the name of that other fellow was, Lewis? The chap who's standing against Storrs?"

"Cornford, Denis Cornford. Married to an American girl."

" 'DC,' Lewis! Do you remember in the manila file? Those four sets of initials?"

Lewis nodded, for in his mind's eye he could see that piece of paper as clearly as Morse:

$$\mathbf{AM}^{\checkmark} \quad \mathbf{DC}^{\checkmark} \quad \mathbf{JS}^{\checkmark} \quad \mathbf{CB}$$

"There they are," continued Morse, "side-by-side in the middle—Denis Cornford and Julian Storrs, flanked on either side by Angela Martin—I've little doubt!—and—might it be?—Sir Clixby Bream."

"So you think Owens might have got something on all—?"

"Slow down!" interrupted Morse. "Just round the corner here."

Lewis turned left at the traffic lights into Marston Ferry Road and stopped immediately outside the Summertown Health Center.

"Wish me well," said Morse as he alighted.

Part Three

Chapter Thirty-Seven

Tuesday, February 27

> The land of Idd was a happy one. Well, almost.
> There was one teeny problem. The King had sleep-
> less nights about it and the villagers were very
> scared. The problem was a dragon called Diabetes.
> He lived in a cave on top of a hill. Every day he
> would roar loudly. He never came down the hill but
> everyone was still very scared just in case he did.
>
> —Victoria Lee, *The Dragon of Idd*

FROM THE WAITING ROOM on the first floor, Morse heard his name called.

"How can I help?" asked Dr. Paul Roblin, a man Morse had sought so earnestly to avoid over the years, unless things were bordering on the desperate.

As they were now.

"I think I've got diabetes."

"Why do you think that?"

"I've got a book. It mentions some of the symptoms."

"Which are?"

"Loss of weight, tiredness, a longing for drink."

"You've had the last one quite a while though, haven't you?"

Morse nodded wearily. "I've lost weight; I could

sleep all the time; and I drink a gallon of tap water a day."

"As *well* as the beer?"

Morse was silent, as Roblin jabbed a lancet into the little finger of his left hand, squeezed the skin until a domed globule appeared, then smeared the blood onto a test strip. After thirty seconds, he looked down at the reading. And for a while sat motionless, saying nothing. "How did you get here, Mr. Morse?"

"Car."

"Is your car here?"

"No, I had a lift. Why?"

"Well, I'm afraid I couldn't let you drive a car now."

"Why's that?"

"It's serious. Your blood sugar level's completely off the end of the chart. We shall have to get you to the Radcliffe Infirmary as soon as we can."

"What are you telling me?"

"You should have seen me way before this. Your pancreas has packed in completely. You'll probably be on three or four injections of insulin a day for the rest of your life. You may well have done God-knows-what damage to your eyes and your kidneys —we shall have to find out. The important thing is to get you in hospital immediately."

He reached for the phone.

"I only live just up the road," protested Morse.

Roblin put his hand over the mouthpiece. "They'll have a spare pair of pajamas and a toothbrush. Don't worry!"

"You don't realize—" began Morse.

"Hello? Hello! Can you get an ambulance here—Summertown Health Center—straightaway, please . . . The Radcliffe Infirmary . . . Thank you."

"You don't realize I'm in the middle of a murder inquiry."

But Roblin had dialed a second number, and was already speaking to someone else.

"David? Ah, glad you're there! Have you got a bed available? . . . Bit of an emergency, yes . . . He'll need an insulin drip, I should think. But you'll know . . . Yes . . . Er, Mr. Morse—initial 'E.' He's a chief inspector in the Thames Valley CID."

✴

Half an hour later—weight (almost thirteen stone), blood pressure (alarmingly high), blood sugar level (still off the scale), details of maternal and paternal grandparents' deaths (ill-remembered), all of these duly recorded—Morse found himself lying supine, in a pair of red-striped pajamas, in the Geoffrey Harris Ward in the Radcliffe Infirmary, just north of St. Giles', at the bottom of the Woodstock Road. A tube from the insulin drip suspended at the side of his bed was attached to his right arm by a Cellotaped needle stuck into him just above the inner wrist, allowing little, if any, lateral movement without the sharpest reminder of physical agony.

It was this tube that Morse was glumly considering when the Senior Consultant from the Diabetes Center came round: Dr. David Matthews, a tall, slim, Mephistophelian figure, with darkly ascetic, angular features.

"As I've told you all, I'm in the middle of a murder inquiry," reiterated Morse, as Matthews sat on the side of the bed.

"And can I tell *you* something? You're going to forget all about that, unless you want to kill yourself. With a little bit of luck you may be all right, do you understand? So far you don't seem to have done yourself all that much harm. Enough, though! But you're going to have to forget everything about work —*everything*—if you're going to come through this business without too much damage. You do know what I mean, don't you?"

Morse didn't. But he nodded helplessly.

"Only here four or five days, if you do as we tell you."

"But, as I say—"

"No 'buts,' I'm afraid. Then you might be home Saturday or Sunday."

"But there's so much to do!" remonstrated Morse almost desperately.

"Weren't those the words of Cecil Rhodes?"

"Yes, I think they were."

"The last words, if I recall aright."

Morse was silent.

And the Senior Consultant continued: "Look, there are three basic causes of diabetes—well, that's an oversimplification. But you're not a medical man."

"Thank you," said Morse.

"Hereditary factors, stress, excessive booze. You'd score five . . . six out of ten on the first. Your father had diabetes, I see."

"Latish in life."

"Well, you're not exactly a youngster yourself."

"Perhaps not."

"Stress? You're not too much of a worryguts?"

"Well, I worry about the future of the human race —does that count?"

"What about booze? You seem to drink quite a bit, I see?"

So Morse told him the truth; or, to be more accurate, told him between one-half and one-third of the truth.

Matthews got to his feet, peered at the insulin drip, and marginally readjusted some control thereon.

"Six out of ten on the second; ten out of ten on the third, I'm afraid. And by the way, I'm not allowing you any visitors. None at all—not even close relatives. Just me and the nurses here."

"I haven't got any close relatives," said Morse.

Matthews now stood at the foot of his bed. "You've already had *somebody* wanting to see you, though. Fellow called Lewis."

After Matthews had gone, Morse lay back and thought of his colleague. And for several minutes he felt very low, unmanned as he was with a strangely poignant gratitude.

Chapter Thirty-Eight

Thursday, February 29

> The relations between us were peculiar. He was a
> man of habits, narrow and concentrated habits, and
> I had become one of them. But apart from this I
> had uses. I was a whetstone for his mind, I stimu-
> lated him. He liked to think aloud in my presence.
>
> —Conan Doyle, *The Adventures of
> the Creeping Man*

"AND 'OW IS 'E TODAY, then?" asked Mrs. Lewis
when her husband finally returned home on Thursday evening, and when soon the fat was set a-sizzling
in the chip pan, with the two eggs standing ready to
be broken in the frying pan.

"On the mend."

"They always say that."

"No. He's genuinely on the mend."

"Why can't 'e 'ave visitors then? Not contagious,
is it, this diabetes?"

Lewis smiled at her. Brought up as she had been in
the Rhondda Valley, the gentle Welsh lilt in her voice
was an abiding delight with him—though not, to be
quite truthful, with everyone.

"He'll probably be out this weekend."

"And back to work?"

Lewis put his hands on his wife's shoulders as she stood watching the pale chips gradually turning brown.

"This weekend, I should think."

"You've always enjoyed working with 'im, 'aven't you?"

"Well . . ."

"I've often wondered why. It's not as if 'e's ever treated you all that well, is it?"

"I'm the only one he's ever treated well," said Lewis quietly.

She turned toward him, laterally shaking the chips with a practiced right hand.

"And 'ow are *you* today, then? The case going okay?"

Lewis sat down at the red Formica-topped kitchen table and surveyed the old familiar scene: lacy white doily, knife and fork, bottle of tomato ketchup, bread and butter on one side, and a glass of milk on the other. He should have felt contented; and as he looked back over another long day, perhaps he did.

❖

Temporarily, Chief Superintendent David Blair from the Oxford City Force had been given overall responsibility for the Rachel James murder inquiry, and he had spent an hour at Kidlington Police HQ earlier that afternoon, where Lewis had brought him up to date with the latest developments.

Not that they had amounted to much . . .

><

The reports from DCs Learoyd and Elton were not destined significantly to further the course of the investigation. Lord Hardiman, aged eighty-seven, a sad victim of Alzheimer's disease, and now confined to his baronial hall in Bedfordshire, was unlikely, it seemed, to squander any more of his considerable substance in riotous living along the Reeperbahn. While the child fondler, recognized immediately by his erstwhile neighbors, was likewise unlikely to disturb the peace for the immediate future, confined as he was at Her Majesty's Pleasure in Reading for the illegal publication and propagation of material deemed likely to deprave and corrupt.

More interestingly, Lewis had been able to report on his own inquiries, particularly on his second interview with Julian Storrs, who had been more willing now to divulge details of dates, times, and hotels for his last three visits to Paddington with Rachel James.

And after that, to report on his interview with Sir Clixby Bream, who had informed Lewis of the imminent election of a new Master, and who had given him a copy of the College Statutes (fortunately, rendered *Anglice*) with their emphasis upon the need for any candidate for the Mastership to be in good physical health (*in corpore sano*).

"Nobody can guarantee good health," Blair had observed.

"No, but sometimes you can almost guarantee *bad* health, perhaps, sir?"

"We're still no nearer to finding how Owens got a copy of that letter?"

"No. I went round to the Harvey Clinic again yesterday. No luck, though. The doc who wrote the letter got himself killed, as you know, and all his records have been distributed around . . . reallocated, sort of thing."

"They're all in a mess, you mean?"

Lewis nodded. "Somehow Owens got to know that he hadn't got much time left, didn't he? So he's got three things on him: He knows a good deal about Angela Storrs' past; he knows he was having an affair with Rachel James; and he knows he's pretty certainly hiding his medical reports from his colleagues in College—from everybody, perhaps."

Quite certainly Morse would have complained about the confusing profusion of third-person pronouns in the previous sentence. But Blair seemed to follow the account with no difficulty.

"From his wife, too?" he asked.

"I wouldn't be surprised."

"You know, Morse once told me that any quack who tells you when you're going to die is a bloody fool."

Lewis grinned. "He's told me the same thing about a dozen times."

"He's getting better, you say?"

"Out by the weekend, they think."

"You hope so, don't you?"

Lewis nodded, and Blair continued quietly:

"You're peculiar companions, you know, you and Morse. Don't you think? He can be an ungrateful, ungracious sod at times."

"Almost always, sir," admitted Lewis, smiling to himself as if recalling mildly happy memories.

"He'll have to take things more easily now."

"Would you care to tell him that?"

"No."

"Just one thing more, sir—about Owens. I really think we ought to consider the possibility that he's in a bit of danger. There must be quite a few people who'd gladly see him join Rachel in the mortuary."

"What do you suggest, Sergeant?"

"That's the trouble, isn't it? We can't just give him a bodyguard."

"There's only one way of keeping an eye on him all the time."

"Bring him in, you mean, sir? But we can't do that —not yet."

"No. No good bringing him in and then having to let him go. We shall need something to charge him with. I don't suppose . . ." Blair hesitated. "I don't suppose there's any chance that *he* murdered Rachel James?"

"I don't think so, myself, no."

"What's Morse think?"

"He *did* think so for a start, but . . . Which reminds me, sir. I'd better make another trip to the newspaper offices tomorrow."

"Don't go and do everything yourself, Sergeant."

"Will you promise to tell the Chief Inspector that?"

"No," replied Blair as he prepared to leave; but hesitantly so, since he was feeling rather worried himself now about what Lewis had said.

"What did Morse think about the possibility of Owens getting himself murdered?"

"Said he could look after himself; said he was a streetwise kid from the start; said he was a survivor."

"Let's hope he's right."

"Sometimes he is, sir," said Lewis.

Chapter Thirty-Nine

We forget ourselves and our destinies in health;
and the chief use of temporary sickness is to
remind us of these concerns.

—Ralph Waldo Emerson, *Journals*

SISTER JANET MCQUEEN—an amply bosomed
woman now in her early forties, single and darkly
attractive to the vast majority of men—had been considerably concerned about her new patient: one E.
Morse. Patently, in spite of his superficial patter, the
man knew nothing whatsoever of medicine, and
appeared unaware, and strangely unconcerned, about
his physical well-being; ill-being, rather.

On several occasions during the following days
she'd spent some time with him, apologizing for the
two-hourly check on his blood sugar levels (even
during the night); explaining the vital role of the
pancreas in the metabolic processes; acquainting him
with the range, color, purpose, and possible efficacy,
of the medication and equipment now prescribed—
single-use insulin syringes, Human Ultratard,
Human Actrapid, Unilet Lancets, Exactech Reagent
Strips, Enalapril Tablets, Frusemide Tablets, Nife-
dipine Capsules . . .

He'd seemed to understand most of it, she thought. And from their first meeting she'd realized that the prematurely white-haired man was most unusual.

"Glad about the pills," he'd said.

"You are?"

"Different colors, aren't they? White, pink, brown-and-orange. Good, that is. Gives a man a bit of psychological confidence. In the past, I've always thought that confidence was a bit overrated. Not so sure now, though, Sister."

She made no answer. But his words were to remain in her mind; and she knew that she would look forward to talking with this man again.

By Tuesday evening, Morse's blood sugar level had fallen dramatically. And at coffee time on Wednesday morning, Sister McQueen came to his bedside, the fingers of her right hand almost automatically feeling his pulse as she flicked the watch from the starched white lapel of her uniform.

"Shall I survive till the weekend?"

"You hardly deserve to."

"I'm okay now, you mean?"

She snorted in derision; but winsomely so.

"You know why we didn't want you to have any visitors?"

"You wanted me all to yourself?" suggested Morse.

She shook her head slowly, her sensitive, slim lips widening into a saddened smile.

"No. Dr. Matthews thought you were probably far

too worried about life—about your work—about other things, perhaps. And he didn't want to take any chances. Visitors are always a bit of a stress."

"He needn't have worried too much about that."

"But you're wrong, aren't you?" She got to her feet. "You've had four people on the phone every day, regular callers—regular as well-adjusted bowels."

Morse looked up at her.

"Four?"

"Somebody called Lewis—somebody called Strange—somebody called Blair. All from the police, I think."

"*Four*, you said?"

"Ah yes. Sorry. And somebody called Jane. She works for you, she said. Sounds awfully sweet."

>‹

As he lay back after Sister had gone, and switched on the headphones to Classic FM, Morse was again aware of how low he had sunk, since almost everything—a kindly look, a kindly word, a kindly thought, even the *thought* of a kindly thought—seemed to push him ever nearer to the rim of tears. Forget it, Morse! Forget yourself and forget your health! For a while anyway. He picked up *The ABC Murders* which he'd found in the meager ward library. He'd always enjoyed Agatha Christie: a big fat puzzle ready for the reader from page one. Perhaps it might help a little with the big fat puzzle waiting for him in the world outside the Radcliffe Infirmary . . .

ABC.
Alexander Bonaparte Cust.
Adèle Beatrice Cecil.
Ann Berkeley Cox . . .

Within five minutes Morse was asleep.

⋈

On Thursday afternoon, a slim, rather prissy young dietitian came to sit beside Morse's bed and to talk quickly, rationally, and at inordinate length, about such things as calories and carrots and carbohydrates.

"And if you ever feel like a pint of beer once a week, well, you just go ahead and have one! It shouldn't do you much harm."

Morse's spirit groaned within him.

⋈

The Senior Consultant himself came round again the following morning. The insulin drip had long gone; blood readings were gradually reverting to a manageable level; blood pressure was markedly down.

"You've been very lucky," said Matthews.

"I don't deserve it," admitted Morse.

"No. You don't."

"When are you going to let me go?"

"Home? Tomorrow, perhaps. Work? Up to you. I'd

take a fortnight off myself—but then I've got far more sense than you have."

>‹

Well before lunchtime on Saturday, already dressed and now instructed to await an ambulance, Morse was seated in the entrance corridor of the Geoffrey Harris Ward when Sister McQueen came to sit beside him.

"I'm almost sorry to be going," said Morse.

"You'll miss us?"

"I'll miss *you*."

"Really?"

"Could I ring you—here?" asked Morse diffidently.

"In those immortal words: 'Don't ring us—we'll ring you.'"

"You mean you *will* ring me?"

She shook her head. "Perhaps not. And it doesn't matter, does it? What matters is that you look after yourself. You're a nice man—a very nice man!—and I'm so glad we met."

"If I did come to see you, would you look after me?"

"Bed and Breakfast, you mean?" She smiled. "You'd always be welcome in the McQueen Arms."

She stood up as an ambulance man came through the flappy doors.

"Mr. Morse?" he asked.

"I'd love to be in the McQueen arms," Morse managed to say, very quietly.

As he was driven past the Neptune fountain in the forecourt of the Radcliffe Infirmary, he wondered if Sister had appreciated that shift in key, from the upper-case Arms to the lower-case arms.

He hoped she had.

Chapter Forty

Sunday, March 3

Important if true.

—Inscription A. W. Kinglake wished
to see on all churches

Forgive us for loving familiar hymns and religious
feelings more than Thee, O Lord.

—From the United Presbyterian Church Litany

"But I'd better not call before the *Archers*' omni-
bus?" Lewis had suggested the previous evening.

"Don't worry about that. I've kept up with events
in Ambridge all week. And I don't want to hear 'em
again. I just wonder when these scriptwriters will
understand that beautiful babies are about as boring
as happy marriages."

"About ten then, sir?"

⊰⊱

Morse, smartly dressed in clean white shirt and semi-
pressed gray flannels, was listening to the last few
minutes of the *Morning Service* on Radio 4 when
Lewis was quickly admitted—and cautioned.

"Sh! My favorite hymn."

In the silence that followed, the two men sat listening with Morse's bleating, uncertain baritone occasionally accompanying the singing.

"Didn't know you were still interested in that sort of thing," volunteered Lewis after it had finished.

"I still love the old hymns—the more sentimental the better, for my taste. Wonderful words, didn't you think?" And softly, but with deep intensity, he recited a few lines he'd just sung:

"I trace the rainbow through the rain
And feel the promise is not vain
That Morn shall tearless be."

But Lewis, who had noted the moisture in Morse's eyes, and who had sensed that the promise of the last line might soon be broken, immediately injected a more joyful note into the conversation.

"It's really good to have you back, sir."

Apparently unaware that any reciprocal words of gratitude were called for, Morse asked about the case; and learned that the police were perhaps "treading water" for the time being, and that Chief Superintendent Blair was nominally i/c pro tem.

"David Blair. Best copper in the county," Lewis was about to nod a partial agreement, "apart from me, of course."

And suddenly Lewis felt very happy that he was back in harness with this arrogant, ungracious, vulnerable, lovable man with whom he had worked so closely for so many years; a man who looked somewhat slimmer, somewhat paler than when he had last seen him, but who sounded not a whit less brusque as he now asked whether Lewis had checked up on the time when Storrs had left home for his last visit with Rachel to Paddington, and the time when the postman had delivered the mail in Polstead Road that same morning.

And Lewis had.

9:45–9:50 A.M.

9:10–9:20 A.M.

Respectively.

"From which, Lewis, we may draw *what* conclusions?"

"Precious few, as far as I can see."

"Absolutely! What other new facts have you got for me?"

So Lewis told him.

➤◄

It was ten minutes short of noon when Morse dropped the mini-bombshell.

"The Cherwell, do you think, Lewis? The landlord there always keeps a decent pint."

"But beer's full of sugar, isn't it? You can't—"

"Lewis! This diabetes business is all about *balance*, that's all. I've got to take all this insulin because I can't produce any insulin *myself*—to counteract any sugar intake. But if I didn't have any sugar intake to counteract, I'd be in one helluva mess. I'd become *hypoglycemic*, and you know what that means."

Not having the least idea, Lewis remained silent as Morse took out a black penlike object from his pocket, screwed off one end, removed a white plastic cap from the needle there, twisted a calibrator at the other end, unbuttoned his shirt, and plunged the needle deep into his midriff.

Lewis winced involuntarily.

But Morse, looking up like some young child expecting praise after taking a very nasty-tasting medicine, seemed wholly pleased with himself.

"See? That'll take care of things. No problem."

>‹

With great care, Lewis walked back from the bar with a pint of Bass and a glass of orange juice.

"I've been waiting a long time for this," enthused Morse, burying his nose into the froth, taking a gloriously gratifying draught of real ale, and showing, as he relaxed back, a circle of blood on his white shirt just above the waist.

After a period of silence, during which Morse several times raised his glass against the window to admire the color of the beer, Lewis asked the key question.

"What have they said about you starting work again?"

"What do you say about us seeing Storrs and Owens this afternoon?"

"You'll have a job with Storrs, sir. Him and his missus are in Bath for the weekend."

"What about Owens?"

"Dunno. Perhaps he's away, too—on another of his personnel courses."

"One easy way of finding out, Lewis. There's a telephone just outside the Gents."

"Look, sir! For heaven's sake! You've been in hospital a week—"

"Five days, to be accurate, and only for observation. They'd never have let me out unless—"

But he got no further.

The double doors of the Cherwell had burst open and there, framed in the doorway, jowls aquiver, stood Chief Superintendent Strange—looking around, spying Morse, walking across, and sitting down.

"Like a beer, sir?" asked Lewis.

"Large single-malt Scotch—no ice, no water."

"And it's the same again for me," prompted Morse, pushing over his empty glass.

"I might have known it," began Strange, after regaining his breath. "Straight out of hospital and straight into the nearest boozer."

"It's *not* the nearest."

"Don't remind me! Dixon's already carted me round to the Friar Bacon—the King's Arms—the Dew Drop—and now here. And it's about time somebody reminded you that you're in the Force to reduce the crime level, not the bloody beer level."

"We were talking about the case when you came in, sir."

"*What* case?" snapped Strange.

"The murder case—Rachel James."

"Ah yes! I remember the case well; I remember the address, too: Number 17 Bloxham Drive, wasn't it? Well, you'd better get off your arse, matey," at a single swallow, he drained the Scotch which Lewis had just placed in front of him, "because if you *are* back at work, you can just forget that beer and get over smartish to Bloxham Drive again. Number 15, this time. Another murder. Chap called Owens—Geoffrey Owens. I think you've heard of him?"

Part Four

Chapter Forty-One

For now we see through a glass darkly; but then
face to face.

—*I Corinthians*, ch. 13, v. 12

DÉJÀ VU.

The street, the police cars, the crowd of curious
onlookers, the SOCOs—repetition almost everywhere, as if nothing was found only once in the
world. Just that single significant shift: the shift from
one terraced house to another immediately adjacent.

Morse himself had said virtually nothing since
Strange had brought the news of Owens' murder; and
said nothing now as he sat in the kitchen of Number
15, Bloxham Drive, elbows resting on the table there,
head resting on his hands. For the moment his job
was to bide his time, he knew that, during the inter-
regnum between the activities of other professionals
and his own assumption of authority: a necessary yet
ever frustrating interlude, like that when an in-flight
stewardess rehearses the safety drill before takeoff.

By all rights he should have felt weary and
defeated; but this was not the case. Physically, he felt
considerably fitter than he hadthe week before; and
mentally, he felt eager for that metaphorical takeoff

to begin. Some people took little or no mental exercise except that of jumping to conclusions; while Morse was a man who took excessive mental exercise and who *still* jumped to dubious conclusions, as indeed he was to do now. But as some of his close colleagues knew—and most especially as Sergeant Lewis knew—it was at times like this, with preconceptions proved false and hypotheses undone, that Morse's brain was wont to function with astonishing speed, if questionable lucidity.

As it did now.

><

Lewis walked through just before 2 P.M.

"Anything I can do for the minute, sir?"

"Just nip out and get me the *Independent on Sunday*, will you? And a packet of Dunhill."

"Do you think—?" But Lewis stopped and waited as Morse reluctantly took a five-pound note from his wallet.

For the next few minutes Morse was aware that his brain was still frustrated and unproductive. And there was something else, too. For some reason, and for a good while now, he had been conscious that he might well have missed a vital clue in the case (cases!) which so far he couldn't quite catch. It was a bit like going through a town on a high-speed train when the eyes had *almost* caught the name of the station as it flashed so tantalizingly across the carriage window.

Lewis returned five minutes later with the cigarettes, which Morse put unopened into his jacket pocket; and with the newspaper, which Morse opened at the Cryptic Crossword ("Quixote"), glanced at 1 across: "Some show dahlias in the Indian pavilion (6)" and immediately wrote in "HOWDAH."

"Excuse me, sir—but how do you get that?"

"Easiest of all the clue types, that. The letters are all there, in their proper, consecutive order. It's called the 'hidden' type."

"Ah, yes!" Lewis looked and, for once, Lewis saw. "Shall I leave you for two or three minutes to finish it off, sir?"

"No. It'll take me at least five. And it's time you sat down and gave me the latest news on things here."

Owens' body Morse had already viewed, howsoever briefly, sitting back, as it had been, against the cushions of the living room settee, the green covers permeated with many pints of blood. His face unshaven, his long hair loose down to the shoulders, his eyes open and staring, almost (it seemed) as if in permanent disbelief; and two bullet wounds showing raggedly in his chest. Dead four to six hours, that's what Dr. Laura Hobson had already suggested—a margin narrower than Morse had expected, though wider than he'd hoped; death, she'd claimed, had fairly certainly been "instant," or "instantaneous," as Morse would have preferred. There were no signs of any forcible entry to the house: the front door had been found still locked and bolted; the tongue of the Yale on the back door still engaged, though not clicked to the locked position from the inside. On the mantelpiece above the electric fire (not switched on) was a small oblong virtually free of the generally pervasive dust.

The body would most probably not have been discovered that day had not John Benson, a garage mechanic from Hartwell's Motors, agreed to earn himself a little untaxed extra income by fixing a few faults on Owens' car. But Benson had been unable to get any answer when he called just after 11:15 A.M.; had finally peered through the open-curtained front window; had rapped repeatedly, and increasingly loudly, against the pane when he saw Owens lying asleep on the settee there.

But Owens was not asleep. So much had become gradually apparent to Benson, who had dialed 999 at about 11:30 A.M. from the BT phone box at the entrance to the Drive.

Thus far no one, it appeared, had seen or heard anything untoward that morning between seven and eight o'clock, say. House-to-house inquiries would soon be under way, and might provide a clue or two. But concerning such a possibility Morse was predictably (though, as it happened, mistakenly) pessimistic. Early Sunday morning was not a time when many people were about, except for dog owners and insomniacs: the former, judging from the warnings on the lampposts concerning the fouling of verges and footpaths, not positively encouraged to parade their pets along the street; the latter, if there were any, not as yet coming forward with any sightings of strangers or hearings of gunshots.

No. On the face of it, it had seemed a typical, sleepy Sunday morning, when the denizens of Bloxham Drive had their weekly lie-in, arose late, walked around their homes in dressing gowns, sometimes boiled an egg, perhaps, and settled down to read in the scandal sheets about the extramarital exploits of the great and the not-so-good.

But one person had been given no chance to read his Sunday newspaper, for the *News of the World* lay unopened on the mat inside the front door of Number 15; and few of the others in the Drive that morning were able to indulge their delight in adulterous liaisons, stunned as they were by disbelief and, as the shock itself lessened, by a growing sense of fear.

⤞⤝

At 2:30 P.M. Morse was informed that few if any of the neighbors were likely to be helpful witnesses—except the old lady in Number 19. Morse should see her himself, perhaps?

"Want me to come along, sir?"

"No, Lewis. You get off and try to find out something about Storrs—*and* his missus. Bath, you say? He probably left details of where he'd be at the Porters' Lodge—that's the usual drill. And do it from HQ. Better keep the phone here free."

⤞⤝

Mrs. Adams was a widow of some eighty summers, a small old lady who had now lost all her own teeth, much of her wispy white hair, and even more of her hearing. But her wits were sharp enough, Morse sensed that immediately; and her brief evidence was of considerable interest. She had slept poorly the previous night; got up early; made herself some tea and toast; listened to the news on the radio at seven o'clock; cleared away; and then gone out the back to empty her wastebasket. *That*'s when she'd seen him!

"Him?"

"Pardon?"

"You're sure it was a *man*?"

"Oh yes. About twenty—twenty-five past seven."

The case was under way.

"You didn't hear any shots or bangs?"

"Pardon?"

Morse let it go.

But he managed to convey his thanks to her, and to explain that she would be asked to sign a short statement. As he prepared to leave, he gave her his card.

"I'll leave this with you, Mrs. Adams. If you remember anything else, please get in touch with me."

He thought she'd understood; and he left her there in her kitchen, holding his card about three or four inches from her pale, rheumy eyes, squinting obliquely at the wording.

She was not, as Morse had quickly realized, ever destined to be called before an identity parade; for although she might be able to spot that all of them were men, any physiognomical differentiation would surely be wholly beyond the capacity of those tired old eyes.

Poor Mrs. Adams!

Sans teeth, sans hair, sans ears, sans eyes—and very soon, alas, sans everything.

><

Seldom, in any investigation, had Morse so badly mishandled a key witness as now he mishandled Mrs. Arabella Adams.

Chapter Forty-Two

> **Alibi** (*adv.*): in another place, elsewhere.
> —*Small's Latin-English Dictionary*

SOME PERSONS IN life eschew all sense of responsibility, and are never wholly at ease unless they are closely instructed as to what to do, and how and when to do it. Sergeant Lewis was not such a person, willing as he was always to shoulder his share of responsibility and, not infrequently, to face some apportionment of blame. Yet, to be truthful, he was ever most at ease when given some specific task, as he had been now; and he experienced a pleasing sense of purpose as he drove up to Police HQ that same afternoon.

One thing only disturbed him more than a little. For almost a week now Morse had foregone, been forced to forego, both beer and cigarettes. And what foolishness it was to capitulate, as Morse *had* done, to both, within the space of only a couple of hours! But that's what life was all about—personal decisions; and Morse had clearly decided that the long-term disintegration of his liver and his lungs was a price well worth paying, even with diabetes, for the short-term pleasures of alcohol and nicotine.

Yet Morse was still on the ball. As he had guessed, Storrs had left details of his weekend whereabouts at the Porters' Lodge. And very soon Lewis was speaking to the Manager of Bath's Royal Crescent Hotel—an appropriately cautious man, but one who was fully cooperative once Lewis had explained the unusual and delicate nature of his inquiries. The Manager would ring back, he promised, within half an hour.

Lewis picked up the previous day's copy of the *Daily Mirror*, and sat puzzling for a few minutes over whether the answer to 1 across—"River (3)"—was CAM, DEE, EXE, FAL, and so on through the alphabet; finally deciding on CAM, when he saw that it would fit neatly enough with COD, the fairly obvious answer to 1 down—"Fish (3)." He had made a firm start. But thereafter he had proceeded little, since the combination which had found favor with the setter of the crossword (EXE/EEL) had wholly eluded him. His minor hypothesis, like Morse's earlier major one, was sadly undone.

But he had no time to return (quite literally) to square one, since the phone rang. It had taken the Manager only fifteen minutes to assemble his fairly comprehensive information . . .

><

Mr. and Mrs. J. Storrs had checked into the hotel at 4 P.M. the previous afternoon, Saturday, March 2: just the one night, at the special weekend-break tariff of £125 for a double room. The purpose of the Storrs' visit (almost certainly) had been to hear the Bath Festival Choir, since one of the reception staff had ordered a taxi for them at 7 P.M. to go along to the Abbey, where the Fauré *Requiem* was the centerpiece of the evening concert. The couple had been back in the hotel by about half past nine, when they had immediately gone into the restaurant for a late, prebooked dinner, the only extra being a bottle of the house red wine.

If the sergeant would like to see the itemized bill . . . ?

No one, it appeared, had seen the couple after about 11 P.M., when they had been the last to leave the restaurant. Before retiring, however, Mr. Storrs had rung through to room service to order breakfast for the two of them, in their room, at 7:45 A.M.: a full English for himself, a Continental one for his wife.

Again, the itemized order was available if the sergeant . . .

Latest checkout from the hotel (as officially specified in the brochure) was noon. But the Storrs had left a good while before then. As with the other details (the Manager explained) some of the times given were just a little vague, since service personnel had changed. But things could very soon be checked. The account had been settled by Mr. Storrs himself on a Lloyds Bank Gold Card (the receptionist recalled this clearly), and one of the porters had driven the Storrs' BMW round to the front of the hotel from the rear garage—being tipped (it appeared) quite liberally for his services.

So that was that.

Or *almost* so—since Lewis was very much aware that Morse would hardly be overjoyed with such findings; and he now asked a few further key questions.

"I know it's an odd thing to ask, sir, but are you completely sure that these people *were* Mr. and Mrs. Storrs?"

"Well, I . . ." The Manager hesitated long enough for Lewis to jam a metaphoric foot inside the door.

"You knew them—know them—*personally*?"

"I've only been Manager here for a couple of years. But, yes—they were here twelve months or so ago."

"People change, though, don't they? *He* might have changed quite a bit, Mr. Storrs, if he'd been ill or . . . or something?"

"Oh, it was *him* all right. I'm sure of that. Well, *almost* sure. And he signed the credit card bill, didn't he? It should be quite easy to check up on that."

"And you're quite sure it was *her*, sir? Mrs. Storrs? Is there any possibility at all that he was spending the night with someone else?"

The laugh at the other end of the line was full of relief and conviction.

"Not—a—chance! You can be one hundred percent certain of that. I think everybody here remembers her. She's, you know, she's a bit sharp, if you follow my meaning. Nothing unpleasant—don't get me wrong! But a little bit, well, *severe*. She dressed that way, too: white trouser-suit, hair drawn back high over the ears, beauty-parlor face. Quite the lady, really."

Lewis drew on his salient reminiscence of Angela Storrs:

"It's not always easy to recognize someone who's wearing sunglasses, though."

"But she wasn't wearing sunglasses. Not when I saw her, anyway. I just happened to be in reception when she booked in. And it was *she* recognized *me*! You see, the last time they'd been with us, *she* did the signing in, while Mr. Storrs was sorting out the luggage and the parking. And I noticed the registration number of their BMW and I mentioned the coincidence that we were both '188J.' She reminded me of it yesterday. She said they'd still got the same car."

"You can swear to all this?"

"Certainly. We had quite a little chat. She told me they'd spent their honeymoon in the hotel—in the Sarah Siddons suite."

Oh.

So that was that.

An alibi—for both of them.

Lewis thanked the Manager. "But please do keep all this to yourself, sir. It's always a tricky business when we're trying to eliminate suspects in a case. Not *suspects*, though, just . . . just people."

A few minutes later Lewis again rang the Storrs' residence in Polstead Road; again listening to Mrs. Storrs on the answer phone: "If the caller will please speak clearly after the long tone . . ." The voice was a little—what had the Manager said?—a little "severe," yes. And quite certainly (Lewis thought) it was a voice likely to intimidate a few of the students if she became the new Master's wife. But after waiting for the "long tone," Lewis put down the phone without leaving any message. He always felt awkward and tongue-tied at such moments; and he suddenly realized that he hadn't got a message to leave in any case.

Chapter Forty-Three

Horse sense is something a horse has that prevents him from betting on people.

—Father Mathew

MORSE WAS STILL seated at the kitchen table in Number 15 when Lewis rang through.

"So it looks," concluded Lewis, "as if they're in the clear."

"Ye-es. How far is it from Oxford to Bath?"

"Seventy, seventy-five miles?"

"Sunday morning. No traffic. Do it in an hour and a half—no problem. Three hours there and back."

"There's a murder to commit in the middle, though."

Morse conceded the point. "Three and a half."

"Well, whatever happened, he didn't use his *own* car. That was in the hotel garage—keys with the porter."

"Haven't you heard of a *duplicate* set of car keys, Lewis?"

"What if he was locked in—or blocked in?"

"He *un*locked himself, and *un*blocked himself, all right?"

"He must have left about four o'clock this morning

then, because he was back in bed having breakfast with his missus before eight."

"Ye-es."

"I just wonder what Owens was doing, sir—up and about and dressed and ready to let the murderer in at half past five or so."

"Perhaps he couldn't sleep."

"You're not taking all this seriously, are you?"

"All right. Let's cross 'em both off the list, I agree."

"Have we *got* a list?"

Morse nodded. "Not too many on it, I know. But I'd like to see our other runner in the Lonsdale Stakes."

"Do you want *me* to see him?"

"No. You get back here and look after the shop till the SOCOs have left—they're nearly through."

With which, Morse put down the phone, got to his feet, and looked cautiously through into the hallway; then walked to the front door, where a uniformed PC stood on guard.

"Has the Super gone?" asked Morse.

"Yes, sir. Five minutes ago."

Morse walked back to the kitchen and opened the door of the refrigerator. The usual items: two pints of Co-op milk, Flora margarine, a packet of unsmoked bacon rashers, five eggs, a carton of grapefruit juice, two cans of Courage's bitter . . .

Morse found a glass in the cupboard above the draining board, and poured himself a beer. The liquid

was cool and sharp on his dry throat; and very soon
he had opened the second can, his fingers almost sensuously feeling the cellophane-wrapped cigarettes in
his pocket, still unopened.

By the time the SOCOs were ready to move into
the kitchen, the glass had been dried and replaced on
its shelf.

"Can we kick you out a little while, sir?" It was
Andrews, the senior man.

"You've finished everywhere else?"

"Pretty well."

Morse got to his feet.

"Ah! Two cans of beer!" observed Andrews. "Think
they may have had a drink together before . . . ?"

"Not at that time of the morning, no."

"I dunno. I used to have a friend who drank a pint
of Guinness for breakfast every morning."

"Sounds a civilized sort of fellow."

"Dead. Cirrhosis of the liver."

Morse nodded morosely.

"Anyway, we'll give the cans a dusting over, just
in case."

"I shouldn't bother," said Morse.

"Won't do any harm, surely?"

"I said, I shouldn't *bother*," snapped Morse.

And suddenly Andrews understood.

>‹

Upstairs there was little to detain Morse. In the front
room the bed was still unmade, a pair of pajamas

neatly folded on the top pillow. The wardrobe appeared exactly as he'd viewed it earlier. Only one picture on the walls: Monet's miserable-looking version of a haystack.

The "study" (Morse's second visit there too!) was in considerable disarray, for the desk drawers, now liberally dusted with fingerprint powder, had been taken out, their contents strewn across the floor, including the book which had stimulated some interest on Morse's previous visit. The central drawer likewise had been removed, and Morse assumed that after discovering the theft of the manila file Owens had seen no reason to repair the damaged lock.

Nothing much else of interest upstairs, as far as Morse could see; just that one, easy conclusion to be drawn: that the murderer had been looking for something—some documents, some papers, some evidence which could have constituted a basis for blackmail.

Exactly what Morse had been looking for.

Exactly what Morse had found.

He smiled sadly to himself as he looked down at the wreckage of the room. Already he had made a few minor blunders in the investigations; and one major, tragic blunder, of course. But how fortunate that he'd been able to avail himself of JJ's criminal expertise, since otherwise the crucial evidence found in the manila file would have vanished now forever.

Downstairs, Morse had only the living room to consider. The kitchen he'd already seen; and the nominal "dining room" was clearly a room where Owens had seldom, if ever, dined—an area thick with dust and crowded with the sorts of items most householders regularly relegate to their lofts and garden sheds: an old electric fire, a coal scuttle, a box of plugs and wires, a traffic cone, an ancient Bakelite wireless, a glass case containing a stuffed owl, a black plastic lavatory seat, six chairs packed together in the soixante-neuf position—and a dog collar with the name "Archie" inscribed on its disc.

Perhaps, after all, there had been some little goodness somewhere in the man?

⇥⇤

Morse had already given permission for the body to be removed, and now for the second time he ventured into the living room. Not quite so dust-bestrewn here, certainly; but manifestly Owens had never been a house-proud man. Surfaces all around were dusted with powder, and chalk marks outlined the body's former configuration on the settee. But the room was dominated by blood—the stains, the smell of blood; and Morse, as was his wont, turned his back on such things, and viewed the contents of the room.

He stood enviously in front of the black, three-decked Revox CD-cassette player which stood on a broad shelf in the alcove to the left of the front window, with dozens of CDs and cassettes below it, including, Morse noted with appreciation, much Gustav Mahler. And indeed, as he pressed the "Play" panel, he immediately recognized *Das Lied von der Erde*.

No man is wholly bad, perhaps . . .

On the shelf beneath was an extended row of videos: *Fawlty Towers*, *Morecambe and Wise Christmas Shows*, *Porridge*, and several other TV classics. And two (fairly obviously) pornographic videos: *Grub Screws*, its crudely lurid, technicolor cover poses hardly promising a course in carpentry with the Open University; and the plain-covered, yet succinctly entitled *Sux and Fux*, which seemed to speak quite unequivocally for itself. Morse himself had no video mechanism on his rented TV set; but he was in the process of thinking about the benefits of such a facility when Lewis came in, the latter immediately instructed to have a look around.

Morse's attention now turned to the single row of books in the opposite alcove. Mostly paperbacks: P. D. James, Jack Higgins, Ruth Rendell, Wilbur Smith, Minette Walters . . . *RAC Handbook*, *World Atlas*, *Chambers Dictionary*, *Pevsner's Oxfordshire* . . .

"See this?" Lewis suddenly raised aloft the *Grub Screws*. "The statutory porn video, sir. Good one, that! Sergeant Dixon had it on at his stag night."

"You'd like to see it again, you mean?"

"*Again?* Not for me, sir. Those things get ever so boring after a while. But don't let me stop you if . . ."

"What? Me? I've got more important things to do

than watch that sort of thing. High time I saw Corn-ford, for a start. Fix something up, Lewis. The sooner the quicker."

><

After Lewis had gone, Morse felt unwilling to face the chorus of correspondents and the battery of cam-eras which awaited those periodically emerging from the front of Number 15. So he sat down, yet again, in the now empty kitchen; and pondered.

Always in his life, he had wanted to know the *answers* to things. In Sunday School he had once asked a question concerning the topographical posi-tion of Heaven, only to be admonished by an un-imaginative middle-aged spinster for being so very silly. And he had been similarly discouraged when as a young grammar school boy he had asked his Divin-ity master who it was, if God had created the Uni-verse, who in turn had created God. And after receiving no satisfactory answer from his Physics master about what sort of thing could possibly exist out there at the end of the world, when space had run out, Morse had been compelled to lower his sights a little, thereafter satisfying his intellectual craving for answers by finding the values of "x" and "y" in (ever more complicated) algebraic equations, and by deci-phering the meaning of (ever more complicated) chunks of choruses from the Greek tragedies.

Later, from his mid-twenties onward, his need to

know had transferred itself to the field of crossword puzzles, where he had so often awaited with almost paranoiac impatience the following day's answer to any clue he'd been unable to solve the day before. And now, as he sat in Bloxham Drive on that overcast, chilly Sunday afternoon in early March, he was aware that there *was* an answer to this present puzzle: probably a fairly simple answer to the question of what exactly had taken place earlier that morning. For a sequence of events *had* taken place, perhaps about 7:30. Someone had knocked on the door; had gained entry; had shot Owens twice; had gone upstairs to try to find something; had left via the kitchen door; had gone away, on foot, on a bike, in a car.

Who?

Who, Morse? For it was *someone*—someone with a human face and with a human motive. If only he could put together all the clues, *he would know*. And even as he sat there some pattern would begin to clarify itself in his mind, presenting a logical sequence of events, a causative chain of reactions. But then that same pattern would begin to blur and fade, since there was destined to be no flash of genuine insight on that afternoon.

Furthermore, Morse was beginning to feel increasingly worried about his present failure—like some hitherto highly acclaimed novelist with a score of best-sellers behind him who is suddenly assailed by a nightmarish doubt about his ability to write that one further winner; by a fear that he has come to the end of his creative output, and must face the possibility of defeat.

Lewis came back into the kitchen once more.

Dr. Cornford would be happy to meet Morse whenever it suited. Five o'clock that afternoon? Before Chapel? In his rooms in Lonsdale?

Morse nodded.

"And I rang the Storrs again, sir. They're back in Oxford. Seems they had a bit of lunch in Burford on the way. Do you want me to go round?"

Morse looked up in some puzzlement.

"What the hell for, Lewis?"

Chapter Forty-Four

The bells would ring to call her
   In valleys miles away:
"Come all to church, good people;
   Good people, come and pray."
But here my love would stay.

       —A. E. Housman,
         A Shropshire Lad XXI

MORSE INQUIRED AT the Lodge, then turned left and walked along the side of the quad to the Old Staircase, where on the first floor he saw, above the door to his right, the Gothic-style white lettering on its black background: DR. D. J. CORNFORD.

"I suppose it's a bit early to offer you a drink, Chief Inspector?"

Morse looked at his wristwatch.

"Is it?"

"Scotch? Gin? Vodka?"

"Scotch, please."

Cornford began to pour an ever increasingly liberal tot of Glenmorangie into a tumbler.

"Say 'when'!"

It seemed that the Chief Inspector may have had some difficulty in enunciating the monosyllable, for

Cornford paused when the tumbler was half filled with the pale-golden malt.

"When!" said Morse.

"No ice here, I'm afraid. But I'm sure you wouldn't want to adulterate it, anyway."

"Yes, I would, if you don't mind. Same amount of water, please. We've all got to look after our livers."

Two doors led off the high-ceilinged, oak-paneled, book-lined room; and Cornford opened the one that led to a small kitchen, coming back with a jug of cold water.

"I would have joined you normally—without the water!—but I'm reading the Second Lesson in Chapel tonight," it was Cornford's turn to consult his wristwatch, "so we mustn't be all that long. It's that bit from the Epistle to the Romans, Chapter thirteen —the bit about drunkenness. Do you know it?"

"Er, just remind me, sir."

Clearly Cornford needed no copy of the text in front of him, for he immediately recited the key verse, with appropriately ecclesiastical intonation:

Let us walk honestly, as in the day; not in rioting and drunkenness, not in chambering and wantonness, not in strife and envying . . .

"You'll be reading from the King James version, then?"

"Absolutely! I'm an agnostic myself; but what a tragedy that so many of our Christian brethren have opted for these newfangled versions! 'Boozing and Bonking,' I should think they translate it."

Morse sat sipping his scotch contentedly. He could have suggested "Fux and Sux"; but decided against it.

Cornford smiled. "What do you want to see me about?"

"Well, in a way it's about that last bit of your text: the 'strife and envying' bit. You see, I know you're standing for the Mastership here . . ."

"Yes?"

Morse took a deep breath, took a further deepish draught, and then told Cornford of the murder that morning of Geoffrey Owens; told him that various documents from the Owens household pointed to a systematic campaign of blackmail on Owens' part; informed him that there was reason to believe that he, Cornford, might have been—almost certainly *would* have been—one of the potential victims.

Cornford nodded quietly. "Are you sure of this?"

"No, not sure at all, sir. But—"

"But you've got your job to do."

"You haven't received any blackmail letters yourself?"

"No."

"I'll be quite blunt, if I may, sir. Is there anything you can think of in the recent past, or distant past, that could have been used to compromise you in some way? Compromise your candidature, say?"

Cornford considered the question. "I've done a few things I'm not very proud of—haven't we all?—but

I'm fairly sure I got away with them. That was in another country, anyway . . ."

Morse finished the quotation for him: ". . . and, besides, the wench is dead."

Cornford's pale gray eyes looked across at Morse with almost childlike innocence.

"Yes."

"Do you want to tell me about them?"

"No. But only because it would be an embarrassment for me and a waste of time for you."

"You're a married man, I understand."

"Yes. And before someone else tells you, my wife is American, about half my age, and extremely attractive." The voice was still pleasantly relaxed, yet Morse sensed a tone of quiet, underlying strength.

"*She* hasn't been troubled by letters, anonymous letters, anything like that?"

"She hasn't told me of anything."

"*Would* she tell you?"

Did Morse sense a hint of uneasy hesitation in Cornford's reply?

"She would, I think, yes. But you'd have to ask *her.*"

Morse nodded. "I know it's a bit of a bother—but I *shall* have to do that, I'm afraid. She's, er, she's not around?"

Cornford again looked at his wristwatch.

"She'll be coming over to Chapel very shortly."

"Has there been much feeling—much tension—between you and the, er, other candidate?"

"The atmosphere on High Table has been a little, let's say, uncomfortable once or twice, yes. To be expected, though, isn't it?"

"But you don't throw insults at each other like those boxers before a big fight?"

"No, we just *think* them."

"No whispers? No rumors?"

"Not as far as I'm aware, no."

"And you get on reasonably well with Mr. Storrs?"

Cornford got to his feet and smiled again, his head slightly to one side.

"I've never got to know Julian all that well, really."

The Chapel bell had begun to ring—a series of monotonous notes, melancholy, ominous almost, like a curfew.

Ten minutes to go.

> *"Come ye to church, good people,*
> *Good people, come and pray,"*

quoted Cornford.

Morse nodded, as he ventured one final question:

"Do you mind me asking you when you got up this morning, sir?"

"Early. I went out jogging—just before seven."

"Just you?"

Cornford nodded vaguely.

"You didn't go out after that—for a paper? In the car, perhaps?"

"I don't have a car, myself. My wife does, but it's garaged out in New Road."

"Quite a way away."

"Yes," repeated Cornford slowly, "quite a way away."

As Morse walked down the stairs, he thought he'd recognized Cornford for exactly what he was: a civilized, courteous, clever man; a man of quiet yet unmistakable resolve, who would probably make a splendid new Master of Lonsdale.

Just two things worried him, the first of them only slightly: if Cornford was going to quote Housman, he jolly well ought to do it accurately.

And he might be wholly wrong about the second . . .

>‹

The bedroom door opened a few moments after Morse had reached the bottom of the creaking wooden staircase.

"And what do you think all *that* was about?"

"Couldn't you hear?"

"Most of it," she admitted.

She wore a high-necked, low-skirted black dress, with an oval amethyst pinned to the bodice—suitably ensembled for a seat next to her husband in the Fellows' pews.

"His hair is whiter than yours, Denis. I saw him when he walked out."

The bell still tolled.

Five minutes to go.

Cornford pulled on his gown and threw his hood back over his shoulders with practiced precision; then repeated Housman (again inaccurately) as he put his arms around his wife and looked unblinkingly into her eyes.

"Have you got anything to pray for? Anything that's worrying you?"

Shelly Cornford smiled sweetly, trusting that such deep dissimulation would mask her growing, now almost desperate, sense of guilt.

"I'm going to pray for you, Denis—for you to become Master of Lonsdale. That's what I want more than anything else in the world," her voice very quiet now, "and that's not for me, my darling—it's for you."

"Nothing else to pray for?"

She moved away from him, smoothing the dress over her energetic hips.

"Such as what?"

"Some people pray for forgiveness, that sort of thing, sometimes," said Denis Cornford softly.

＞＜

Morse had walked to the Lodge, where he stood in the shadows for a couple of minutes, reading the various notices about the College's sporting fifteens, and elevens, and eights; and hoping that his presence there was unobserved—when he saw them. An academically accoutred Cornford, accompanied by a woman in black, had emerged from the foot of the

Old Staircase, and now turned away from him toward the Chapel in the inner quad.

The bell had stopped ringing.

And Morse walked out into Radcliffe Square; then across into the King's Arms in Broad Street, where he ordered a pint of bitter, and sat down in the back bar, considering so many things—including a wholly unprecedented sense of gratitude to the Tory Government for its reform of the Sunday licensing laws.

Chapter Forty-Five

I'd seen myself a don,
Reading old poets in the library,
Attending chapel in an MA gown
And sipping vintage port by candlelight.

—John Betjeman,
Summoned by Bells

IN THE HILARY Term, in Lonsdale College, on Sunday evenings only, it had become a tradition for the electric lighting to be switched off, and for candles in their sconces to provide the only means of illumination in the Great Hall. Such a procedure was popular with the students, almost all of whom had never experienced the romance of candlelight except during power cuts, and particularly enjoyable for those on the dais whereon the High Table stood, constantly aware as they were of flickering candles reflected in the polished silver of saltcellars and tureens, and the glitter of the cutlery laid out with geometrical precision at every place.

On such evenings, no particular table plan was provided, although it was the regular custom for the visiting preacher (on this occasion a black bishop from Central Africa) to sit on the right side of the Master, with the College Chaplain on the left. The other occupants of High Table (which was usually fully booked on Sunday evenings) were regularly those who had earlier attended the Chapel service, often with their wives or with a guest; and in recent years, one student invited by each of the Fellows in rotation.

That evening the student in question was Antony Plummer, the new organ scholar, who had been invited by Julian Storrs for the very good reason that the two of them had attended the same school, the Services School, Dartmouth, to which establishment some members of the armed forces were wont to send their sons while they themselves were being shunted from one posting to another around the world—in former colonies, protectorates, mandated territories, and the few remaining overseas possessions.

Plummer had never previously been so honored, and from his new perspective, seated between Mr. and Mrs. Storrs, he looked around him lovingly at the gilded, dimly illuminated portraits of the famous alumni—the poets and the politicians, the soldiers and the scientists—who figured so largely in the lineage of Lonsdale. The rafted timbers of the ceiling were lost in darkness, and the shadows were deep on the somber paneling of the walls, as deftly and deferentially the scouts poured wine into the sparkling glasses.

Storrs, just a little late in the proceedings perhaps, decided it was time to play the expansive host.

"Where *is* your father now, Plummer?"

"Last I heard he was running some NATO exercise in Belgium."

"Colonel now, isn't he?"

"Brigadier."

"My goodness!"

"You were with him in India, I think."

Storrs nodded: "Only a captain, though! I followed my father into the Royal Artillery there, and spent a couple of years trying to teach the natives how to shoot. Not much good at it, I'm afraid."

"Who—the natives?"

Storrs laughed good-naturedly. "No—*me*. Most of 'em could have taught me a few things, and I wasn't really cut out for service life anyway. So I opted for a gentler life and applied for a Fellowship here."

Angela Storrs had finished the bisque soup, and now complimented Plummer on the anthem through which he had conducted his largely female choir during the Chapel service.

"You enjoyed it, Mrs. Storrs?"

"Er, yes. But to be quite truthful, I prefer boy sopranos."

"Can you say why that is?"

"Oh, yes! One just *feels* it, that's all. We heard the Fauré *Requiem* yesterday evening. Absolutely wonderful—especially the 'In Paradisum,' wasn't it, Julian?"

"Very fine, yes."

"And you see," continued Angela, "I would have *known* they were boys, even with my eyes shut. But don't ask me *why*. One just *feels* that sort of thing, as I said. Don't you agree? One shouldn't try to *rationalize* everything."

Three places lower down the table, one of the other dons whispered into his neighbor's ear:

"If that woman gets into the Lodge, I'll go and piss all over her primroses!"

⭰⭲

By coincidence, colonialism was a topic at the far end of the table, too, where Denis Cornford, his wife beside him, was listening rather abstractedly to a visiting History Professor from Yale.

"No. Don't be too hard on yourselves. The Brits didn't treat the natives all that badly, really. Wouldn't you agree, Denis?"

"No, I wouldn't, I'm afraid," replied Cornford simply. "I haven't made any particular study of the subject, but my impression is that the British treated most of their colonials quite abominably."

Shelly slipped her left hand beneath the starched white tablecloth, and gently moved it along his thigh. But she could feel no perceptible response.

⭰⭲

At the head of the splendid oak plank that constituted the High Table at Lonsdale, over the roast lamb, served with St. Julien '93, Sir Clixby had been seeking to mollify the bishop's bitter condemnation of the English Examination Boards for expecting Rwandan refugees to study the Wars of the Roses. And soon after the profiteroles, the atmosphere seemed markedly improved.

All the conversation which had been crisscrossing the evening—amusing, interesting, pompous, spiteful—ceased abruptly as the Master banged his gavel, and the assembled company rose to its feet.

Benedictus benedicatur.

The words came easily and suavely, from lips that were slightly overred, slightly overfull, in a face so smooth one might assume that it seldom had need of the razor.

Those who wished, and that was most of them, now repaired to the SCR where coffee and port were being served (though wholly informally) and where the Master and Julian Storrs stood side-by-side, buttocks turned toward the remarkably realistic gas fire.

"Bishop on his way back to the railway station then?" queried Storrs.

"On his way back to *Africa*, I hope!" said the Master with a grin. "Bloody taxi *would* have to be late tonight, wouldn't it? And none of you lot with a car here."

"It's this drink-driving business, Master. I'm all in favor of it. In fact, I'd vote for random checks myself."

"And Denis there—hullo, Denis!—he was no help either."

Cornford had followed their conversation and now edged toward them, sipping his coffee.

"I sold my old Metro just before Christmas. And if you recall, Master, I only live three hundred yards away."

The words could have sounded lighthearted, yet somehow they didn't.

"Shelly's got a car, though?"

Cornford nodded cautiously. "Parked a mile away."

The Master smiled. "Ah, yes. I remember now."

Half an hour later, as they walked across the cobbles of Radcliffe Square toward Holywell Street, Shelly Cornford put her arm through her husband's and squeezed it. But, as before, she could feel no perceptible response.

Chapter Forty-Six

But she went on pleading in her distraction; and
perhaps said things that would have been better left
to silence.

"Angel!—Angel! I was a child—a child when it
happened! I knew nothing of men."

"You were more sinned against than sinning, that
I admit."

"Then you will not forgive me?"

"I do forgive you, but forgiveness is not all."

"And love me?"

To this question he did not answer.

—Thomas Hardy, *Tess of the d'Urbervilles*

"COFFEE?" SHE suggested, as Cornford was hanging
up his overcoat in the entrance hall.

"I've just had some."

"I'll put the kettle on."

"No! Leave it a while. I want to talk to you."

They sat together, if opposite is together, in the
lounge.

"What did you do when the Chaplain invited us all
to confess our manifold sins and wickedness?"

The measured, civilized tone of Cornford's voice
had shifted to a slightly higher, yet strangely quieter
key; and the eyes, normally so kindly, seemed to
concentrate ever narrowingly upon her, like an

ornithologist focusing binoculars on an interesting species.

"Pardon?"

" 'In thought, word, and deed'—wasn't that the formula?"

She shook her head in apparent puzzlement. "I haven't the faintest—"

But his words cut sharply across her protestation. "Why are you lying to me?"

"What—?"

"Shut up!" The voice had lost its control. "You've been unfaithful to me! *I* know that. *You* know that. Let's start from there!"

"But I haven't—"

"Don't lie to me! I've put up with your infidelity, but I can't put up with your *lies*!"

The last word was hissed, like a whiplash across his wife's face.

"Only once, really," she whispered.

"Recently?"

She nodded, in helpless misery.

"Who with?"

In great gouts, the tears were falling now. "Why do you have to know? Why do you have to torture yourself? It didn't mean anything, Denis! It didn't *mean anything.*"

"Hah!" He laughed bitterly. "Didn't you think it might mean something to *me*?"

"He just wanted—"

"Who was it?"

She closed her eyes, cheeks curtained with mascara'd tears, unable to answer him.

"*Who was it?*"

But still she made no answer to the piercing question.

"Shall I tell *you*?"

He knew—she realized he knew. And now, her eyes still firmly shut, she spoke the name of the adulterer.

"He didn't come here? You went over to the Master's Lodge?"

"Yes."

"And you went to his bedroom?"

"Yes."

"And you undressed for him?"

"Yes."

"You stripped naked for him?"

"Yes."

"And you got between the sheets with him?"

"Yes."

"And you had sex? The pair of you had sex together?"

"Yes."

"How many times?"

"Only once."

"*And you enjoyed it!*"

Cornford got to his feet and walked back into the entrance hall. He felt stunned, like someone who has just been kicked in the teeth by a recalcitrant shire horse.

"Denis!" Shelly had followed him, standing beside him now as he pulled on his overcoat.

"You know *why* I did it, Denis? I did it for *you*. You *must* know that!"

He said nothing.

"How did you know?" Her voice was virtually inaudible.

"It's not what people say, is it? It's the *way* they say it. But I knew. I knew tonight . . . I knew before tonight."

"How *could* you have known? Tell me! Please!"

Cornford turned up the catch on the Yale lock, and for a few moments stood there, the half-opened door admitting a draft of air that felt bitterly cold.

"I *didn't* know! Don't you see? I just hoped you'd deny everything—even if it meant you had to lie to me. But you hadn't even got the guts to *lie* to me! You didn't even want to spare me all this pain."

The door banged shut behind him; and Shelly Cornford walked back into the lounge where she poured herself a vast gin with minimal tonic.

And wished that she were dead.

Chapter Forty-Seven

Virgil G. Perkins, author of international best-
seller *Enjoying Jogging* (Crown Publications NY,
1992) collapsed and died while jogging with a
group of fellow enthusiasts in St. Paul yesterday.
Mr. Perkins, aged 26, leaves behind his wife,
Beverley, their daughter, Alexis, and seven other
children by previous marriages.

—*Minnesota Clarion*, December 23, 1995

IN THE KING'S ARMS, that square, cream-painted
hostelry on the corner of Parks Road and Holywell
Street, Morse had been remarkably abstemious that
evening. After his first pint, he had noticed on the
door the pub's recommendation in the *Egon Ronay
Guide* (1995); and after visiting the loo to inject himself, he had ordered a spinach-and-mushroom
lasagne with garlic bread and salad. The individual
constituents of this particular offering had never
much appealed to him; yet the hospital dietitian (as
he recalled) had been particularly enthusiastic about
such fare. And, let it be said, the meal had been marginally enjoyed.

It was 7:45 P.M.

A cigarette would have been a paradisal plus; and
yet somehow he managed to desist. But as he looked

around him, at the college crests, the colored prints, the photographs of distinguished local patrons, he was debating whether to take a few more calories in liquid form when the landlord was suddenly beside him.

"Inspector! I hadn't seen you come in. This is for you—it's been here a couple of weeks."

Morse took the printed card:

> Let me tell you of a moving experience—very moving! The furniture van is fetching my effects from London to Oxford at last. And on March 18th I'll be celebrating my south-facing patio with a shower of champagne at 53 Morris Villas, Cowley. Come and join me!
>
> RSVP (at above address)
>
> Deborah Crawford

Across the bottom was a handwritten note: "Make it, Morse! DC."

Morse remembered her well . . . a slim, unmarried blonde who'd once invited him to stay overnight in her north London flat, following a comparatively sober Metropolitan Police party; when he'd said that after such a brief acquaintance such an accommodation might perhaps be inappropriate.

Yes, that was the word he'd used: "inappropriate."

Pompous idiot!

But he'd given her his address, which she'd vowed she'd never forget.

Which clearly she had.

"She was ever so anxious for you to get it," began the landlord—but even as he spoke the door that led to Holywell Street had opened, and he turned his attention to the newcomer.

"Denis! I didn't expect to see you in tonight. No good us both running six miles on a Sunday morning if we're going to put all the weight back on on a Sunday night."

Morse looked up, his face puzzled.

"You mean—you went jogging—together—this morning? What time was that?"

"Far too early, wasn't it, David!"

The landlord smiled. "Stupid, really. On a Sunday morning, too."

"What time?" repeated Morse.

"Quarter to seven. We met outside the pub here."

"And where did the pair of you run?"

"*Five* of us actually, wasn't it, Denis? We ran up to the Plain, up the Iffley Road, across Donnington Bridge, along the Abingdon Road up to Carfax, then through Cornmarket and St. Giles' up to the Woodstock Road as far as North Parade, then across to the Banbury, South Parks, and we got back here . . ."

"Just before eight," added Cornford, pointing to Morse's empty glass.

"What's it to be?"

"No, it's my round—"

"Nonsense!"

"Well, if you insist."

In fact, however, it was the landlord who insisted, and who now walked to the bar as Cornford seated himself.

"You told me earlier," Morse was anxious to get things straight, "you'd been on your own when you went out jogging."

"No. If I did, you misunderstood me. You said, I think, 'Just you?' And when I said yes, I'd assumed that you were asking if both of us had gone—Shelly and me."

"And she didn't go?"

"No. She never does."

"She just stayed in bed?"

"Where else?"

Morse made no suggestion.

"Do you ever go jogging, Inspector?" The question was wearily mechanical.

"Me? No. I walk a bit, though. I sometimes walk down to Summertown for a newspaper. Just to keep fit."

Cornford almost grinned. "If you're going to be Master of Lonsdale, you're supposed to be fit. It's in the Statutes somewhere."

"Makes you wonder how Sir Clixby ever managed it!"

Cornford's answer was unexpected.

"You know, as you get older it's difficult for young people to imagine you were ever young yourself—good at games, that sort of thing. Don't you agree?"

"Fair point, yes."

"And the Master was a very fine hockey player—had an England trial, I understand."

The landlord came back with two pints of bitter; then returned to his bartending duties.

Cornford was uneasy, Morse felt sure of that. Something regarding his wife, perhaps? Had *she* had anything to do with the murder of Geoffrey Owens? Unlikely, surely. One thing looked an odds-on certainty, though: if Denis Cornford had ever figured on the suspect list, he figured there no longer.

><

Very soon, after a few desultory passages of conversation, Morse had finished his beer, and was taking his leave, putting Deborah's card into the inside pocket of his jacket, and forgetting it.

Forgetting it only temporarily, though; for later that same evening he was to look at it again—more carefully. And with a sudden, strange enlightenment.

Chapter Forty-Eight

Is it nothing to you, all ye that pass by? Behold and
see if there be any sorrow like unto my sorrow,
which is done unto me, wherewith the Lord hath
afflicted me in the day of his fierce anger.

—Lamentations, ch. 1, v. 12

FEELING A WONDERFUL sense of relief, Shelly Cornford heard the scratch of the key in the front door at
twenty-five past eleven. For over two hours she had
been sitting upright against the pillows, a white bed
jacket over her pajamas, her mind tormented with the
terrifying fear that her husband had disappeared into
the dark night, never to return: to throw himself over
Magdalen Bridge, perhaps; to lay himself across the
railway lines; to slash his wrists; to leap from some
high tower. And it was to little avail that she'd listened to any logic that her tortured mind could
muster: that the water was hardly deep enough, perhaps; that the railway lines were inaccessible; that he
had no razor in his pocket; that Carfax Tower, St.
Mary's, St. Michael's—all were now long shut . . .

Come back to me, Denis! I don't care what happens
to *me*; but come back tonight! Oh, God—*please*, God
—let him come back safely. Oh, God, put an end to
this, my overwhelming misery!

His words before he'd slammed the door had pierced their way into her heart. "You hadn't even got the guts to lie to me . . . You didn't even want to spare me all this pain."

Yet how wrong he'd been, with both his accusations!

Her mother had never ceased recalling that Junior High School report: "She's such a gutsy little girl." And the simple, desperately simple, truth was that she loved her husband far more than anything or anyone she'd ever loved before. And yet . . . and yet she remembered so painfully clearly her assertion earlier that same evening: that more than anything in the world she wanted Denis to be Master.

And now? The center of her life had fallen apart. Her heart was broken. There was no one to whom she could turn.

Except, perhaps . . .

><

And again and again she recalled that terrible conversation:

"Clixby?"

"Shelly!"

"Are you alone?"

"Yes. What a lovely surprise. Come over!"

"Denis knows all about us!"

"What?"

"Denis knows all about us!"

"'All' about us? What d'you mean? There's nothing for him *to* know—not really."

"*Nothing?* Was it nothing to you?"

"You sound like the book of *Proverbs*—or is it *Ecclesiastes*?"

"It *didn't* mean anything to you, did it?"

"It was only the *once*, properly, my dear. For heaven's sake!"

"You just don't understand, do you?"

"How did he find out?"

"He didn't."

"I don't follow you."

"He just guessed. He was talking to you tonight—"

"After Hall, you mean? Of course he was. You were there."

"Did you say anything? Please, tell me!"

"What? Have you taken leave of your senses?"

"Why did he say he *knew*, then?"

"He was just guessing—you just said so yourself."

"He must have had some reason."

"Didn't you deny it?"

"But it was true!"

"What the hell's that got to do with it? Don't you see? All you'd got to do was to deny it."

"That's exactly what Denis said."

"Bloody intelligent man, Denis. I just hope you appreciate him. He was right, wasn't he? All you'd got to do was to deny it."

"And that's what you wanted me to do?"

"*You're* not really being very intelligent, are you?"

"I just can't believe what you're saying."

"It would have been far kinder."

"Kinder to *you*, you mean?"

"To me, to you, to Denis—to everybody."

"God! You're a shit, aren't you?"

"Just hold your horses, girl!"

"What are you going to do about it?"

"What do you mean—'do' about it? What d'you expect me to do?"

"I don't know. I've no one to talk to. That's why I rang you."

"Well, if there's anything—"

"But there is! I want help. This is the worst thing that's ever happened to me."

"But don't you see, Shelly? This is something you and Denis have got to work out for yourselves. Nobody else—"

"God! You *are* a shit, aren't you! Shit with a capital 'S.'"

"Look! Is Denis there?"

"Of course he's not, you fool."

"Please don't call me a fool, Shelly! Get a hold on yourself and put things in perspective—and just remember who you're talking to!"

><

"Denis!"

"You get back to bed. I'll sleep in the spare room."

"No. *I'll* sleep in there—"

"I don't give a sod who sleeps where. We're just not sleeping in the same room, that's all."

His eyes were still full of anger and anguish,

though his voice was curiously calm. "We've got to talk about this. For a start, you'd better find out the rights and wrongs and the rest of it about people involved in divorce on the grounds of adultery. Not tonight, though."

"Denis! Please let's talk *now*—please!—just for a little while."

"What the hell about? About *me*? You know all about me, for Christ's sake. I'm half-pissed—and soon I'm going to be fully pissed—and as well as that I'm stupid—and hurt—and jealous—and possessive—and old-fashioned—and faithful . . . You following me? I've watched most of your antics, but I've never been too worried. You know why? Because I knew you *loved* me. Deep down I knew there was a bedrock of love underneath our marriage. Or I *thought* I knew."

In silence, in abject despair, Shelly Cornford listened, and the tears ran in furrows down her cheeks.

"We're finished. The two of us are finished, Shelly —do you know, I can hardly bring myself to call you by your name? Our marriage is over and done with —make no mistake about that. You can feel free to do what you want now. I just don't care. You're a born flirt! You're a born prick teaser! And I just can't live with you any longer. I just can't live with the picture of you lying there naked and opening your legs to another man. Can you try to get that into your thick skull?"

She shook her head in utter anguish.

"You said," Cornford continued, "you'd have given anything in life to see me become Master. Well, *I* wouldn't—do you understand that? But I'd have given anything in life for you to be faithful to me— whatever the prize."

He turned away from her, and she heard the door of the spare bedroom close; then open again.

"When was it? Tell me that. *When?*"

"This morning."

"You mean when I was out jogging?"

"Yes," she whispered.

He turned away once more; and she beheld and could see no sorrow like unto her own sorrow.

The keys to her car lay on the mantelpiece.

Chapter Forty-Nine

Monday, March 4

> I work all day, and get half-drunk at night.
> Waking at four to soundless dark, I stare.
> In time the curtain-edges will grow light.
> Till then I see what's really always there:
> Unresting death, a whole day nearer now,
> Making all thought impossible but how
> And where and when I shall myself die.
>
> —Philip Larkin, *Aubade*

NEVER, IN HIS lifetime of muted laughter and occasional tears, had Morse spent such a horrifying night. Amid fitful bouts of semi-slumber—head weighted with pain, ears throbbing, stomach in spasms, gullet afire with bile and acidity—he'd imagined himself on the verge of fainting, of vomiting, of having a stroke, of entering cardiac arrest. One of Ovid's lovers had once besought the Horses of the Night to slacken their pace and delay thereby the onset of the Dawn. But as he lay turning in his bed, Morse longed for a sign of the brightening sky through his window. During that seemingly unending night, he had consumed several glasses of cold water, Alka-Seltzer tablets, cups of black coffee, and the equivalent of a weekly dosage of Nurofen Plus.

No alcohol, though. Not one drop of alcohol.

At last Morse had decided to abandon alcohol.

⋗⋖

Lewis looked into Morse's bedroom at 7:30 A.M. (Lewis was the only person who had a key to Morse's flat.)

In the prestigious area of North Oxford, most householders had long since fitted their homes with antiburglar devices, with neighbors holding the keys to the alarm mechanism. But Morse had little need of such a device, for the only salable, stealable items in his flat were the CDs of all the operas of the man he regarded as a towering genius, Richard Wagner; and his earnestly assembled collection of first editions of the greatest hero in his life, the pessimistic poet A. E. Housman, who, like Morse, had left St. John's College, Oxford, without obtaining a degree.

But not even North Oxford burglars had tastes that were quite so esoteric.

And in any case, Morse seldom spoke to either of his immediate neighbors.

"You look awful, sir."

"Oh, for Christ's sake, Lewis! Don't you know if somebody says you *look* awful, you *feel* awful?"

"Didn't you feel awful *before* I said it?"

Morse nodded a miserable agreement.

"Shall I get you a bit of breakfast?"

"No."

"Well, I reckon we can eliminate the Storrs—both of 'em. I've checked with the hotel as far as possible. And unless they hired a helicopter . . ."

"We can cross off the Cornfords, too—*him*, anyway. He's got four witnesses to testify he was running around Oxford pretending to be Roger Bannister."

"What about *her*?"

"I can't really see why . . . or how."

"Owens could have been blackmailing her?"

Morse fingered his stubbled chin. "I don't think so somehow. But there's *something* there . . . something Cornford didn't want to tell me about."

"What d'you think?"

But Morse appeared unable to answer, as he swung his legs out of bed and sat for a while, alternately turning his torso to left and right.

"Just easing the lumbago, Lewis. Don't *you* ever get it?"

"No."

"Just nip and get me a glass of orange juice from the fridge. The *unsweetened* orange juice."

As he walked into the kitchen, Lewis heard the post slither through the letter-box.

So did Morse.

"Lewis! Did you find out what time the postman usually calls in Polstead Road?"

"I've already told you. You were right."

"About the only bloody thing I *have* been right about."

"Arrghh! Cheer up, sir!"

"Just turn out those pockets, will you?" Morse pointed to the suit and shirt thrown carelessly over the only chair in the bedroom. "Time I had a change of clothes—maybe bring me a change of luck."

"Who's your new girlfriend?" Lewis held up the invitation card. " 'Make it, Morse! DC.' "

"That card is wholly private and—"

But Morse got no further.

He felt the old familiar tingling across the shoulders, the hairs on his lower arms standing up, as if a conductor had invited his orchestra to arise after a concert.

"Christ!" whispered Morse irreverently. "Do you know what, Lewis? I think you've done it again!"

Chapter Fifty

Monday–Tuesday, March 4–5

> The four-barreled Lancaster Howdah pistol is of
> .577 in caliber. Its name derived from the story that
> it was carried by tiger hunters who traveled by ele-
> phant and who kept the pistol as a defense against
> any tiger that might leap on to the elephant's back.
>
> *—Encyclopedia of Rifles and Handguns,*
> ed. SEAN CONNOLLY

FOR THE RELATIVES, for the statement takers and the
form fillers, for the boffins at ballistics and forensics,
the murder of Geoffrey Owens would be a serious
business. No less than for the detectives. Yet for Morse
himself the remainder of that Monday had been unproductive and anticlimactic, with a morning of euphoria
followed by an afternoon of blood trouble.

Hospital instructions had been for him to take four
daily readings of his blood sugar level, using a slim,
penlike appliance into which he inserted a test strip
duly smeared with a drop of his blood, with each
result appearing, after only thirty seconds, in a small
window on the side of the pen. While the average
blood sugar level of the healthy person is about 4.5,
the pen is calibrated from 1 to 25, since the levels of

diabetic patients often vary very considerably. Any level higher than 25 is registered as "HI."

Now thus far readings had been roughly what Morse had been led to expect (the highest 15.5): it would take some little while—and then only if he promised to do as he was told—to achieve that "balance," which is the aim of every diabetic. More than disappointing to him therefore had been the "HI" registered at lunchtime that day. In fact, more of a surprise than a disappointment, since momentarily he was misled into believing that "HI" was analogous to the greeting from a fruit machine: "Hello And Welcome!"

But it wasn't; and Morse was rather worried about himself; and returned to his flat, where he took two further Nurofen Plus for his persisting headache, sat back in his armchair, decided he lacked the energy to do *The Times* crossword or even to turn on the CD player—and fairly soon fell fast asleep.

At six o'clock he rang Lewis to say he would be doing nothing more that day. Just before seven o'clock he measured his blood sugar once again; and finding it somewhat dramatically reduced, to 14.3, had decided to celebrate with a small glass of Glenfiddich before he listened to *The Archers*.

✦

The following morning, feeling much refreshed, feeling eager to get on with things, Morse had been at his desk in Police HQ for half an hour before Lewis entered, holding a report.

"Ballistics, sir. Came in last night."

Morse could no more follow the technical terminology of ballistics reports than he could understand a paragraph of Structural Linguistics or recall the configuration of the most recent map of Bosnia. To be sure he had a few vague notions about "barrels" and "grooves" and "cylinders" and "calibers"; but his knowledge went no further, and his interest not quite so far as that. Cursorily glancing therefore through the complex data assembled in the first five pages, he acquainted himself with the short, simply written summary on page six:

Rachel James was fatally shot by a single bullet fired from a range of c. 45 cms.; Geoffrey Owens was fatally shot by two bullets fired from a range of c. 100 cms. The pistol used in each case, of .577 in. caliber, was of the type frequently used by HM Forces. Quite certainly the same pistol was used in each killing.

ASH: 3-4-96

Morse sat back in the black-leather armchair and looked mildly satisfied with life.

"Ye-es. I think I'm beginning to wake up at last in this case, Lewis. You know, it's high time we got together, you and me. We've been doing our own little things so far, haven't we? *You've* gone off to see somebody—*I've* gone off to see somebody—and we've not got very far, have we? It's the same as always, Lewis. We need to do things together from now on."

"No time like the present."

"Pardon?"

Lewis pointed to the ballistics report. "What do you think?"

"Very interesting. Same revolver."

"*Pistol*, sir."

"Same difference."

"I think most of us had assumed it was the same, anyway."

"Really?"

"Well, it's what most of the lads think."

Morse's smile was irritatingly benign. "Same revolver—same murderer. Is that what, er, most of the lads think as well?"

"I suppose so."

"Do you?"

Lewis considered the question. It either was—or it wasn't. Fifty-fifty chance of getting it right, Lewis. Go for it!

"Yes!"

"Fair enough. Now let's consider a few possibilities. Rachel was shot through the kitchen window when she was standing at the sink. The blind was old and made of thinnish material and the silhouette was pretty clear, perhaps; but the murderer was taking a risk. Revolvers," Lewis had given up, "are notoriously inaccurate even at close range, and the bullet's got to penetrate a reasonably substantial pane of glass —enough perhaps to knock the aim off course a bit and hit her in the neck instead of the head. Agreed?"

Lewis nodded at what he saw as an analysis not particularly profound. And Morse continued:

"Now the shooting of Owens took place *inside* the house—from a bit further away; but no glass this time, and a very clear target to aim at. And Owens is shot in the chest, not in the head. A *modus operandi* quite different from the first."

Lewis smiled. "So we've got two *moduses operandi*."

"Modi, Lewis! So it *could* be that we've two murderers. But that would seem on the face of it highly improbable, because it's not difficult to guess the reason for the difference . . . Is it?"

"Well, as I see things, sir, Owens was probably murdered by somebody he knew. He probably invited whoever it was in. Perhaps they'd arranged to meet anyway. Owens was dressed and—" Lewis stopped a moment. "He hadn't shaved though, had he?"

"He was the sort of fellow who always looked as if he needed a shave."

"Perhaps we should have checked more closely."

"You don't expect *me* to check that sort of thing, do you? I'm a necrophobe—you've known me long enough, surely."

"Well, that's it then, really. But *Rachel* probably didn't know him."

"Or *her*."

"She must have been really scared if she heard a tap on the window that morning and went to open the blind—"

"You're still assuming that both murders were committed by the same person, Lewis."

"And *you* don't think so?"

Morse shrugged. "Could have been two lovers or partners or husband and wife—or two completely separate people."

Lewis was beginning to sound somewhat exasperated. "You know, I shall be much happier when we've got a bit more of the routine work done, sir. It's all been a bit ad hoc so far, hasn't it?" (Morse raised his eyebrows at the Latinism.) "Can't we leave a few of the ideas until we've given ourselves a chance to check everything a bit?"

"Lewis! You are preaching to the converted. That's exactly what we've got to do. Go back to the beginning. 'In our beginning is our end,' somebody said— Eliot, wasn't it? Or is it 'In our end is our beginning'?"

"Where do you suggest we begin then, sir?"

Morse considered the question.

"What about you fetching me a cup of coffee? No sugar."

Chapter Fifty-One

Tuesday, March 5

> The overworked man who agrees to any division
> of labor always gets the worst share.
>
> —Hungarian proverb

"WHERE DO YOU suggest we begin then?" repeated Lewis, as Morse distastefully sipped his unsweetened coffee.

"When we *do* start again, we'll probably find that we've been looking at things from the wrong angle. We've been assuming—*I* have, anyway—that it was Owens who was pulling all the strings. As a journalist, he'd often been in a privileged position with regard to a few juicy stories; and as a man he pretty clearly gloried in the hold he could have on other people: blackmail. And from what we learned, I thought it was likely that the two candidates for the Mastership at Lonsdale were being blackmailed; I thought that they'd have as good a motive, certainly Storrs, as anybody for wishing Owens out of the way. But I never dreamed that Owens was in danger of being murdered, as you know . . .

"There's just the one trouble about following up

that particular hypothesis though, isn't there? It's now clear that neither of those two, neither Storrs nor Cornford—nor their wives for that matter—could have been responsible for *both* murders. And increasingly unlikely, perhaps, that any of them could have been responsible even for *one* of the murders. So where does this all leave us? It's a bit like a crossword clue you sometimes get stuck with. You think one bit of the clue's the definition, and the other bit's a buildup of the letters. Then suddenly you realize you've got things *the wrong way round*. And perhaps I'm reading the clue the wrong way round here, Lewis. What if someone was blackmailing *Owens*— the exact opposite of our hypothesis? What if— we've spoken about it before—what if Rachel James came to discover something that would upset his carefully loaded applecart? And blackmailed *him*?"

"Trying to climb aboard the gravy train herself?"

"Exactly. Money! You said right at the start that we needed a *motive* for Rachel's murder; and I suspect she'd somehow got to know about his own blackmailing activities and was threatening to expose him."

Lewis was looking decidedly impatient.

"Sir! Could we *please* get along to Owens' office first, and get a few simple *facts* established?"

"Just what I was about to suggest. We shall have to get down there and find out everything we can about him. See the editor, the subeditor, his colleagues, that personnel fellow—especially him! Go through his desk and his drawers. Get hold of his original application, if we can. Try to learn something about his men friends, his girlfriends, his enemies, his habits, what he liked to eat and drink, his salary, any clubs he belonged to, his political leanings—"

"We know he voted Conservative, sir."

"—the newspaper he took, where he usually parked his car, what his job prospects were—yes, plenty to be going on with there."

"Quite a list. Good job there's two of us, sir."

"Pardon?"

"Hefty agenda—that's all I'm saying."

"Not all that much really. Far easier than it sounds. And if you get off straightaway . . ." Morse looked at his wristwatch: 10:45 A.M.

Lewis frowned. "You mean you're not joining me?"

"Not today, no."

"But you just said—"

"One or two important things I've got to do after lunch."

"Such as?"

"Well, to be truthful, I've been told to take things a bit more gently. And I suppose I'd better take a bit of notice of my medical advisers."

"Of course."

"Don't get me wrong, mind! I'm feeling fine. But I think a little siesta this afternoon . . ."

"*Siesta?* That's what they have in Spain in the middle of the summer when the temperature's up in the nineties—but we're in England in the middle of winter and it's freezing outside."

Morse looked down at his desk, a little sheepishly, and Lewis knew that he was lying.

"Come on, sir! It's something to do with that invite you had, isn't it? Deborah Crawford?"

"In a way."

"Why are you being so secretive about it? You wouldn't tell me yesterday either."

"Only because it needs a bit more thinking about, that's all."

" 'You and me together'—isn't that what you said?"

Morse fingered the still-cellophaned cigarettes, almost desperately.

"Si' down then, Lewis."

Chapter Fifty-Two

It is the nature of an hypothesis, when once a man has conceived it, that it assimilates every thing to itself as proper nourishment, and, from the first moment of your begetting it, it generally grows the stronger by every thing you see, hear, read, or understand.

—Laurence Sterne, *Tristram Shandy*

"IT WASN'T DEBORAH Crawford, Lewis—it was her initials, 'DC.' When we found that list in the manila file, I jumped the gun. I automatically assumed that 'JS' was Julian Storrs—I think I was right about that —and I assumed that 'DC' was Denis Cornford— and I think I was *wrong* about that. As things have turned out I don't believe Owens ever knew Cornford at all, *or* his missus, for that matter. But he knew another 'DC': the woman at Number 1 Bloxham Close—Adèle Beatrice Cecil—the ABC lass Owens knew well enough to call by her nickname, 'Della.' 'DC.' And the more I think about *her*, the more attractive a proposition I find it."

"Well, most men would, sir. Lovely looker!"

Ignoring the pleasantry, Morse continued: "Just consider for a minute what an important figure she is in the case. She's the prime witness, really. *She's* the one who sees Owens leave for work about sevenish on the morning Rachel was murdered; *she's* the one who rings Owens an hour or so later to tell him the police are in Bloxham Close" (again Lewis let it go) "and gives him a headstart on all the other news-hounds. That's what she says, isn't it? But she might not be telling the truth!"

Lewis sat in silence.

"Now, as I recall it, your objection to Owens himself ever being a suspect was the time factor. You argued that he couldn't have gone to work that morning, parked his car, been seen in the newspaper offices, got in his car again, driven back to Kidlington, murdered Rachel, driven back to Osney Mead *again*, taken the phone call from Della Cecil, driven back to Kidlington *again*, to be on hand with his mobile and his notebook while the rest of the press are pulling their socks on. He could *never* have done all that in such a short space of time, you said. Impossible! And of course you were right—"

"Thank you, sir."

"—in one way; and quite wrong in another. Let's stick to our original idea that the list of initials we found was a blackmail list, and that *she's* on it— Della Cecil. He's got something on her, too. So when he asks her to help him in his plan to get Rachel out of the way, she's little option but to cooperate."

"Have you any idea what this 'plan' was, sir?"

"That's the trouble. I've got far too many ideas."

"Want to try me?"

"All right. They're all the same sort of plan, really —any plan to cut down that *time* business you're so worried about. Let me just outline a possible plan, and see what you think of it. Ready? Owens drives out to work, at ten to seven, let's say—and *she follows him*, in her own car. When he's parked the car, when his entry's recorded, he goes into the building, makes sure he's seen by somebody—doesn't matter who it is—then immediately leaves via a side door and gets into *her* car, parked along the street in front of the offices. Back in Kidlington, he murders Rachel James, about half past seven, *and doesn't return to work at all*. He's got a key and he goes into *Della*'s house—and waits. At the appropriate time, when the police arrive, a call is made to his own office—he knows there'll be no one there!—and a message is left *or isn't left* on the answer phone. All that matters is that a telephonic communication is established, and gets recorded on those BT lists we all get, between *her* phone and Owens' phone in his office. Then all he's got to do is to emerge amid all the excitement once the murder's reported—the police, the local people, the Press, the TV . . . Well?"

"You make it up as you go along, sir."

Morse's face betrayed some irritation. "Of *course* I bloody do! That's what I'm here for. I just told you. If once we accept there could be *two* people involved —*two* cars—there are *dozens* of possibilities. It's like permutating your selection on the National Lottery. I've just given you *one* possibility, that's all."

"But it just couldn't—"

"What's wrong with it? Come on! Tell me!"

"Well, let's start with the car—"

"*Cars*, plural."

"All right. When he's parked his car—"

"I didn't say that. I deliberately said parked *the* car, if you'd been listening. It could have been his—it could have been hers: it's the *card* number that's recorded there, not the *car* number. She could have driven his car—he could have driven hers—and at any point they could have swapped. Not much risk. Very few people around there at seven. Or eight, for that matter."

"Is it my turn now?" asked Lewis quietly.

"Go on!"

"I'm talking about Owens' car, all right? That was parked in Bloxham Drive—'Drive' *please*, sir—when Owens was there that morning. The street was cordoned off, but the lads let him in—because he told them he lived there. And I saw the car myself."

"So? He could have left it—or she could have left it—in a nearby street. Anywhere. Up on the main road behind the terrace, say. That's where JJ—"

But Morse broke off.

"It *still* couldn't have happened like you say, sir!"

"No?"

"No! He was seen in his office, Owens was, remember? Just at the time when Rachel was being murdered! Seen by the Personnel Manager there."

"We haven't got a statement from him yet, though."

"He's been away, you know that."

"Yes, I *do* know that, Lewis. But you spoke to him."

Lewis nodded.

"On the phone?"

"On the phone."

"You did it through the operator, I suppose?"

Lewis nodded again.

"Do you know who she probably put you through to?" asked Morse slowly.

The light dawned in Lewis's eyes. "You mean . . . she could have put me through to Owens himself?"

Morse shrugged his shoulders. "That's what we've got to find out, isn't it? Owens was *deputy* Personnel Manager, we know that. He was on a management course only last weekend."

"Do you really think that's what happened?"

"I dunno. I know one thing, though: it *could* have happened that way."

"But it's all so—so airy-fairy, isn't it? And you said we were going to get some *facts* straight first."

"Exactly."

Lewis gave up the struggle. "I'll tell you something that *would* be useful: some idea where the gun is."

"The 'pistol,' do you mean?"

"Sorry. But if only we knew where *that* was . . ."

"Oh, I think I know where we're likely to find the pistol, Lewis."

Part Five

Chapter Fifty-Three

Wednesday, March 6

> A good working definition of Hell on Earth is a forced attendance for a couple of days or even a couple of hours at a Young Conservatives' Convention.
>
> —Cassandra, in the *Daily Mirror*, June 1952

MISS ADÈLE CECIL (she much preferred "Miss" to "Ms." and "Adèle" to "Della") had spent the previous evening and night in London, where she had attended, and addressed, a meeting of the chairmen, chairwomen, and chairpersons of the Essex Young Conservative Association. Thirty-eight such personages had assembled at Durrants, in George Street, a traditional English hotel just behind Oxford Street, with good facilities, tasteful cuisine, and comfortable beds. Proceedings had been businesslike, and the majority of delegates (it appeared) had ended up in the rooms originally allocated to them.

It was at a comparatively early breakfast in the restaurant that over her fresh grapefruit, with Full English to follow, the headwaiter had informed Adèle of the telephone message, which she had taken in one of the hooded booths just outside the breakfast room.

"How did you know I was here?"

"Don't you remember me? I'm a detective."

Yes, she remembered him—the white-haired, supercilious, sarcastic police officer she didn't want to meet again.

"I shan't be back in Oxford till lunchtime."

"The Trout? Half past twelve?"

As she started on her eggs, bacon, mushrooms, and sausages, she accepted the good-natured twitting of her three breakfast companions, all male:

"Boyfriend?"

"Couldn't he wait?"

"What's *he* got . . . ?"

→←

During her comparatively young life, Adèle had been companionably attached to a couple of dozen or so men, of varying ages, with many of whom she had slept—though seldom more than once or twice, and never without some satisfactory reassurance about the availability and reliability of condoms, and a relatively recent checkup for AIDS.

They were all the same, men. Well, most of them. Fingers fumbling for hooks at the backs of bras, or at the front these days. So why was she looking forward just a little to her lunchtime rendezvous? She wasn't really, she told herself, as she parked the Rover, crossed the narrow road just below the bridge, and entered the bar.

"What'll you have?"

"Orange juice and lemonade, please."

They sat facing each other at a low wooden table, and Morse was immediately (and again) aware of her attractiveness. She wore a slimly tailored dark-gray outfit, with a high-necked Oxford blue blouse, her ash-blonde hair palely gleaming.

Morse looked down at his replenished pint of London Pride.

"Good time at the Conference?"

"I had a lovely time," she lied.

"I'm glad it went well," he lied.

"Do you mind?" She waved an unlit cigarette in the air.

"Go ahead, please."

She offered the packet across.

"Er, not for the minute, thank you."

"Well?"

"Just one or two questions."

She smiled attractively: "Go ahead."

Morse experienced a sense of paramnesia. *Déjà vu.* "You've already signed a statement—about the morning Rachel was murdered?"

"You know that, surely?"

"And it was the truth?" asked Morse, starkly. "You couldn't have been wrong?"

"Of course not!"

"You told me you 'had a heart-to-heart' with Rachel once in a while. I think those were your words?"

"So?"

"Does that mean you spoke about boyfriends—men friends?"

"And clothes, and money, and work—"

"Did you know she was having an affair with Julian Storrs?"

She nodded slowly.

"Did you mention this to Mr. Owens?" Morse's eyes, blue and unblinking, looked fiercely into hers.

And her eyes were suddenly fierce, too, as they held his. "What the hell do you think I'd do that for?"

Morse made no direct answer as he looked down at the old flagstones there. And when he resumed, his voice was very quiet.

"Did *you* ever have an affair with Julian Storrs?"

She thought he looked sad, as if he hadn't really wanted to ask the question at all; and suddenly she knew why she'd been looking forward to seeing him. So many hours of her life had she spent seeking to discover what lay beneath the physical looks, the sexual prowess, the masculine charms of some of her lovers; and so often had she discovered the selfsame answer—virtually nothing.

She looked long into the blazing log fire before finally answering:

"I spent one night with him—in Blackpool—at one of the Party Conferences."

She spoke so softly that Morse could hardly hear

the words, or perhaps it was he didn't wish to hear the words. For a while he said nothing. Then he resumed his questioning:

"You told me that when you were at Roedean there were quite a few daughters of service personnel there, apart from yourself?"

"Quite a few, yes."

"Your own father served in the Army in India?"

"How did you know that?"

"He's in *Who's Who*. Or he was. He died two years ago. Your mother died of cancer twelve years ago. You were the only child of the marriage."

"Orphan Annie, yeah!" The sophisticated, upper crust veneer was beginning to crack.

"You inherited his estate?"

"*Estate?* Hah!" She laughed bitterly. "He left all his money to the bookmakers."

"No heirlooms, no mementos—that sort of thing?"

She appeared puzzled. "*What* sort of thing?"

"A pistol, possibly? A service pistol?"

"Look! You don't seriously think *I* had anything to do with—"

"My job's to ask the questions—"

"Well, the answer's 'no,'" she snapped. "Any more questions?"

One or two clearly:

"Where were you on Sunday morning—last Sunday morning?"

"At home. In bed. Asleep—until the police woke me up."

"And *then?*"

"Then I was frightened. And you want me to tell you the truth? Well, I'm *still* bloody frightened!"

Morse looked at her again: so attractive; so vulnerable; and now just a little nervous, perhaps? Not frightened though, surely.

Was she hiding something?

"Is there anything more," he asked gently "anything at all, you can tell me about this terrible business?"

And immediately he sensed that she could.

"Only one thing, and perhaps it's got nothing . . . Julian asked me to a Guest Night at Lonsdale last November, and in the SCR after dinner I sat next to a Fellow there called Denis Cornford. I only met him that once—but he was really nice—lovely man, really—the sort of man I wish I'd met in life."

"Bit old, surely?"

"About your age."

Morse's fingers folded round the cellophane, and he sought to stop his voice from trembling.

"What about him?"

"I saw him in the Drive, that's all. On Thursday night. About eight. He didn't see me. I'd just driven in and he was walking in front of me—no car. He kept walking along a bit, and then he turned into Number 15 and rang the bell. Geoff Owens opened the front door—and let him in."

"You're quite sure it was him?"

"Oh, yes," replied Adèle.

Chapter Fifty-Four

> He looked into her limpid eyes: "I will turn this
> Mozart off, if you don't mind, my love. You see,
> I can never concentrate on two beautiful things at
> the same time."
>
> —Passage quoted by Terence Benczik in
> *The Good and the Bad in Mills and Boon*

WITH SUSPICIOUSLY extravagant caution Morse drove
the Jaguar up toward Kidlington HQ, again conscious
of seeing the nameplate of that particular railway station flashing, still unrecognizably, across his mind.
At the Woodstock Road roundabout he waited patiently for a gap in the Ring Road traffic; rather too
patiently for a regularly hooting hooligan somewhere
behind him.

Whether he believed what his ABC girl had told
him, he wasn't really sure. And suddenly he realized
he'd forgotten to ask her whether indeed it was *she*
who occasionally extended her literary talents
beyond her humdrum political pamphlets into the
fields of (doubtless more profitable) pornography.

But it was only for a few brief minutes that Morse
considered the official confiscation of the titillatingly
titled novel, since his car phone had been ringing as
he finally crossed into Five Mile Drive. He pulled

over to the side of the road, since seldom had he been able to discharge two simultaneous duties at all satisfactorily.

It was Lewis on the line—an excited Lewis.

Calling from the newspaper offices.

"I just spoke to the Personnel Manager, sir. It was him!"

"Lew-is! Your pronouns! *What* exactly was *who*?"

"It wasn't Owens I spoke to on the phone. It was the Personnel Manager himself!"

Morse replied only after a pause, affecting a tone of appropriate humility: "I wonder why I don't take more notice of you in the first place."

"You don't sound all that surprised?"

"Little in life surprises me any longer. The big thing is that we're getting things straight at last. Well done!"

"So your girl *wasn't* involved."

"I don't think so."

"Did she tell you anything important?"

"I'm not sure. We know Owens had got something on Storrs, and perhaps . . . it might be he had something on Cornford as well."

"Cornford? How does he come into things?"

"She tells me, our Tory lass, that she saw him going into Owens' house last Thursday."

"Phew!"

"I'm just going back to HQ, and then I'll be off to see our friends the Cornfords—both of 'em—if I can park."

"Last time you parked on the pavement in front of the Clarendon Building."

"Ah, yes. Thank you, Lewis. I'd almost forgotten that."

"Not forgotten your injection, I hope?"

"Oh no. That's now become an automatic part of my lifestyle," said Morse, who had forgotten all about his lunchtime jab.

>‹

The phone was ringing when Morse opened the door of his office.

"Saw you coming in," explained Strange.

"Yes, sir?"

"It's all these forms I've got to fill in—retirement forms. They give me a headache."

"They give *me* a headache."

"At least you know how to fill 'em in."

"Can we leave it just a little while, sir? I don't seem able to cope with two things at once these days, and I've got to get down to Oxford."

"Let it wait! Just don't forget *you*'ll be filling in the same forms pretty soon."

>‹

Bloxham Drive was still cordoned off, the police presence still pervasively evident. But Adèle Beatrice Cecil—alias Ann Berkeley Cox, author of *Topless in Torremolinos*—was waved through by a sentinel PC, just as Geoffrey Owens had been waved through over a fortnight earlier, on the morning that Rachel James had been murdered.

As she let herself into Number 1, she was immediately aware that the house was (literally) almost freezing. Why hadn't she left the heating on? How good to have been able to jump straight into a hot bath; or into an electric-blanketed bed; or into a lover's arms . . .

For several minutes she thought of Morse, and of what he had asked her. What on earth had he suspected? And suddenly, alone again now, in her cold house, she found herself shivering.

Chapter Fifty-Five

To an outsider it may appear that the average Oxbridge don works but twenty-four weeks out of the annual fifty-two. If therefore at any point in the academic year it is difficult to locate the where-abouts of such an individual, most assuredly this circumstance may not constitute any adequate cause for universal alarm.

—*A Workload Analysis of University Teachers*, ed. HARRY JUDGE

JUST AFTER 4 P.M. that same day, Morse rang the bell beside the red-painted front door of an elegant, ash-lared house just across from the Holywell Music Room. It was the right house, he knew that, with the Lonsdale Crest fixed halfway between the neatly paned windows of the middle and upper stories.

There was no answer.

There were no answers.

Morse retraced his steps up to Broad Street and crossed the cobbles of Radcliffe Square to the Porters' Lodge at Lonsdale.

"Do you know if Dr. Cornford's in College?"

The duty porter rang a number; then shook his head.

"Doesn't seem to be in his rooms, sir."

"Has he been in today?"

"He was in this morning. Called for his mail—what, ten? Quarter past?"

"You've no idea where he is?"

The porter shook his head. "Doesn't come in much of a Wednesday, Dr. Cornford. Usually has his Faculty Meeting Wednesdays."

"Can you try him for me there? It's important."

The porter rang a second number; spoke for a while; put down the phone.

"They've not seen him today, sir. Seems he didn't turn up for the two o'clock meeting."

"Have you got his home number?"

"He's ex-directory, sir. I can't—"

"So am *I* ex-directory. You know who I am, don't you?"

The young porter looked as hopefully as he could into Morse's face.

"No, sir."

"Forget it!" snapped Morse.

He walked back up to Holywell Street, along to the red door, and rang the bell.

There was no answer.

There were no answers.

><

An overlipsticked middle-aged traffic warden stood beside the Jaguar.

"Is this your vehicle, sir?"

"Yes, madam. I'm just waiting for the Chief Constable. He's," Morse pointed vaguely toward the Sheldonian, "nearly finished in there. At any rate, I hope he bloody has! And if he hasn't, put the bill to 'im, love—not to me!"

"Sorry!"

Morse wandered across to the green-shuttered Blackwell's, and browsed awhile; finally purchasing the first volume of Sir Steven Runciman's *History of the Crusades*.

He wasn't quite sure why.

Then, for the third time, he walked up to the red door in Holywell Street and rang the bell.

>‹

Morse heard the news back in HQ.

From Lewis.

A body had been found in a car, in a narrow lane off New Road, in a garage rented under the name of Dr. Cornford.

For a while Morse sat silent.

"I only met him the once you know, Lewis. Well, the twice, really. He was a good man, I think. I liked him."

"It isn't Dr. Cornford though, sir. It's his wife."

Chapter Fifty-Six

Thursday, March 7

Is it sin
To rush into the secret house of death
Ere death dare come to us?

—Shakespeare, *Antony and Cleopatra*

"Tell me about it," said Morse.

Seated opposite him, in the first-floor office in St. Aldates Police Station, Detective Chief Inspector Peter Warner told the story sadly and economically.

Mrs. Shelly Cornford had been found in the driving seat of her own car, reclining back, with a hosepipe through the window. The garage had been bolted on the inside. There could be little doubt that the immediate cause of death was carbon monoxide poisoning from exhaust fumes. A brief handwritten note had been left on the passenger seat: "I'm so sorry, Denis, I can't forgive myself for what I did. I never loved anyone else but you, my darling—S." No marks of violence; 97 mg blood alcohol—the equivalent (Warner suggested) of two or three stiffish gins. Still a few unanswered questions, of course: about her previous whereabouts that day; about the purchase of the green hosepipe and the connector, both new. But suspicion of foul play? None.

"I wonder where she had a drink?" asked Morse.

"Well, if she'd walked up from Holywell Street, there'd be the King's Arms, the White Horse, The Randolph. . . . But you're the expert."

Morse asked no more questions; but sat thinking of the questionnaire he had set for the *Police Gazette* (it seemed so long ago): "If you could gladden your final days with one of the following . . ." Yes, without a doubt, if he'd been honest, Morse would have applauded Shelly Cornford's choice. And what the hell did it matter *where* she'd had those few last glasses of alcohol—few last "units" rather—the measurements into which the dietitian had advised him to convert his old familiar gills and pints and quarts.

"Do you want to see her?"

Morse shook his head.

"You'd better see *him*, though."

Morse nodded wearily. "Is he all right?"

"We-ell. His GP's been in—but he refuses to take any medication. He's in the canteen with one of the sergeants. We've finished with him, really."

⟶⟵

"Tell me about it," urged Morse.

Denis Cornford's voice was flat, almost mechanical, as he replied:

"On Sunday just before I met you in the pub she told me she'd been to bed with another man that morning. I hardly spoke to her after that. I slept in the spare room the last three nights."

"The note?" asked Morse gently. "Is that what she was referring to?"

"Yes."

"Nothing to do with anything else?"

"No."

"She was there, in your rooms, just before Chapel on Sunday, wasn't she?"

Cornford evinced no surprise.

"We'd had a few harsh words. She didn't want to see you."

"Do you know who the other man was?"

"Yes. Clixby Bream."

"*She* told you that, sir?"

"Yes."

"So—so she couldn't have had anything to do with the Owens murder?"

"No. Nor could the Master."

"Did *you* have anything to do with it?"

"No."

"Why did you go to see Owens last Thursday?"

"I knew Owens a bit through various things I did for his newspaper. That night I had to go to Kidlington—I went on the bus—the Kidlington History Society—held at the school—'Effects of the Enclosure Acts in Oxfordshire'—seven o'clock to eight. He lived fairly near—five minutes' walk away. I'd done a three-part article for him on Medieval Oxford —Owens said it needed shortening a bit—we discussed some changes—no problems. I got a bus back to Oxford—about nine."

"Why didn't you tell me you knew Owens?"

"I didn't want to get involved."

"What will you do now?"

"I left a note for the Master about the election." The voice was still monotonous; the mouth dry. "I've withdrawn my nomination."

"I'm so sorry about everything," said Morse very quietly.

"Yes, I think you are, aren't you?"

Morse left the pale, bespectacled historian staring vaguely into a cup of cold tea, like a man who is temporarily anesthetized against some overwhelming pain.

✹

"It's a terrible business—terrible!"

The Master poured himself a single-malt scotch.

"Drink, Chief Inspector?"

Morse shook his head.

"Won't you sit down?"

"No. I've only called to say that Dr. Cornford has just told me everything—about you and his wife."

"Mmm."

"We shall have to get a statement from you."

"Why is that?"

"The *time* chiefly, I suppose."

"Is it really necessary?"

"There *was* a murder on that Sunday morning."

"Mmm. Was she one of your suspects?"

Morse made no direct answer. "She couldn't have been making love to you and murdering someone else at the same time."

"No." The bland features betrayed no emotion; yet Morse was distastefully aware that the Master was hardly displeased with such a succinct, such an unequivocal assertion of Shelly Cornford's innocence, since by implication it was an assertion of his own.

"I understand that Dr. Cornford has written to you, sir."

"Exited from the lists, poor Denis, yes. That just leaves Julian Storrs. Good man though, Julian!"

Morse slowly walked to the door.

"What do you think about suicide, Sir Clixby?"

"In general?" The Master drained his tumbler, and thoughtfully considered the question. "Aristotle, you know, thought suicide a form of cowardice—running away from troubles oneself and leaving all the heartache to everybody else. What do *you* think?"

Morse was conscious of a deep loathing for this smooth and odious man.

"I don't know what your particular heartache is, sir. You see I never met Mrs. Cornford myself. But I'd be surprised if she was a coward. In fact, I've got the feeling she was a bit of a gutsy girl." Morse stood beside the study door, his face drawn, his nostrils distended. "And I'll tell you something else. She probably had far more guts in her little finger than you've ever had in the whole of your body!"

⇥⇤

Lewis was waiting in the Jaguar outside the Porters' Lodge; and Morse quickly climbed into the passenger seat. His voice was still vicious:

"Get—me—out—of—here, Lewis!"

Chapter Fifty-Seven

Friday, March 8

> Those who are absent, by its means become pre-
> sent: correspondence is the consolation of life.
>
> —Voltaire,
> *Philosophical Dictionary*

SERGEANT LEWIS had himself only just entered Morse's office when Jane came through with the post: six official-looking letters, opened, with appropriate previous correspondence paper-clipped behind them; one square white envelope, unopened, marked "Private," and postmarked Oxford; and an airmail letter, also unopened, marked "Personal," and post-marked "Washington."

Jane smiled radiantly at her boss.

"Why are you looking so cheerful?" queried Morse.

"Just nice to have you back, sir, that's all."

Inside the white envelope was a card, the front showing an auburn-haired woman, in a white dress, reading a book; and Morse read the brief message inside:

Geoffrey Harris Ward
Radcliffe Infirmary
March 7, 1996

   We all miss your miserable presence in the
ward. If you <u>haven't</u> finished smoking, we shall
never meet for that G&T you promised me.
Look after yourself!

Affectionately,
Janet (McQueen)

P.S. I looked through your old hospital records
from many years ago. Know something? I
found your Christian name!

"Why are *you* looking so cheerful?" asked Lewis.
   But Morse made no answer, and indeed appeared
to be reading the message again and again. Then he
opened the letter from America.

Washington
March 4

Dear Morse,
   Just read your thing in the Police Gazette.
How did I know it was yours? Ah, I too was a
detective! I'd have had the champagne myself.
And I think the Fauré Requiem's a bit light-
weight compared with the Verdi—in spite of
the imprimatur of the Papacy. I know you've
always wept to Wagner but I've always wept to

Verdi myself—and the best Xmas present I had
was the Karajan recording of Don Carlos.

I know you're frightened of flying, but a visit
here—especially in the spring, they say—is
something not to be missed in life. We'll get
together again for a jar on my return (April)
and don't leave it too long before you take your
pension.

As aye,
Peter (Imbert)

Morse handed the letter across to Lewis.
"The old Metropolitan Commissioner!"
Morse nodded, rather proudly.
"Washington, D.C., that'll be, sir."
"Where else?"
"Washington, C.D.—County Durham, near enough."
"Oh."
"What's your program today, sir?"
"Well, we've done most of the spadework—"
"Except the Harvey Clinic side of things."
"And that's in hand, you say?"
"Seeing the woman this morning. She's just back
from a few days' holiday."
"Who's she again? Remind me."
"I told you about her: Dawn Charles."
"Mrs. or Miss or Ms.?"
"Not sure. But she's the main receptionist there.
They say if anybody's likely to know what's going
on, she is."

"What time are you seeing her?"

"Ten o'clock. She's got a little flat out at Bicester on the Charles Church Estate. You joining me?"

"No, I don't think so. Something tells me I ought to see Storrs again."

Lovingly Morse put the "Girl Reading" (Perugini, 1878) back into her envelope, then looked through Sir Peter's letter once again.

Don Carlos.

The two words stood out and stared at him, at the beginning of a line as they were, at the end of a paragraph. Not an opera Morse knew well, *Don Carlos*. Another "DC," though. It was amazing how many DCs had cropped up in their inquiries—and still another one just now in the District of Columbia. And suddenly in Morse's mind the name of the Verdi opera merged with a name he'd just heard: the "Don" chiming in with the "Dawn," and the "Carlos" with the "Charles."

Was it *Dawn Charles* (Mrs. or Miss or Ms.) who held the key to the mystery? Did they belong to *her*, that pair of initials in the manila file?

Morse's eyes gleamed with excitement.

"I think," he said slowly, "Mr. Julian Storrs will have to wait a little while. I shall be coming with you, Lewis—to Bicester."

Part Six

Chapter Fifty-Eight

The best liar is he who makes the smallest amount of lying go the longest way.

      —Samuel Butler, *Truth and Convenience*

DAWN CHARLES looked nervous when she opened the door of her flat in Woodpecker Way and let the two detectives through into the gray-carpeted lounge, where the elder of the two, the white-haired one, was already complimenting her on such an attractive residence.

"Bit unlucky though, really. I bought it at the top of the property boom for fifty-eight thousand. Only worth thirty-four now."

"Oh dear!"

The man made her feel uneasy. And her mind went back to the previous summer when on returning from France she'd put the Green Channel sticker on the windscreen—only to be diverted into the Red Channel; where pleasantly, far too pleasantly, she'd been questioned about her time abroad, about the weather, about anything and everything—except those extra thousand cigarettes in the back of the boot. It had been as if they were just stringing her along; knowing the truth all the time.

But these men couldn't possibly know the truth, that's what she was telling herself now; and she thought she could handle things. On Radio Oxford just before Christmas she'd heard P. D. James's advice to criminal suspects: "Keep it short! Keep it simple! Don't change a single word unless you have to!"

"Please sit down. Coffee? I've only got instant, I'm afraid."

"We both prefer instant, don't we, Sergeant?"

"Lovely," said Lewis, who would much have preferred tea.

Two minutes later, Dawn held a jug suspended over the steaming cups.

"Milk?"

"Please," from Lewis.

"Thank you," from Morse.

"Sugar?"

"Just the one teaspoonful," from Lewis.

But a shake of the head from Morse; a slight raising of the eyebrows as she stirred two heaped teaspoonfuls into her own coffee; and an obsequious comment which caused Lewis to squirm inwardly: "How on earth do you manage to keep such a beautiful figure —with all that sugar?"

She colored slightly. "Something to do with the metabolic rate, so they tell me at the clinic."

"Ah, yes! The clinic. I'd almost forgotten."

Again he was sounding too much like the Customs man, and Dawn was glad it was the sergeant who now took over the questioning.

A little awkwardly, a little ineptly (certainly as Morse saw things) Lewis asked about her training, her past experience, her present position, her relationships with employers, colleagues, clients . . .

The scene was almost set.

She knew Storrs (she claimed) only as a patient; she'd known Turnbull (she claimed) only as a consultant; she knew Owens (she claimed) not at all.

Lewis produced the letter stating Julian Storrs' prognosis.

"Do you think this photocopy was made at the clinic?"

"I didn't copy it."

"Someone must have done."

"I didn't copy it."

"Any idea who might have done?"

"*I* didn't copy it."

It was hardly a convincing performance, and she was aware that both men knew she was lying. And quietly—amid a few tears, certainly, but with no hysteria—the truth came out.

Owens she had met when the Press had come along for the clinic's 25th anniversary—he must have seen something, heard something that night, about Mr. Storrs. After Mr. Turnbull had died, Owens had telephoned her—they'd met in the Bird and Baby in St. Giles'—he'd asked her if she could copy a letter for him—yes, *that* letter—he'd offered her £500—and she'd agreed—copied the letter—been paid in cash. That was it—that was all—a complete betrayal of trust, she knew that—something she'd never done before—would never have done in the normal course of events. It was just the money—nothing else—she'd desperately needed the money . . .

Morse had been silent throughout the interrogation, his attention focused, it seemed, on the long, black-stockinged legs.

"Where does that leave me—leave us?" she asked miserably.

"We shall have to ask you to come in to make an official statement," said Lewis.

"Now, you mean?"

"That'll be best, yes."

"Perhaps not," intervened Morse. "It's not *all* that urgent, Miss Charles. We'll be in touch fairly soon."

⤞⤝

At the door, Morse thanked her for the coffee: "Not the best homecoming, I'm afraid."

"Only myself to blame," she said, her voice tight as she looked across at the Visitors' parking lots, where the Jaguar stood.

"Where did you go?" asked Morse.

"I didn't go anywhere."

"You stayed here—in your flat?"

"I didn't go anywhere."

⤞⤝

"What was that about?" asked Lewis as he drove back along the A34 to Oxford. "About her statement?"

"I want you to be with me when we see Storrs this afternoon."

"What did you think of her?"

"Not a very good liar."

"Lovely figure, though. Legs right up to her armpits! She'd have got a job in the chorus line at the Windmill."

Morse was silent, his eyes gleaming again as Lewis continued:

"I read somewhere that they all had to be the same height and the same build—in the chorus line there."

"Perhaps I'll take you along when the case is over."

"No good, sir. It's been shut for ages."

→←

Dawn Charles closed the door behind her and walked thoughtfully back to the lounge, the suspicion of a smile about her lips.

Chapter Fifty-Nine

Everything in life is somewhere else, and you get there in a car.

—E. B. White, *One Man's Meat*

LEWIS HAD BACKED into the first available space in Polstead Road, the tree-lined thoroughfare that leads westward from Woodstock Road into Jericho; and now stood waiting while Morse arose laboriously from the low passenger seat of the Jaguar.

"Seen *that* before, sir?" Lewis pointed to the circular blue plaque on the wall opposite: "This house was the home of T. E. Lawrence (Lawrence of Arabia) from 1896–1921."

Morse grunted as he straightened up his aching back, mumbling of lumbago.

"What about a plaque for Mr. Storrs, sir? 'This was the home of Julian Something Storrs, Master of Lonsdale, 1996 to . . . 1997'?"

Morse shrugged indifferently:

"Perhaps just 1996."

The two men walked a little way along the short road. The houses here were of a pattern: gabled, red-bricked, three-storied properties, with ashlared, mullioned windows, the frames universally painted white; interesting and amply proportioned houses built toward the end of the nineteenth century.

"Wouldn't mind living here," volunteered Lewis.

Morse nodded. "Very civilized. Small large houses, these, Lewis, as opposed to large small houses."

"What's the difference?"

"Something to do with the number of bathrooms, I think."

"Not much to do with the number of garages!"

"No. Clearly nothing whatever to do with the number of garages, since the reason for the continuum of cars on either side of the road was becoming increasingly obvious: there *were* no garages here, nor indeed any room for such additions. To compensate for the inconvenience, the front areas of almost all the properties had been cemented, cobbled, graveled, or paved, in order to accommodate the parking of motor cars; including the front of the Storrs' residence, where on the gravel alongside the front window stood a small, pale gray, D-registration Citroën, a thin pink stripe around its bodywork.

"Someone's in?" ventured Morse.

"Mrs. Storrs, perhaps—he's got a BMW. A woman's car, that, anyway."

"Really?"

Morse was still peering through the Citroën's front window (perhaps for some more eloquent token of femininity) when Lewis returned from his ineffectual ringing.

"No one in. No answer, anyway."

"On another weekend break?"

"I could ring the Porters' Lodge."

"You do that small thing, Lewis. I'll be . . ." Morse pointed vaguely toward the hostelry at the far end of the road.

⊰⊱

It was at the Anchor, a few minutes later, as Morse sat behind a pint of John Smith's Tadcaster bitter, that Lewis came in to report on the Storrs: away again, for the weekend, the pair of them, this time though their whereabouts not vouchsafed to the Lodge.

Morse received the news without comment, appearing preoccupied; *thinking* no doubt, supposed Lewis, as he paid for his orange juice. Thinking and drinking . . . drinking and thinking . . . the twin activities which in Morse's view were ever and necessarily concomitant.

Not wholly preoccupied, however.

"I'll have a refill while you're at the bar, Lewis. Smith's please."

⊰⊱

After a period of silence, Morse asked the question:

"If somebody came to you with a letter—a photocopied letter, say—claiming your missus was having a passionate affair with the milkman—"

Lewis grinned. "I'd be dead worried. We've got a woman on the milk float."

"—what would you do?"

"Read it, obviously. See who'd written it."

"Show it to the missus?"

"Only if it was a joke."

"How would you know that?"

"Well, you wouldn't really, would you? Not for a start. You'd try to find out if it was genuine."

"Exactly. So when Storrs got a copy of that letter, a letter he'd pretty certainly not seen before—"

"Unless Turnbull showed it to him?"

"Doubt it. A death certificate, wasn't it? He'd want to let Storrs down a bit more gently than that."

"You mean, if Storrs tried to find out if it *was* genuine, he'd probably go along to the clinic . . ."

Morse nodded, like some benevolent schoolmaster encouraging a promising pupil.

"And show it to . . . Dawn Charles?"

"Who else? She's the sort of Practice Manager there, if anybody is. And let's be honest about things. You're not exactly an expert in the Socratic skills yourself, are you? But how long did it take *you* to get the truth out of her? Three or four minutes?"

"You think Storrs did it as well?"

"Pretty certainly, I'd say. He's nobody's fool; and he's not going to give in to blackmail just on somebody's vague say-so. He's an academic, and if you're an academic you're trained to *check*—check your sources, check your references, check your evidence."

"So perhaps Storrs has been a few steps in front of us all the time."

Morse nodded. "He probably rumbled our receptionist straightaway. Not *many* suspects there at the clinic."

Slowly Lewis sipped his customary orange juice, his earlier euphoria fading.

"We're not exactly galloping toward the finishing post, are we?"

Morse looked up, his blue eyes betraying some considerable surprise.

"Why do you say that, Lewis? That's exactly what we *are* doing."

Chapter Sixty

Saturday, March 9

Hombre apercebido medio combatido
(A man well prepared has already half fought the
battle).

—Cervantes, *Don Quixote*

SOMEWHAT CONCERNED about the adequacy of the
Jaguar's petrol allowance, Morse had requisitioned
an unmarked police car, which just before 10 A.M.
was heading south along the A34, with Sergeant
Lewis at the wheel. As they approached Abingdon,
Morse asked Lewis to turn on Classic FM, and
almost immediately asked him to turn it off, as he
recognized the Brandenburg Concerto No. 2.

"Somebody once said, Lewis, that it was not impossible to get bored even in the presence of a mistress,
and I'm sorry to say I sometimes get a little bored
even in the company of Johann Sebastian Bach."

"Really. I thought it was rather nice."

"Lew-is! He may be terrific; he may be terrible—
but he's never *nice*. Not Bach!"

Lewis concentrated on the busy road ahead as
Morse sank back into his seat and, as was ever his

wont in a car, said virtually nothing for the rest of the journey.

And yet Morse had said so many things—things upon which Lewis's mind intermittently focused again, as far too quickly he drove down to the Chieveley junction with the M4. . . .

><

Once back from Polstead Road, Friday afternoon had been very busy and, for Lewis, very interesting. It had begun with Morse asking about their present journey.

"If you had a posh car, which way would you go to Bath?"

"A34, M4, A46—probably the best; the quickest, certainly."

"What if you had an old banger?"

"Still go the same way, I think."

"What's wrong with the Burford–Cirencester way?"

"Nothing at all, if you like a bit of scenery. Or if you don't like motorway driving."

Then another question:

"How do we find out which bank the Storrs use?"

"Could be they have different banks, sir. Shouldn't be too difficult, though: Lloyds, Barclays, NatWest, Midland . . . Shall I ring around?"

Morse nodded. "And try to find out how they've been spending their money recently—if it's possible."

"May take a bit of time, but I don't see why not. Let me find out anyway."

Lewis turned to go, but Morse had a further request.

"Before you do, bring me the notes you made about the Storrs' stay in Bath last weekend. I'm assuming you've typed 'em up by now?"

"All done. Maybe a few spelling mistakes—a few grammatical lapses—beautifully typed, though."

>‹

It had taken Lewis only ten minutes to discover that Mr. Julian Storrs and Mrs. Angela Storrs both banked at Lloyds. But there had been far greater difficulty in dealing with Morse's supplementary request.

The Manager of Lloyds (Headington Branch) had been fully cooperative but of only limited assistance. It was very unusual of course, but not in cases such as this *unethical*, for confidential material concerning clients to be disclosed. But Lewis would have to contact Lloyds Inspection Department in Bristol.

Which Lewis had promptly done, again receiving every cooperation; also, however, receiving the disappointing news that the information required was unlikely as yet to be fully ready. With credit card facilities now almost universally available, the volume of transactions was ever growing; and with receipt items sometimes irregularly forwarded from retail outlets, and with a few inevitable checks and delays in processing and clearance—well, it would take a little time.

"Later this afternoon?" Lewis had queried hopefully.

"No chance of that, I'm afraid."

"Tomorrow morning?"

Lewis heard a deep sigh at the other end of the line. "We don't usually . . . It *is* very urgent, you say?"

><

The phone had been ringing in Morse's office—an office minus Morse—and Lewis had taken the brief call. The postmortem on Shelly Cornford confirmed death from carbon monoxide poisoning, and completely ruled out any suspicion of foul play.

A note on yellow paper was Cellotaped to the desk:

Lewis!
—Just off to the Diab. Center (3.45)
—Yr notes on Bath most helpful, but try to get Sarah Siddons right—two d's, please.
—Good job we're getting a few facts straight before jumping too far ahead. Reculer pour mieux sauter!
—We'll be jumping tomorrow A.M. *tho' to Bath. Royal Crescent informs me the Storrs—Herr und Frau—are staying there again!*
—I need yr notes on Julian Storrs.
—Ring me at home—after the Archers. M

And on the side of the desk, a letter from the Thame and District Diabetic Association addressed to Det. Chief Inspector Morse:

Dear sir,

Welcome to the Club! Sorry to be so quick off the mark but news travels fast in diabetic circles.

We meet on the first Thursday of each month 7:30 P.M. in the Town Hall in Thame and we shall be delighted if you can come to speak to us. We can offer no fee but we can offer a warmhearted and grateful audience.

During this last year we have been fortunate to welcome several very well-known people. For example our last six speakers have been Dr. David Matthews, Lesley Hallett, Professor Harry Keane, Angela Storrs, Dr. Robert Turner, and Willie Rushton.

Please try to support us if you can. For our 1996/97 program we are still looking for speakers for October '96 and February '97. Any hope of you filling one of these slots?

I enclose SAE and thank you for your kind consideration. . . .

But Lewis read only the first few lines, for never, except in the course of a criminal investigation, had he wittingly read a letter meant for the eyes of another person. . . .

><

From the passenger seat Morse had still said nothing until Lewis, after turning off the M4 at Junction 18 onto the A46, was within a few miles of Bath.

"Lewis! If you had a mistress—"

"Not the milk-lady, sir. She's far too fat for me."

"—and, say, you were having a weekend away together and you told your missus that you were catching the train but in fact this woman was going to pick you up in her car somewhere—The Randolph, say . . ."

"Yes, sir?" (Was Morse getting lost?)

"Would you still *go* to the railway station? Would you make sure she picked you up *at* the railway station—not The Randolph?"

"Dunno, sir. I've never—"

"I know you haven't," snapped Morse. "Just *think*, man!"

So Lewis thought. And *thought* he saw what Morse was getting at.

"You mean it might make you feel a bit better in your own mind—feel a bit less guilty, like—if you did what you *said* you'd be doing—before you went?" (Was Lewis getting lost?)

"Something like that," said Morse unenthusiastically as a sign welcomed the two detectives to the Roman City of Bath.

><

As soon as Lewis had stopped outside the Royal Crescent Hotel, Morse rang through on the mobile phone to the Deputy Manager, as had been agreed. No problem, it appeared. The Storrs had gone off somewhere an hour or so earlier in the BMW. The coast was clear; and Morse got out of the car and walked round to the driver's window.

"Good luck in Bristol!"

Lewis raised two crossed fingers of his right hand,

like the logo of the National Lottery, as Morse continued:

"If you find what I *hope* you're going to find, the battle's half won. And it's mostly thanks to you."

"No! It was you who figured it all out."

"Wouldn't have done, though, without all those visits of yours to Soho."

"Pardon, sir?"

"To see the chorus line, Lewis! The chorus line at the Windmill."

"But I've never—"

" 'Legs right up to her armpits,' you said, right? And that was the *second* time you'd used those words, Lewis. Remember?"

Chapter Sixty-One

Life, within doors, has few pleasanter prospects
than a neatly arranged and well-provisioned breakfast table.

> —Nathaniel Hawthorne,
> *The House of the Seven Gables*

MORSE STOOD FOR some while on the huge slabs that
form the wide pavement stretching along the whole
extent of the great 500-foot curve of cinnamon-
colored stone, with its identical facades of double
Ionic columns, which comprise Bath's Royal Crescent. It seemed to him a breathtaking architectural
masterpiece, with the four-star hotel exactly at its
center: Number 16.

He walked between the black spiked railings,
through the white double doors, into the black-and-
white floor-tiled, high-ceilinged entrance hall, and
then to reception, where he was immediately ushered
into the beige-carpeted, pine-furnished office of the
Deputy Manager, just beyond.

Sara Hickman was from Leicestershire, a tall,
slimly attractive woman in her mid-thirties, with
green eyes (just like Sister McQueen) and dark curly
hair. She was dressed in a businesslike suit; she spoke
in a businesslike manner; and so very clearly was she

part of an extremely businesslike hotel, since manifold awards—RAC Blue Ribbons, AA Rosettes,
Egon Ronay Stars—vied with each other for space
around the walls.

After hesitating, finally capitulating, over the offer
of coffee, Morse soon found himself listening very
carefully.

Sara had, she told him, been able to reinterview
almost all of the service personnel who had been on
duty the previous weekend, most of whom, as it happened, were performing similar duties that present
weekend. But there seemed little to add, at least in
general terms, to the details earlier communicated by
the Manager himself to the Thames Valley Police.
One minor correction: the room the Storrs had slept
in was a Standard Twin, not a Standard Double; and
in fact the couple had asked for the same room again,
if it was available. Which, by some strange coincidence, it was: the only Standard Twin still available
in the hotel that weekend. Registration? She passed
to Morse the card dated the previous Saturday, 3-2-
96: Guest's Name; Address; Telephone No.; Arrival
Date; Departure Date; Nationality; Payment Type;
Passport No.; Signature; Car Reg. No.—and more.
All filled in with a neat, feminine, slightly forward-
leaning script, in black Biro; and signed "Angela
Storrs." It would be comparatively easy to check, of
course; but Morse had little or no doubt that the signature was genuine.

"The Manager told my sergeant, when he rang

about last weekend, that we might be able to see some itemized bills?"

Sara Hickman smiled.

"I thought somehow you might ask for them," she said, and now read aloud from a small sheaf of bills in front of her.

"Last Saturday night they ate at Table twenty-six, in the far corner of the restaurant. He had the Carpaccio of Beef, Truffled Noodles, and Parmesan, for his starter; for his main course, the Seabass served with Creamed Celeriac and Fennel Liqueur; Passion Fruit Mousse for sweet. *She* wasn't quite so adventurous, I'm afraid: Consommé; with Baked Plaice and Green Salad for her main course; and then cream crackers and Edam—the waiter particularly remembers her asking for the Edam."

"Good low-fat cheese they tell me," mumbled Morse, recalling his own hard-nosed dietitian's homily in the Geoffrey Harris Ward. And he was smiling vaguely to himself as the Deputy Manager continued:

"Now, Sunday morning. Mr. Storrs had ordered breakfasts for the two of them over the phone the previous night—at about eleven, half past—can't be sure. He said he thought he was probably too late with the form, but he obviously had it in front of him —the night porter remembers that. He said he'd have a Full English for himself, no kidney though, with the tomato well grilled, and two fried eggs. Said his wife would go for a Continental: said she'd like cereal,

Ricicles, if we'd got some—Chief Inspector, we've got a bigger selection of cereals than Sainsbury's!—some brown toast and honey, the fresh fruit compote, and orange juice. Oh, yes," Sara checked the form again, "and hot chocolate."

"The time?" asked Morse.

"It would have been between seven-thirty and eight. We don't serve Full English until after seven-thirty—and both breakfasts went up together."

"And last night for dinner?"

"They didn't eat here."

"This morning?"

"They had breakfast in their room again. This time they filled in the form early, and left it on the doorknob outside the room. Same as before for Mr. Storrs—"

"How do you know it wasn't for *her*?"

"Well, it's exactly what he ordered before. Here, look for yourself."

She passed the room service order across the desk; and Morse saw the instructions: "Well grilled" against "Tomato"; no tick against "Kidney"; the figure "2" against "Eggs (fried)."

"I see what you mean," admitted Morse. "Not even married couples have exactly the same tastes, I suppose."

"*Especially* married couples," said Sara Hickman quietly.

Morse's eyes continued down the form, to the Continental section, and saw the ticks against "Weetabix" ("semi-skimmed milk" written beside it), "Natural

Yogurt," "Toast (brown)," "Coffee (decaffeinated)." The black-Biro'd writing was the same as that on the registration form. Angela Storrs' writing. Certainly.

"I shall have to have copies of these forms," said Morse.

"Of course." Sara got to her feet. "I'll see that's done straightaway. Shall we go over to the bar?"

The day was brightening.

But for Morse the day had already been wonderfully bright; had been for the past hour or so, ever since the Deputy Manager had been speaking with him.

And indeed was very shortly to be brighter still.

Chapter Sixty-Two

Queen Elizabeth the First Slept Here.

—Notice which according to the British Tourist
Board is to be observed in approximately
2400 residences in the United Kingdom

THEY WALKED ACROSS the splendidly tended garden
area behind the main complex to the Dower House,
an elegant annex wherein were situated most of the
hotel's suites and bedrooms, as well as the restaurant,
the main lounge—and the bar.

Immediately inside the entrance, Morse saw the
plaque (virtually a statutory requirement in Bath) com-
memorating a particularly eminent royal personage:

**George IV
1820–1830
Resided here
1799
as
Prince of Wales**

In the lounge, Morse sat down amid the unashamedly luxurious surroundings of elaborate wall
lights, marble busts—and courteously prompt ser-

vice, for a uniformed waitress was already standing beside them.

"What would you like to drink, sir?"

Lovely question.

As he waited for his beer, Morse looked around him; and in particular at the portrait above the fireplace there: "Lord Ellmore, 1765–1817," the inscription read, a fat-cheeked, smooth-faced man, with a protruding lower lip, who reminded Morse unhappily of Sir Clixby Bream.

Then he walked through to the Gents in the corridor just off the lounge where the two loos stood side by side, the Men's and the Ladies' logos quite unequivocally distinct on their adjacent doors.

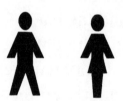

It would have been difficult even for the myopic Mrs. Adams to confuse the two, thought Morse, as he smiled and mouthed a few silent words to himself:

"Thank you! Thank you, Mrs. Arabella Adams!"

It wasn't that she could have been certain—from some little distance? with her failing eyesight?—that the person she had seen was a man or a woman. Certainly not so far as the recognition of any facial features was concerned. Faces were notoriously difficult to distinguish, appearing so different when seen in profile, perhaps, or in the shadows, or wearing glasses. No! It was just that old Mrs. Adams had always known what men looked like, and what women looked like, since habitually the men wore trousers and the women wore skirts. But of course if someone wore trousers, that certainly didn't prove that the wearer was a man, now did it, Morse? In fact it proved one thing and one thing *only*: that the person in question was wearing trousers!

><

Ten minutes later, as he worked his way with diminishing enthusiasm through an over-generous plateful of smoked-salmon sandwiches, Morse saw Sergeant Lewis appear in the doorway—a Lewis looking almost as self-satisfied as the oily Lord Ellmore himself—and raise his right thumb, before being introduced to Sara Hickman.

"Something to drink, Sergeant?"

"Thank you. Orange juice, please."

"Something to eat?"

"What have you got?"

She smiled happily. "Anything. Anything you like. Our Head Chef is at your command."

"Can he rustle up some eggs and chips?"

She said she was sure—well, almost sure—that he could, and departed to investigate.

"Lew-is! This is a cordon bleu establishment."

"Should taste good then, sir."

The buoyant Lewis passed a note to Morse, simultaneously (and much to Morse's relief) helping himself to a couple of sandwiches.

"You don't mind, sir? I'm half starving."

><

At 2:30 P.M. Marilyn Hudson, a small, fair-complexioned young woman, was called into Sara's office. Marilyn had been a chamber-cum-kitchenmaid at the hotel for almost three years; and it was soon clear that she knew as much as anyone was likely to know about the day-to-day—and night-by-night—activities there.

Morse now questioned her closely about the morning of the previous Sunday, March 3.

"You took them breakfast?"

"Yes, sir. About quarter to eight."

"You knocked on the door?"

"Like I always do, yes. I heard somebody say 'Come in' so I—"

"You had a key?"

"I've got a master key. So I took the tray in and put it on the dressing table."

"Were they in bed together?"

"No. Twin beds it is there. She was on the far side. Difficult to miss her, though."

"Why do you say that?"

"Well, it was her *pajamas*—yellow an' black an' green stripes—up an' down."

"Vertical stripes, you mean?"

"I'm not sure about that, sir. Just up an' down, like I said. An' she's got the same pair now. I took their breakfast again this morning. Same room—thirty-six." Marilyn gave a nervous little giggle. "Perhaps it's time she changed them."

"She may have got two pairs," interposed Lewis—not particularly helpfully, judging from the scowl on Morse's face.

"Do you think it *could* have been anybody else—except Mrs. Storrs?"

"No, sir. Like I say, she was there in the bed. But . . ."

"But what?"

"Well, I saw *her* all right. But I didn't really see *him*. He was in the bathroom having a shave—electric razor it was—and the door was open a bit and I saw he was still in his pajamas and he said thank you but . . ."

"Would you have recognized him if he'd turned his head?"

For the first time Marilyn Hudson seemed unsure of herself.

"Well, I'd seen them earlier in the hotel, but I didn't notice him as much as her really. She was, you know, ever so dressy and smart—dark glasses she wore—and a white trouser-suit. Same thing as she's got on today."

Morse turned to Lewis. "Do you think she's got *two* white trouser-suits, Sergeant?"

"Always a possibility, sir."

"So," if Morse was experiencing some disappointment, he gave no indication of it, "what you're telling us is that you're pretty sure it was her, but not quite so sure it was *him*?"

Marilyn considered the question a while before replying:

"No. I'm *pretty* sure it was both of them, sir."

><

"Good girl, our Marilyn," confided Sara, "even if her vocabulary's a bit limited."

Morse looked across at her quizzically:

"Vertical and horizontal, you mean? I shouldn't worry about that. I've always had trouble with east and west myself."

"Lots of people have trouble with right and left," began Lewis—but Morse was already making a further request:

"You've still got the details of who was staying here last Saturday?"

"Of course. Just a minute."

She returned shortly with a sheaf of registration cards; and Morse was looking through, flicking them over one at a time—when suddenly he stopped, the familiar tingling of excitement across his shoulders.

He handed the card to Lewis.

And Lewis whistled softly, incredulously, as he read the name.

Morse turned again to Sara. "Can you let us have a

copy of the bill—account, whatever you call it—for Room fifteen?"

"You were right then, sir!" whispered Lewis excitedly. "You always said it was 'D.C.'!"

Sarah came back and laid the account in front of Morse.

"Single room—number fifteen. Just the one night. Paid by credit card."

Morse looked through the items.

"No evening meal?"

"No."

"No breakfast either?"

"No."

"Look! Can we use your phone from here?"

"Of course you can. Shall I leave you?"

"Yes, I think so," said Morse, "if you don't mind."

⊁⊀

Morse and Lewis emerged from the office some twenty minutes later; and were walking behind reception when one of the guests came through from the entrance hall and asked for the key to Room 36.

Then he saw Morse.

"Good God! What are *you* doing here?" asked Julian Storrs.

"I was just going to ask you exactly the same question," replied Morse, with a curiously confident smile.

Chapter Sixty-Three

"Why did you murder those workmen in 1893?"
"It wasn't in 1893. It was in '92."

—Quoted by H. H. Asquith

"DO YOU WANT my wife to be here as well? I dropped her in the city center to do a bit of shopping. But she shouldn't be long—if that's what you want?"

"We'd rather talk to you alone, sir."

"What's this bloody 'sir' got to do with things?"

The three of them—Storrs, Morse, Lewis—were seated in Room 36, a pleasingly spacious room, whose windows overlooked the hotel's pool and the sodden-looking croquet green.

"What's all this about anyway?" Storrs' voice was already sounding a little weary, increasingly tetchy. "Can we get on with it?"

So Morse got on with it, quickly sketching in the background to the two murders under investigation:

Storrs had been having an affair with Rachel James —and Rachel James had been murdered.

Storrs had been blackmailed by Owens—and Owens had been murdered.

The grounds for this blackmail were threefold: his extramarital relationship with Ms. James; his dishonest concealment of his medical prognosis; and his wife's earlier career as striptease dancer and Soho call girl. For these reasons, it would surely have been very strange had Storrs not figured somewhere near the top of the suspect list.

As far as the first murder was concerned, Storrs—both the Storrs—had an alibi: they had been in bed with each other. How did one break that sort of alibi?

As far as the second murder was concerned, Storrs—again *both* Storrs—had their alibis: but this time not only were they in the same bedroom together, but also eighty-odd miles away from the scene of the crime. In fact, in the very room where they were now. But alibis could be fabricated; and if so, they could be broken. Sometimes they *were* broken.

(Storrs was listening in silence.)

Means? Forensic tests had established that both murders had been committed with the same weapon—a pistol known as the Howdah, often used by senior ranks in the armed forces, especially in India, where Storrs had served until returning to Oxford. He had acquired such a pistol; probably still had it, unless he had got rid of it recently—*very* recently.

The predominant cause—the Prime Mover—for the whole tragic sequence of events had been his obsessive, overweening ambition to gain the ultimate honor during what was left to him of his lifetime—the Mastership of Lonsdale, with the virtually inevitable accolade of a knighthood.

Motive, then? Yes.

Means? Yes.

Opportunity, though?

For the first murder, transport from Polstead Road to Kidlington was easy enough—there were *two* cars. But the target had not been quite so easy. In fact, it might well have been that Rachel James was murdered mistakenly, because of a mix-up over house numbers and a ponytailed silhouette.

But for the second murder, planning had to be far more complicated—and clever. Perhaps the "in-bed-together" alibi might sound a little thin the second time. But not if he was in a bed in some distant place; not if he was openly *observed* in that distant place at the time the murder must have been committed. No one had ever been in two places at the same time: that would be an affront to the rules by which the Almighty had established the universe. But the distance from Oxford to Bath was only eighty-odd miles. And in a powerful car, along the motorway, on a Sunday morning, early . . . An hour, say? Pushing it, perhaps? An hour and a quarter, then —two and a half hours on the road. Then there was a murder to be committed, of course. Round it up to three hours, say.

><

During the last few minutes of Morse's exposition, Storrs had walked across to the window, where he stood looking out over the garden. The afternoon had clouded, with the occasional spatter of rain across the panes. Storrs was humming quietly to himself; and Morse recognized the tune of "September," one of Richard Strauss's *Four Last Songs*:

> *Der Garten trauert*
> *Kühl sinkt in die Blumen der Regen . . .*

Then, abruptly, Storrs turned round.

"You do realize what you're saying?" he asked quietly.

"I think I do," replied Morse.

"Well, let's get a few things straight, shall we? Last Sunday my wife Angela and I had breakfast here, in this room, at about a quarter to eight. The same young girl brought us breakfast this morning, as it happens. She'll remember."

Morse nodded. "She's not quite sure it was *you*, though, last Sunday. She says you were shaving at the time, in the bathroom."

"Who the hell *was* it then? If it wasn't me?"

"Perhaps you'd got back by then."

"Back? Back from Oxford? How did I manage that? Three hours, you say? I must have left at half past four!"

"You had a car—"

"Have you checked all this? You see, my car was in the hotel garage—and God knows where *that* is. I left it outside when we booked in, and gave the keys to one of the porters. That's the sort of thing you pay for in places like this—didn't you know that?"

Again Morse nodded. "You're right. The garage wasn't opened up that morning until ten minutes to nine."

"So?" Storrs looked puzzled.

"You could have driven someone else's car."

"Whose, pray?"

"Your wife's, perhaps?"

Storrs snorted. "Which just *happened* to be standing outside the hotel—is that it? A helicopter lift from Polstead Road?"

"I don't know," admitted Morse.

"All right. Angela's car's there waiting for me, yes? How did I get out of the hotel? There's only the one exit, so I must have slipped unnoticed past a sleeping night porter—" He stopped. "Have you checked up whether the front doors are locked after midnight?"

"Yes, we've checked."

"And are they?"

"They are."

"So?" Again Storrs appeared puzzled.

"So the only explanation is that you weren't in the hotel that night at all," said Morse slowly.

"Really? And who signed the bloody bill on Sunday—what—ten o'clock? Quarter past?"

"Twenty past. We've tried to check everything. You signed the bill, sir, using your own Lloyds Visa Card."

Suddenly Storrs turned his back and stared out of the rain-flecked window once more:

"Look! You must forgive me. I've been leading you up the garden path, I'm afraid. But it was extremely interesting hearing your story. Outside, just to the left —we can't quite see it from here—is what the splendid brochure calls its 'outdoor heated exercise plunge pool.' I was there that morning. I was there just after breakfast—about half past eight. Not just me, either. There was a rich American couple who were staying in the Beau Nash suite. They came from North Carolina, as I recall, and we must have been there together for twenty minutes or so. Want to know what we were talking about? Bosnia. Bloody Bosnia! Are you satisfied? You say you've tried to check everything. Well, just—check—that! And now, if you don't mind, my dear wife appears to be back. I just hope she's not spent— Good God! She's bought herself *another* coat!"

Lewis, who had himself remained silent throughout the interview, walked across to the rain-flecked window, and saw Mrs. Storrs standing beneath the porchway across the garden, wearing a headscarf, dark glasses, and a long expensive-looking white mackintosh. She appeared to be having some little difficulty unfurling one of the large gaudy umbrellas which the benevolent management left in clumps around the buildings for guests to use when needed—needed as now, for the rain had come on more heavily.

Morse, too, got to his feet and joined Lewis at the window, where Storrs was quietly humming that tune again.

Der Garten trauert . . .
The garden is mourning . . .
"Would you and your good lady like to join me for a drink, sir? In the bar downstairs?"

Chapter Sixty-Four

Hypoglycemia (n): abnormal reduction of sugar content of the blood—for Diabetes sufferers a condition more difficult to spell than to spot.

—*Small's Enlarged English Dictionary*,
17th Edition

"WHAT DO YOU think they're talking about up there, sir?"

"He's probably telling her what to say."

Morse and Lewis were seated side-by-side in the Dower House lounge—this time with their backs turned on Lord Ellmore, since two dark-suited men sat drinking coffee in front of the fireplace.

Julian Storrs and a black-tied waiter appeared almost simultaneously.

"Angela'll be down in a minute. Just changing. Got a bit wet shopping."

"*Before* she bought the coat, I hope, sir," said Lewis.

Storrs gave a wry smile, and the waiter took their order.

"Large Glenfiddich for me," said Storrs. "Two pieces of ice."

Morse clearly approved. "Same for me. What'll you have, Lewis?"

"Does the budget run to an orange juice?"

"And," Morse turned to Storrs, "what can we get for your wife?"

"Large gin and slim-line tonic. And put 'em all on my bill, waiter. Room thirty-six."

Morse made no protestation; and Lewis smiled quietly to himself. It was his lucky day.

"Ah! 'Slim-line tonic,'" repeated Morse. "Cuts out the sugar, I believe."

Storrs made no comment, and Morse continued:

"I know your wife's diabetic, sir. We checked up. We even checked up on what you both had to eat last weekend."

"Well done!"

"Only one thing puzzles me really: your wife's breakfast on Sunday morning." He gestured to Lewis, the latter now reading from his notebook:

"Ricicles—that's sort of sugar-frosted toasted rice —my kids used to love 'em, sir—toast and honey, a fruit cocktail, orange juice, and then some hot chocolate."

"Not, perhaps," added Morse, "the kind of breakfast a diabetic would normally order, is it? All that sugar? Everything else she ate here was out of the latest diabetic cookbook."

"Do you know anything *about* diabetes, Chief Inspector?"

It was a new voice, sharp and rather harsh—for Angela Storrs, dressed in the inevitable trouser-suit (lime green, this time), but most unusually minus the dark glasses, had obviously caught some (most?) of the previous conversation.

"Not much," admitted Morse as he sought to rise from his deep, low chair. "I've only been diagnosed a week."

"Please don't get up!" It sounded more an order than a request.

She took a seat next to her husband on the sofa. "I've had diabetes for ten years myself. But you'll learn soon enough. You see, one of the biggest dangers for insulin-dependent diabetics is not, as you might expect, excessively high levels of blood sugar, but excessively *low* levels: hypoglycemia, it's called. Are you on insulin yourself?"

"Yes, and they did try to tell me something about—"

"You're asking about last weekend. Let me tell you. On Saturday evening my blood sugar was low—*very* low; and when Julian asked me about breakfast I decided to play things safe. I did have some glucose with me; but I was still low on Sunday morning. And if it's of any interest, I thoroughly enjoyed my sugary breakfast. A rare treat!"

The drinks had arrived.

"Look!" she continued, once the waiter had asked for her husband's signature on the bill. "Let me be honest with you. Julian has just told me why you're here. He'd already told me about everything else anyway: about his ridiculous affair with that young Rachel woman; about that slimy specimen Owens."

"Did you hate him enough to murder him?"

"*I* did," interrupted Storrs vehemently. "God rot his soul!"

"And about this Mastership business?" Morse looked from one to the other. "You were in that together?"

It was Julian Storrs who answered. "Yes, we were. I told Angela the truth immediately, about my illness, and we agreed to cover it all up. You see," suddenly he was looking very tired, "I wanted it so much. I wanted it more than anything—didn't I, Angela?"

She smiled, and gently laid her own hand over his. "And *I* did too, Julian."

Morse drained his whiskey and thirsted for another.

"Mrs. Storrs, I'm going to ask you a very blunt question—and you must forgive me, because that's my job. What would you say if I told you that you didn't sleep with your husband last Saturday night—that you slept with another man?"

She smiled again; and for a few moments the angularity of her face had softened into the lineaments of a much younger woman.

"I'd just hope he was a good lover."

"But you'd deny it?"

"A childish accusation like that? It's hardly worth denying!"

Morse turned to Storrs. "And you, sir? What would you say if I told you that *you* didn't sleep with your wife last Saturday night—that you slept with another woman?"

"I'd just hope *she* was a good lover, I suppose."

"But you'd deny it, too?"

"Of course."

"Anything *else* you want to check?" asked Angela Storrs.

"Well, just the one thing really, because I'm still not quite sure that I've got it right." Morse took a deep breath, and exhaled rather noisily. "You say you came here with your husband in his BMW, latish last Saturday afternoon—stayed here together overnight —then drove straight back to Oxford together the next morning. Is that right, Mrs. Storrs?"

"Not quite, no. We drove back via Cirencester and Burford. In fact, we had a bite of lunch at a pub in Burford and we had a look in two or three antiques shops there. I nearly bought a silver toast rack, but Julian thought it was grossly overpriced."

"I see . . . I see . . . In that case, it's about time we told you something else," said Morse slowly. "Don't you think so, Sergeant Lewis?"

Chapter Sixty-Five

"Is this a question?"

—from an Oxford entrance examination

"If it is, this could be an answer."

—one candidate's reply

APART FROM themselves and the two men still drinking coffee, the large lounge was now empty.

"Perhaps we could all do with another drink?" It was Morse's suggestion.

"Not for me," said Angela Storrs.

"I'm all right, thank you," said Julian Storrs.

"Still finishing this one," said Lewis.

Morse felt for the cellophaned packet and almost fell. He stared for a while out of the windows: heavy rain now, through which a hotel guest occasionally scuttled across to the Dower House, head and face wholly indistinguishable beneath one of the gay umbrellas. How easy it was to hide when it was raining!

Almost reluctantly, it seemed, Morse made the penultimate revelation:

"There was someone else staying here last Saturday night, someone I think both of you know. She was staying—yes, it was a woman!—in the main part of the hotel, across there in Room fifteen. That woman was Dawn Charles, the receptionist at the Harvey Clinic in Banbury Road."

Storrs turned to his wife. "Good heavens! Did you realize that, darling?"

"Don't be silly! I don't even *know* the woman."

"It's an extraordinarily odd coincidence, though," persisted Morse. "Don't you think so?"

"Of course it's odd," replied Angela Storrs. "*All* coincidences are odd—by definition! But life's full of coincidences."

Lewis smiled inwardly. How often had he heard those selfsame words from Morse.

"But this *wasn't* a coincidence, Mrs. Storrs."

It was Julian Storrs who broke the awkward, ominous silence that had fallen on the group.

"I don't know what that's supposed to mean. All I'm saying is that *I* didn't see her. Perhaps she's a Fauré fan herself and came for the Abbey concert like we did. You'll have to ask *her*, surely?"

"If we do," said Morse simply, confidently, "it won't be long before we learn the truth. She's not such a competent liar as you are, sir—as the *pair* of you are!"

The atmosphere had become almost dangerously tense as Storrs got to his feet. "I am *not* going to sit here one minute longer and listen—"

"Sit down!" said his wife, with an authority so assertive that one of the coffee drinkers turned his head briefly in her direction as Morse continued:

"You both deny seeing Miss Charles while she was here?"

"Yes."

"Yes."

"Thank you. Sergeant? Please?"

Lewis reopened his notebook, and addressed Mrs. Storrs directly:

"So it couldn't possibly have been you, madam, who filled a car with petrol at Burford on that Saturday afternoon?"

"*Last* Saturday? Certainly not!" She almost spat the words at her new interlocutor.

But Lewis appeared completely unabashed. "Have you lost your credit card recently?"

"Why do you ask that?"

"Because someone made a good job of signing your name, that's all. For twelve pounds of Unleaded Premium at the Burford Garage on the A40 at about three o'clock last Saturday."

"What exactly are you suggesting?" The voice sounded menacingly calm.

"I'm suggesting that you drove here to Bath that day in your own car, madam—"

But she had risen to her feet herself now.

"You were right, Julian. We are *not* going to sit here a second longer. Come along!"

But she got no further than the exit, where two men stood barring her way: two dark-suited men who had been sitting for so long beneath the portrait of the bland Lord Ellmore.

She turned round, her nostrils flaring, her wide naked eyes now blazing with fury; and perhaps, as Morse saw them, with hatred, too, and despair.

But she said nothing further, as Lewis walked quietly toward her.

"Angela Miriam Storrs, it is my duty as a police officer to arrest you on the charge of murder. The murder of Geoffrey Gordon Owens, on Sunday, the third of March 1996. It is also my duty to warn you that anything you now say may be taken down in writing and used in evidence at any future hearing."

She stood where she was and still said nothing.

Chief Inspector Morse, too, stood where *he* was, wondering whether his sergeant had got the wording quite right, as Detective Inspector Briggs and Detective Constable Bott, both of the Avon CID, led Angela Miriam Storrs away.

Part Seven

Chapter Sixty-Six

Twas the first and last time that I'd iver known
women to use the pistol. They fear the shot as a rule,
but Di'monds-an'-Pearls she did not—she did not.

     —Rudyard Kipling, *Love-o'-Women*

BEING THE tape-recorded statement made by Angela
Storrs at Thames Valley Police HQ, Kidlington,
Oxon, on the morning of March 11, 1996; transcribed
by Detective Sergeant Lewis; and subsequently
amended—for minor orthographic and punctuational
vagaries—by Detective Chief Inspector Morse.

I murdered both of them, Rachel James and Geof-
frey Owens. I'm a bit sorry about Rachel.
 I was seventeen when I first started working as a
stripper in Soho and then as a prostitute and in
some porno flicks. Julian Storrs came along several
times to the club where I was performing seven or
eight times a night, and he arranged to see me, and
we had sex a few times in the West End. He was a
selfish sod as I knew from the start, especially in
those early days, as far as I was concerned. Which
was fine by me. He was obsessively jealous about
other men and this was something I wasn't used to.
He wanted me body and soul, he said, and soon he
asked me to marry him. Which was fine by me too.

I came from no family at all to speak of, but Julian came from a posh family and he had plenty of money. And he was a don at Oxford University and my mum was proud of me. She just wanted me to be somebody important like she'd never been.

I was unfaithful a few times after a few years, especially with some of the other dons who were about as pathetic as the old boys in the Soho basement who used to stick the odd fiver up your panties.

I enjoyed life at Oxford. But nobody took to me all that much. I wasn't quite in the same bracket as the others and I used to feel awkward when they asked me about where I'd been to university and all that jazz, because I couldn't even pretend I was one of them. I wanted to be one of them, though—God knows why! Ours wasn't a tight marriage even from the start. It wasn't too long before Julian was off with other women, and soon, as I say, I was off with other men. Including the Master. He needs his sheets changing every day, that man, like they do in the posh hotels. But he was going at last and that started things really, or is it finished things? Julian desperately wanted to be Master and only one person wanted that more than he did. Me!

In London I'd lived a dodgy, dangerous sort of life like any woman on the sex circuit does. I'd been mauled about quite a few times, and raped twice, once by a white and once by a black, so I can't be accused of racial prejudice. One of the other girls had a water pistol that fired gentian blue dye over anybody trying it on. I don't know why it was that

*color but I always remember it from the paint box I
had when I was a little girl, next to burnt Siena and
crimson Lake. But Julian had something far better
than that. He'd kept a pistol from his Army days
and after I had a bit of trouble late one Saturday
night in Cornmarket with some football thugs, he
said he didn't mind me carrying it around sometimes if it made me feel better. Which it did. I had a
newfound sense of confidence, and one weekend
Julian took me with some of his TA friends out to
the shooting range on Otmoor and for the first time
ever I actually fired a pistol. I was surprised how
difficult it was, with the way it jerked back and
upward, but I managed it and I loved it. After that I
got used to carrying it around with me—loaded!—
when I was out alone late at night. I felt a great
sense of power when I held it.*

*Then came our big opportunity. Julian was
always going to be a good bet for the Master's job,
and we only had Cornford to beat. I always quite
liked Denis but he never liked me, and to make up
for it I detested his American wife. But this one
thing that stood in the way suddenly became two
things, because we learned that Julian would probably be dead within a year or so although we
agreed never to say anything about it to anyone.
Then there was that third thing—that bloody man
Owens.*

*He'd written to Julian not to me, and he'd done
his homework properly. He knew I'd been a call girl
(sounds better, doesn't it?). He knew about Julian's
latest floozie. And he knew about Julian's illness*

and guessed he was hiding it from the College. He said he'd be ringing and he did, and they met in the Chapters' Bar at The Randolph. All Owens wanted was money, it seems, and Julian's never been short of that. But Julian played it cool and he went back to the bar later on and had a bit of luck because one of the barmaids knew who Owens was because he'd covered quite a few functions there for the newspapers. We didn't need to hire a detective to find his address because it was in the phone book!

I knew what I was doing that morning because I'd already driven round the area twice and I'd done my homework too. I parked on the main road above the terrace and got through a gap in the fence down to the back. I don't think I meant to shoot him but just frighten him to death if I could and let him know that he'd never be able to feel safe in life again if he kept on with his blackmail. Then I saw him behind the kitchen blind, and I suddenly realized how ridiculously easy it would be to solve all our problems. It wouldn't take more than a single second. I knew he lived alone, and I knew this must be him. His head was only a couple of feet away and I saw the ponytail that Julian had told me about. I'd planned to knock on the door and go in and sort things out. But I didn't. I just fired point-blank and that was that. There was a huge thud and a splintering noise and lots of smoke, but only for a second it seemed. Next thing I remember I was sitting in the car trembling all over and expecting to see people rushing around and police sirens and all that. But there was nothing. A few cars drove by and a paperboy rode past on his bicycle.

It was all a bit like a nightmare I've often had—standing on top of some high building with no rail in front of me and knowing it would be so easy to jump off, and if I did jump off, that would be the end of everything. In the nightmare I was always just about going to jump off when I woke up sweating and terrified. It was the same sort of thing at that window. It was like somebody saying "Do it!" And I did it. Julian knew what happened but he didn't have anything to do with it.

We planned the second murder together, though. Nothing to lose, was there?

Julian knew someone must have shopped him down at the clinic and he soon found out it was Dawn Charles. So we had the hold on her now and it wasn't difficult to get her to cooperate. She'd got money problems and Julian promised to help if she did what we wanted. Which wasn't much really.

Things went as we planned them. Julian drove down to Bath in the BMW and I followed in my car. He went M4. I went Burford way. He booked in and left his car in the hotel garage. I left my car in one of the side streets behind the hotel. Dawn Charles went by train to Bath changing at Didcot, so Julian told me. She booked into the hotel as herself of course. After we got back from the Abbey, Julian and I had dinner together, and then I left. Julian rang Dawn Charles on the internal phone system and all she had to do was to walk across the garden. I drove back to Oxford and then up to Bicester where I'd got the key to Dawn's flat. It would have been far too risky to go back to Polstead Road.

Unless Julian persuaded her to sleep in the raw

*Dawn wore my pajamas, and the hotel girl took
them breakfast in bed the next morning. Mistake
about all that sugar, I agree! Dawn Charles is my
sort of height and shape, so Julian tells me, and if
she wore something that was obviously mine there
wouldn't be much of a problem. The whole thing
was very neat really. It didn't matter if she was seen
round the hotel or if I was, because both of us were
staying there officially.*

*I'd phoned Owens to arrange everything and last
Sunday morning I drove round to Bloxham Drive
again. Probably he'd have been more wary if I'd
been a man instead of a woman but I told him I'd
have the money with me. So he said he'd meet me
and have a signed letter ready promising he would-
n't try any more blackmail. I went down the slope at
the back like before and knocked on the right door
this time. It was about a quarter past seven when
he let me in and we went through to his front room.
I don't think either of us spoke. He was standing
there in front of the settee and I took the pistol out
of my shopping bag and shot him twice and left him
there for dead.*

Angela Storrs
3-11-96

As it happened, Lewis was not to read this final version. Had he done so, he might have felt rather surprised—and a little superior?—to notice that his own
"burnt sienna" had been amended to "burnt Siena,"
since he had taken the trouble to look up that color in
Chambers, and had spelled it accordingly.

Chapter Sixty-Seven

Belbroughton Road is bonny, and pinkly burst the
 spray
Of prunus and forsythia across the public way,
For a full spring-tide of blossom seethed and
 departed hence,
Leaving land-locked pools of jonquils by a sunny
 garden fence.

—John Betjeman, *May-Day Song for North Oxford*

SPRING WAS particularly beautiful, if late, in North
Oxford that year, and even Morse, whose only potential for floral exhibitionism was a small window box,
much enjoyed the full-belled daffodils and the short-
lived violets, though not the crocuses.

>‹

Sir Clixby Bream received a letter from Julian Storrs
on Tuesday, March 12. Both contestants had now
withdrawn from the Mastership Stakes. At an Extraordinary General Meeting held the next day in the
Stamper Room, the Fellows of Lonsdale had little
option but to extend yet again the term of the incumbent Master; and by a majority vote to call in the
"Visitor," that splendidly titled dignitary (usually an
archbishop) whose right and duty it was, and is, peri-

odically to inspect and to report on College matters, and to advise and to intervene in any such disputatious circumstances as Lonsdale, *omnium consensu*, now found itself in. An outside appointment seemed a certainty. But Sir Clixby accepted the situation philosophically, as was his wont . . . and the College lawns were beginning to look immaculate again. Life had to go on, even if Denis Cornford was now a broken man, with Julian Storrs awaiting new developments—and death.

><

Adèle Beatrice Cecil had recently learned that the membership of the Young Conservatives had fallen from 500,000 twenty years earlier to 5,000 in January 1996; and anyway she had for several weeks been contemplating a change in her lifestyle. Morse may have been right in one way, she thought—*only* one way, though—in suggesting that it was the personnel rather than the policies which were letting the Party down. Yes, it might be time for a change; and on Wednesday, March 13, she posted off her resignation to Conservative Central Office. She did so with deep regret, yet she knew she was never destined to be idle. She could write English competently, she knew that; as indeed did Morse; as did also her publishers, Erotica Press, who had recently requested an equally sexy sequel to *Topless in Torremolinos*. And already a nice little idea was burgeoning in her brain almost as vigorously as the wallflowers she'd planted the previous autumn: an idea about an older man—well, say a whitish-haired man who wasn't *quite* so old as he looked—and a woman who was considerably younger, about her own age, say. Age difference, in heterosexual encounters, was ever a guaranteed "turn-on," so her editor confided

✦

One man was to continue his officially unemployed status for the remainder of the spring; and probably indefinitely thereafter, although he was a little troubled by the rumor that the Social Security system was likely to be less sympathetic in the future. For the moment, however, he appeared to be adequately funded, judging from his virtually permanent presence in the local pubs and betting shops. It was always going to be difficult for any official down in the Job Center to refute his claim that the remuneration offered for some of their "employment opportunities" could never compensate for his customary lifestyle: he was a recognized artist; and if anyone doubted his word, there was a man living in North Oxford who would always be willing to give him a reference. . . .

On the mantelpiece in his bedroom, the little ormolu clock ticked on, keeping excellent time.

✦

In the immediate aftermath of Mrs. Storrs' arrest, Sergeant Lewis found himself extremely busy, happily i/c the team of companionable DCs assigned to him. So many inquiries remained to be made; so many statements to be taken down and duly typed; so many places to be visited and revisited: Soho, Bloxham Drive, the newspaper offices, the Harvey Clinic, Polstead Road, Lonsdale College, Woodpecker Way, The Randolph, the Royal Crescent Hotel. . . . He had met Morse for lunch on the Wednesday and had listened patiently as a rather self-congratulatory Chief Inspector remembered a few of the more crucial moments in the case: when, for example, he had associated that photograph of the young Soho stripper with that of the don's wife at Lonsdale; when the elegantly leggy Banbury Road receptionist had so easily slipped alongside that same don's wife in a chorus line at the Windmill. That lunchtime, however, Lewis's own crucial contributions to such dramatic developments were never even mentioned, let alone singled out for special praise

>‹

Late on Thursday evening, Morse was walking home from the Cotswold House after a generous measure of Irish whiskey (with an "e," as the proprietor ever insisted) when a car slowed down beside him, the front passenger window electronically lowered.

"Can I give you a lift anywhere?"

"*Hello!* No, thank you. I only live . . ." Morse gestured vaguely up toward the A40 roundabout.

"Everything okay with you?"

"Will be—if you'd like to come along and inspect my penthouse suite."

"I thought you said it was a flat."

⊁⊰

Though clearly surprised to find Morse in his office over the Friday lunch period, Strange refrained from his usual raillery.

"Can you nip in to see me a bit later this afternoon about these retirement forms?"

"Let's do it now, sir."

"What's the rush?"

"I'm off this afternoon."

"Official, is that?"

"Yes, sir."

Strange eyed Morse shrewdly. "Why are you looking so bloody cheerful?"

"Well, another case solved . . . ?"

"Mm. Where's Lewis, by the way?"

"There's still an awful lot of work to do."

"Why aren't you helping him then?"

"Like I say, sir, I'm off for the weekend."

"You're lucky, matey. The wife's booked *me* for the lawn mower."

"I've just got the window box myself."

"Anything in it?"

Morse shook his head, perhaps a little sadly.

"You, er, going anywhere special?" asked Chief Superintendent Strange.

Chapter Sixty-Eight

They fuck you up, your mum and dad.
They may not mean to, but they do.
They fill you with the faults they had
And add some extra, just for you.

—Philip Larkin, *This Be the Verse*

FOR SEVERAL SECONDS after she opened her eyes, Janet McQueen had no idea whatsoever about where she was or what she'd been doing. Then, as she lay there in the green sheets, gradually it flooded back . . .

➳❁

"Ah! Can I perhaps begin to guess our destination?" she'd asked, as the car turned left at Junction 18 and headed south along the A46. "B&B in Bath—is that what it's going to be?"

"You'll see."

As she *had* seen, for soon the Jaguar turned into the Circus, into Brock Street, and finally straight across a cobbled road, where it stopped beside a large magnolia tree. She looked at the hotel, and her green eyes widened as she brought her ringless, manicured fingers together in a semblance of prayer.

"Beautiful!"

Morse had turned toward her then, as she sat beside

him in her navy pin-striped suit; sat beside him in her
V-necked emerald-silk blouse.

"You're beautiful, too, Janet," he said simply, and
quietly.

"You've booked rooms for us *here*?"

Morse nodded. "Bit over the top, I know—but, yes,
I've booked the Sarah Siddons suite for myself."

"What have you booked for me?"

"That's also called the Sarah Siddons suite."

She was smiling contentedly as the Concierge
opened the passenger-seat door.

"Welcome to the Royal Crescent Hotel, madam!"

She'd felt important then.

And she'd loved it.

➤✦

Morse was already up—dressed, washed, shaved—
and sitting only a few feet from her, reading *The
Times*.

"Hello!" she said, softly.

He leaned over and kissed her lightly on the mouth.
"Headache?"

"Bit of one!"

"You know your trouble? You drink too much
champagne."

She smiled (she would always be smiling that
weekend) as she recalled the happiness of their night
together. And throwing back the duvet, she got out of
bed and stood beside him for several seconds, her
cheek resting on the top of his head.

"Shan't be long. Must have a shower."

"No rush."

"Why don't you see if you can finish the crossword before I'm dressed? Let's make it a race!"

But Morse said nothing—for he had already finished the crossword, and was thinking of the Philip Larkin line that for so many years had been a kind of mantra for him:

Waiting for breakfast while she brushed her hair.

❖

It was late morning, as they were walking arm-in-arm down to the city center, following the signs to the Roman Baths, that she asked him the question:

"Shall I just keep calling you 'Morse'?"

"I'd prefer that, yes."

"Whatever you say, sir!"

"You sound like Lewis. He always calls me 'sir.'"

"What do you call him?"

"'Lewis.'"

"Does *he* know your Christian name?"

"No."

"How come you got lumbered with it?"

Morse was silent awhile before answering:

"They both had to leave school early, my parents—and they never had much of a chance in life themselves. That's partly the reason, I suppose. They used to keep on to me all the time about trying as hard as I could in life. They wanted me to do that. They expected me to do that. Sort of emotional blackmail, really—when you come to think of it."

"Did you love them?"

Morse nodded. "Especially my father. He drank and gambled far too much . . . but I loved him, yes. He knew nothing really—except two things: he could recite all of Macaulay's *Lays of Ancient Rome* by heart; and he'd read everything ever written about his greatest hero in life, Captain Cook—'Captain James Cook, 1728 to 1779,' as he always used to call him."

"And your mother?"

"She was a gentle soul. She was a Quaker."

"It all adds up then, really?" said Janet slowly.

"I suppose so," said Morse.

"Do you want to go straight to the Roman Baths?"

"What are you thinking of?"

"Would you like a pint of beer first?"

"I'm a diabetic, you know."

"I'll give you your injection," she promised. "But only if you do me one big favor . . . I shan't be a minute."

Morse watched her as she disappeared into a souvenir shop alongside; watched the shapely straight legs above the high-heeled shoes, and the dark, wavy hair piled high at the back of her head. He thought he could grant her almost any favor that was asked of him.

>‹

She produced the postcard as Morse returned from the bar.

"What's that for?" he asked.

"*Who's* that for, you mean. That's for Sergeant Lewis . . . He means a lot to you, doesn't he?"

"What? Lewis? Nonsense!"

"He means a lot to you, doesn't he?" she repeated.

Morse averted his eyes from her penetrating, knowing gaze; looked down at the frothy head on his beer; and nodded.

"Christ knows why!"

"I want you to send him this card."

"What for? We're back at work together on Monday!"

"I want you to send him this card," she repeated. "You can send it to his home address. You see, I think he deserves to know your Christian name. Don't you?"

Envoi

Monday, March 18

This list is not for every Tom, Dick, and Harry. It's
been compiled by Everett Williams, director of the
Florida Bureau of Vital Statistics, and on it are the
150 most unusual names he's encountered in 34
years with the bureau. Examples are: Tootsie Roll,
Curlee Bush, Emancipation Proclamation
Cogshell, Candy Box, Starlight Cauliflower Shaw,
and Determination Davenport. But he never
encountered a fourth quadruplet called Mo!
Williams figures that some parents have a sense of
humor—or else a grudge against their offspring.

—*Gainesville Gazette*, February 16, 1971

ON THE FOLLOWING Monday evening, Mrs. Lewis
handed the card to her husband:

"This is for you—from Inspector Morse."

"You mean, you've read it?"

"Course I 'ave, boy!"

Smelling the chips, Lewis made no protestation as
he looked at the front of the card: an aerial view of
Bath, showing the Royal Crescent and the Circus.
Then, turning over the card, he read Morse's small,
neat handwriting on the back. What he read moved
him deeply; and when Mrs. Lewis shouted through

from the kitchen that the eggs were ready, he took a handkerchief from his pocket and pretended he was wiping his nose.

The card read as follows:

For philistines like you, Lewis, as well as for classical scholars like me, this city with its bath and temples must rank as one of the finest in Europe. You ought to bring the missus here some time.

Did I ever get the chance to thank you for the few(!) contributions you made to our last case together? If I didn't, let me thank you now—let me thank you for everything, my dear old friend.

Yours aye,

Endeavour Morse

American Heart Association, *American Heart Association Cookbook, 5th Edition Abridged*

Ben Artzi-Pelossof, Noa, *In the Name of Sorrow and Hope*

Benchley, Peter, *White Shark*

Berendt, John, *Midnight in the Garden of Good and Evil*

Bradford, Barbara Taylor, *Angel*

Brando, Marlon with Robert Lindsey, *Brando: Songs My Mother Taught Me*

Brinkley, David, *David Brinkley*

Buscaglia, Leo, Ph.D., *Born for Love*

Byatt, A. S., *Babel Tower*

Ciaro, Joe, editor, *The Random House Large Print Book of Jokes and Anecdotes*

Crichton, Michael, *Disclosure*

Crichton, Michael, *The Lost World*

Cruz Smith, Martin, *Rose*

Daley, Rosie, *In the Kitchen with Rosie*

Doctorow, E. L., *The Waterworks*

Dunne, Dominick, *A Season in Purgatory*

Flagg, Fannie, *Daisy Fay and the Miracle Man*

Flagg, Fannie, *Fried Green Tomatoes at the Whistle Stop Cafe*

Follett, Ken, *A Place Called Freedom*

Fulghum, Robert, *From Beginning to End: The Rituals of Our Lives*

Fulghum, Robert, *It Was on Fire When I Lay Down on It*

Fulghum, Robert, *Maybe (Maybe Not): Second Thoughts from a Secret Life*

García Márquez, Gabriel, *Of Love and Other Demons*

(continued)

Gilman, Dorothy, *Mrs. Pollifax and the Lion Killer*
Grimes, Martha, *The Horse You Came In On*
Grimes, Martha, *Rainbow's End*
Grimes, Martha, *Hotel Paradise*
Halberstam, David, *The Fifties* (2 volumes)
Hepburn, Katharine, *Me*
James, P. D., *The Children of Men*
James, P. D., *Original Sin*
Koontz, Dean, *Dark Rivers of the Heart*
Koontz, Dean, *Icebound*
Koontz, Dean, *Intensity*
Krantz, Judith, *Dazzle*
Krantz, Judith, *Lovers*
Krantz, Judith, *Scruples Two*
Krantz, Judith, *Spring Collection*
Landers, Ann, *Wake Up and Smell the Coffee!*
le Carré, John, *Our Game*
Lindbergh, Anne Morrow, *Gift from the Sea*
Ludlum, Robert, *The Road to Omaha*
Mayle, Peter, *Anything Considered*
McCarthy, Cormac, *The Crossing*
Meadows, Audrey with Joe Daley, *Love, Alice*
Michener, James A., *Mexico*
Michener, James A., *Miracle in Seville*
Michener, James A., *Recessional*
Mother Teresa, *A Simple Path*
Nuland, Sherwin B., *How We Die*
Patterson, Richard North, *Eyes of a Child*
Patterson, Richard North, *The Final Judgment*
Pavarotti, Luciano and William Wright, *Pavarotti: My World*
Phillips, Louis, editor, *The Random House Large Print Treasury of Best-Loved Poems*
Pope John Paul II, *Crossing the Threshold of Hope*
Pope John Paul II, *The Gospel of Life*

(continued)

Powell, Colin with Joseph E. Persico, *My American Journey*
Rendell, Ruth, *Simisola*
Riva, Maria, *Marlene Dietrich* (2 volumes)
Rooney, Andy, *My War*
Shaara, Jeff, *Gods and Generals*
Truman, Margaret, *Murder at the National Gallery*
Tyler, Anne, *Ladder of Years*
Tyler, Anne, *Saint Maybe*
Updike, John, *Rabbit at Rest*